Today there is both a new eroticism and a new conservatism about sex. Here are some of the best, brightest and bravest writers delving into the conflicts between romance and lust, purity and decadence, and desire and love.

If sex is the most intimate of personal relationships, then city life is the most conglomerate. Neither banishes loneliness or the vagaries of the unconscious, as many of these stories show. Some fantasise about the underbelly of the new materalist city; some respond to its fast changing social institutions, others ask whether the individual voice is stronger and more powerful, or is it sinking behind the glitter of communications technology?

Marsha Rowe

SEX AND THE CITY

A Serpent's Tail Compilation

Edited by Marsha Rowe

SERPENT'S
TAIL

Sex and the City is the first of an occasional series of short story compilations published by Serpent's Tail. Spelling is either English or American. Thanks to Harriett Gilbert and Malcolm Imrie for their early persistence in encouraging some of these new writers. Contributions to future compilations are welcome.

British Library Cataloguing in Publication Data

Sex and the city

   1. Short stories in English - Anthologies
   I. Rowe, Marsha
   823'01'08

ISBN 1–85242–165–7

First published in 1989 by
Serpent's Tail, 4 Blackstock Mews, London N4

Layout and design by Fiona Keating
Cover illustration of 'Tallie Landa is Distracted During Her Daily Jog Round the Park' by Pamela Shoemaker, mixed media construction © 1986

Typeset in 10/12pt Ehrhardt by Selectmove, London

Printed on acid-free paper by
Nørhaven A/S, Viborg, Denmark

Contents

SEX AND THE CITY

BILLETS DOUX

Elizabeth Cook

I was thirty last January and am old enough to enjoy the fact that my lover thinks of me as a younger woman. My lover is fifty but looks much younger, perhaps because he is slightly fat – not paunchy, but sleek – and this keeps his skin from getting that crêpey look that some skin gets. I, on the other hand, am rather thin. I used to think that I looked better with clothes on than off – I can wear almost anything – but my lover doesn't agree. I am not particularly beautiful but I have got the most astonishing red hair. It is very long and full and it springs out of my head like fiery thoughts.

My lover's wife is thirty-eight but she doesn't look it. She is really beautiful. She looks like a Swede but she isn't one. She is statuesque and, without being at all fat, everything about her goes in curves. She is like cream and her hair is ice-blonde. She is a famous cookery writer and I am always seeing her on television, tasting things or talking about the food she's eaten abroad. Needless to say she's a wonderful cook. Apart from seeing her on television I don't really know her, but she does come into the library where I work sometimes. The books she gets out are usually for some kind of research she's doing on food in the past. My lover says he's always having to eat things she's trying out from fourteenth-century recipes. But he wouldn't look so plush and well if they were bad.

I cook very badly indeed. My father used to say that no one

would ever marry me for my cooking. And he was right I'm glad to say. But my lover likes dressing me up and taking me out for meals. With his wife cooking at home all the time it's his only chance to eat out. And he likes spending money on me. He's always giving me underclothes. He says he likes it when he's sitting opposite me in a restaurant and he knows what I've got on underneath: probably silk camiknickers and some kind of lacey suspender belt. Men are very traditional when it comes to underwear.

A few months ago my lover took me to a new Indonesian restaurant about thirty miles from here (we never go out in this town because we don't want anyone to see us). The food was very good – all sorts of little bits, very beautifully presented and not overcooked and not at all filling. This was important because we were going back to my house to make love and nothing spoils love-making more than being stuffed.

We had been looking forward to this night because his wife would be on an aeroplane to Singapore and there was no way she could phone him to make sure he was at home like he'd said. So he was going to spend the whole night with me and, even though we wouldn't sleep as much as an ordinary couple would, we would have breakfast together (that means instant coffee) before we both went out to work.

We were as careful about not drinking too much as about the eating. But when we got home I asked my lover to bath me and then he produced a bottle of champagne which was just right. He soaped me all over very carefully in a kind of neutral way – not lingering anywhere except to massage my nipples where they poked out through the cream of the lather. And then when I stepped out he dried me in a big towel as if he were my mother.

He had wanted to get in the bath too but he was always so clean I didn't want him to get any cleaner. I wanted there to be something to taste when I started on him. After he had rubbed me dry he found some oil I had in the bathroom and I lay on my tummy on a towel on the bed while he went over me with his hands, very slowly and deliberately, kneading the oil in. He started off at my shoulders and then moved inwards to my spine and then down over my hips and buttocks and then instead of sliding his hand in, he moved on down my legs one at a time, until he had massaged even the soles of my feet.

By that time I was ready to eat him in one gulp but he still had all his clothes on and he looked very calm and reflective. So then it was my turn to work on him. I made out like I wasn't in a hurry either. I behaved more like a valet than a lover as I took his clothes off and hung them neatly over the back of my chair. I didn't even pause when I unzipped his fly. I just let him step out of his trousers and then I folded them too. And then I pulled his socks over his heels and pushed them into the toes of his shoes and put the shoes together in a pair.

And then I held out my hand to invite him over to the bed. He lay down and I began the feast down at the nape of his left heel. And then I made my way round to the inside of his shin and went up, just dabbing at him with my tongue at first and then as I got up higher licking more wetly so as I got to the inside of his thigh I could really feel the hairs of his leg dragging against the grain of my tongue. But I didn't move on beyond the crease at the top of his thigh; I moved straight down to the toes on his right foot and moved slowly up that leg. Careful as a cat I was. I didn't want to miss one scrap of cream.

It wasn't till I'd nearly reached the top of his right thigh that I found her message to me. But I couldn't have missed it because it stood out like a rose in full bloom. It really was a beautiful print she had made. I would not have expected less from such expert teeth. And it was very well placed – like a stylish tattoo – about an inch below where his balls would graze his thigh when he was standing.

I paused for a moment in my work, my tongue inert a few centimetres off from the rose. My lover groaned a little – it was not so much from pleasure as a nudge to go on. So I did; moving inwards this time, licking the wiry hair on his balls and feeling the weight of his balls as they lolled against my tongue, and then moving up in the crease between balls and thigh wondering whether to start in at the root of his But all the time I was thinking about her messa I should do about it. Should I ignore it? I ignore him, if that was what she'd been thinking. Or should I respond in kind? My tongue was still toying with the crown of hair at the base of his cock when I made up my mind. I moved up a few inches to where his belly began, soft and hairless. I found a spot I liked and nuzzled my nose in it first; and then I took it between my lips and held on like a clam and sucked. But then I thought NO. He'll see that. I stopped at once. It wasn't much of a mark I'd made so far. If I rubbed his belly a bit the blood would flow away. I gave the spot a perfunctory kiss and moved down.

Not to her side (she'd taken right). My mouth moving like a metal detector over him I made for a place that felt right. It was almost in the crease where it begins to be sweaty and to smell like Brie, and this time I used my teeth. I could feel his balls tighten with excitement and this excitement communicated itself to me pretty fast. I only glimpsed the rose I'd made as I took my mouth away. But I was pleased to see that it was brighter than hers.

And to be honest I didn't give it another thought. Not until about three weeks later when, without wishing to be repetitive, I found myself lingering on the same area of my lover's anatomy. And she'd done it again. Not once, but many many times. Some had bloomed and faded, born to blush unseen. But three new ones stood out proud and bright. Mine had of course disappeared by then; but I felt sure she must have seen it. Why else would she have been so assiduous in replacing each paling print with one that was fresh and new and couldn't be missed? She had to be answered.

Quality rather than quantity I thought – and was sure that she'd agree since her quantity had only been a matter of securing visibility. I decided to match the best of her new ones. A little lower than my last, but still high up on the inside of his left thigh. My print was exactly opposite hers: like a lipstick kiss where his thighs would touch each other. He'd moaned, and pressed down on my head as I was doing it. He was having a good time these days.

We managed to see quite a lot of each other at that time. She was working on a new series and making a lot of short trips to Italy and Spain. (She has a great deal of energy – she can get off an aeroplane and just carry on.) And my lover's a bit of a baby – he doesn't care for being on his own. And I think he probably assumes that she goes off with all kinds of men when she's away. But I know better. She has told me of her constancy and I have told her of mine. Yes. She and I continued to speak to each other. We became increasingly exact and resourceful in our markings. Quite witty really: as I prized his buttocks apart to place a mark she'd have to hunt for, I saw she'd got there first. My reply simply meant 'touché'. But sometimes I was the leader. In an attempt to break with the genital fixation we'd got into, I sucked out a beautiful cupid's bow on the sole of his (right) foot. And sure enough – five days later – it was kiss for kiss: a mark to match on his left sole. We'd swapped grounds. It was free for all.

My lover's inner thighs were by now speckled with bites. He reminded me of an old chair the painters had found to stand on when they were decorating the library. Cigarettes had been stubbed out all over it making weals in the paint, and the men went on squashing their fags out on it till it was stippled like a steel band's drum. I began to pity his poor thighs and let them be.

Besides, there are other things to do than bite. Licking and touching for instance. I think people make too much fuss over genitals. They limit their possibilities by assuming that cocks are the only things that can go anywhere and that cunts are the only places to go. But the way I look at it each pore of any body's skin can be a cock or a cunt depending on its mood. Haven't you felt your skin when it's up and searching, pressing out and straining to get into every dent and cranny your lover's skin might offer? But then at other times each pore softens and opens into an eyelet longing to be filled. Skin's like velcro: hooks and loops, whichever one at will, and it can play the game of man and woman, fucker and fucked, in a much more nimble way than genitals can. That was one of the things I'd liked about my lover. He knew about skin. Touching for him was not a cursory business to be undergone because women liked it – get them horny so the real show could start. With us any part could become our sexual centre and it could be hooked or looped or slippery as silk.

But that began to change after the biting correspondence began. As my tongue tip played with the hairs above his belly, feeling the energy that hovered to meet me, his palm would push down on my scalp and force me under to nose in on his cock and balls. And he'd go on pressing me, forcing my face closer and closer in till I'd submit and make yet another mark with my lips and teeth. And then he'd groan and I could imagine his cock arching out into a stretch and then ready to go into me. I expect it was the same for his wife.

After a while the bites I gave were sulky and obliging and not for her in any way. I just wanted him to stop holding my head down and I'd bite to get it over with though I could hardly bear to do it with the skin down there so bruised and tender. But he loved it. He wanted nothing else but to be gnawed at in his bruised parts and then to ram in his cock and fuck.

Other things changed about him too. There was something driven and distracted about him which left me feeling there was not much point in saying anything at all. In the past we'd had crazy, fantasy conversations: we'd choose characters for an evening and then see how far we could go with them, using them on the other people we met and keeping straight faces. But I stopped when he began to smile like he was humouring me. Whatever we did – for we went on going for drives and walks as well as out for meals – I began to get the feeling that he was mentally drumming his fingers until the time we could get home and into bed. It's hard to explain why it was so unpleasant: it wasn't like the old, shared excitement when we took pleasure in everything we did together and, even though we were longing to touch each other more, there was a fineness in the waiting. No; it was different. Worse. I'd begun to feel like an adjunct. Something to be endured and put up with because what he wanted – which was not me – couldn't be had without me.

Which explains why I haven't seen him for a month. He's been persistent – even urgent – in his attempts to see me but he hasn't found the right tone of voice yet. One touch of the old lightness and I'd be back like a shot. I miss that, but he seems to have lost it.

But I've seen more of her recently. She's been using the library quite a lot and I've had to help her over some inter-library loans. She's looking a bit drawn. Perhaps the pace of her life is catching up with her, but I don't like to see it. And her creamy skin isn't glowing in quite the old way. She was talking to me the other day when it was time for my tea break. So I said why didn't she join me. We went to the old-fashioned tea rooms down the road and sat among the old ladies with their hats. I was so pleased to have her with me that I ordered a plate of mixed cakes. It upset me to see her wasting away and I wanted to watch her tuck in.

Elizabeth Cook lives in East London and teaches part-time in London prisons. Her book on Renaissance poetry, *Seeing Through Words*, was published in 1986. She has translated Seneca's play *Thyestes* and has recently completed an edition of the works of John Keats.

A FAMILY FOR CLOTILDE

Luisa Valenzuela

Rolo spent that morning, like so many others, watching Rolando. For his father, taking a rest meant exhausting himself physically: long jogs down the deserted beach, racing, leaping, one exercise after another. He was forty-six and still physically fit. Rolo was about to turn seventeen; it was a serious age, and unlike his father, he felt sick and tired of the world.

Standing at the top of a dune, or drinking an orangeade, Rolo watched the sun glistening on his father's golden back as he conscientiously did his callisthenics. Rolando was a good athlete and he knew it. Rolo looked at his own pale body, narrow at the shoulders, and understood why he was ashamed to walk next to his father when they were both in bathing suits. Even so, as the season progressed, and they rented a cabana, Rolo preferred going to the beach with his father to sitting in a beach chair next to his mother all day long. She was unusually emphatic in her attitudes, and if in November and December she was busy in the house and didn't take a moment's rest, for the remainder of the vacation she would forget the house and family and dedicate herself entirely to sunbathing. She wanted to return to Buenos Aires looking as if she had had a good time.

That afternoon there was nothing to do, as usual, and Rolo sat on the fence and dreamed about dancing, about girls in bikinis, about friends he missed. At four o'clock Don Luis clambered up from the beach along the path between the dunes that led to Rolando's house. Don Luis's cart was massive, and corroded by the sea.

'Good afternoon,' said the driver.

'Hi,' said Rolo.

'You could make that sound more cheerful. I have the suitcases of the lady who's going to stay in the cottage in back of your house. Your family's lucky, I told your father, because at this time of year nobody rents or sells.'

The horses pulling the cart rested after the hard trek. Only the pony was impatient and breathing hard.

'Uh huh,' Rolo mumbled without enthusiasm, but he looked intently at the white leather bags and the enormous old-fashioned trunk.

'Looks like the lady's going to stay a long time, eh?'

'Uh huh.'

'All summer?'

'All summer, part of autumn, the rest of her life. That goes for us, too; we'll never move away from here. Buried.'

He dug his penknife into the trunk of a pine tree. He wanted to go away, anywhere. If only Pinamar were a port, then he could at least imagine trips. . .

It was Sunday morning. With his jacket over his shoulder, Rolo walked through the trees surrounding the house, along the border of thickly clustered acacias, to the garden of the rear cottage. He had forgotten about the new tenant, but there she was reclining on a deck chair in the shade, showing a great deal of white flesh and gleaming red hair. Rolo stopped short.

'Hi, darling. Where're you off to?' She had a warm, soft voice.

'To Mass,' he answered grudgingly.

'To Mass?' Coming from her, the word sounded new and mysterious.

The sun was burning bright. Rolo wanted to stretch out in the cool air under the pines and simply listen to her. Instead he said, 'Yes, to Mass. You may think our chapel small and

ugly and unfinished, but that's not what counts if you want to
go to Mass.'

'Hmm. And if you were to stay here at my side and sip a gin
and tonic, wouldn't that be nicer than going to church?'

'No.'

'Well, your good father would prefer to sit here with me. He
isn't like you. He doesn't go to Mass. Yesterday afternoon he
passed by here on horseback five times. Just a little while ago
I saw him in a bathing suit; he must be off for a swim. . .
Stay a bit.'

She had deep-set dark-grey eyes. Rolo ran off without
answering her.

I'll show that wild woman I'm not like my father, he thought.
Who does the old man think he is, coming through here all hot
and excited? I'll teach them. . .

As the days passed, Rolando grew pensive. Rolo followed
him all over the house, taunting him whenever he could. But
Rolando didn't complain; in fact, it was practically impossible
to drag a word out of him on any subject.

'Dear, don't put your feet on the sofa, you'll dirty the
cretonne.'

'Dear, move a little so I can open the windows and air the
place a bit.'

And the dear did as he was asked, without protest. Astonishing.

Rolo first became suspicious when he noticed that his father
no longer got up at seven o'clock to take his early-morning
swim. Then, one afternoon during siesta, he saw Rolando
sneaking out through the kitchen door. Rolo raced upstairs to
the attic and peered out of the small window just as Rolando
entered Clotilde's house – without knocking, as if she were
one of the family.

They're going to find out what I can do, and they'll have to
learn the hard way, Rolo thought. They'll see. No one plays
dirty with me. I was invited first.

Rolo had never thought of himself as patient, but sometimes
virtues surface in time of need. Squatting on the dry, brittle

leaves behind the bank of acacias, he waited two long hours for
Rolando to abandon her body that must be so white between
the sheets, so soft to sink one's hands into. He thought of the
other poor bodies he had known, withered and worn, smelling
of his friends who had been there before him.

Clotilde must be different, he thought, and he had her in
the palm of his hand. Now that he knew their secret and could
denounce them. Soon he would show those two he also was a
man. Rolo, little Rolo, would follow his father's footsteps to
Clotilde's flesh. He would put his mouth where his father's
had been, he would carefully imitate each of his gestures.
The wait was long and tortuous, but the compensation of
Clotilde's hot, slippery body would come.

A blossoming azalea exuded a subtle smell that Rolo was
not prepared to appreciate. Beyond the flowers, beyond the
walls of the house, he imagined his naked father on the white
Clotilde, and he knew his turn would come.

Rolando wouldn't take long. The door with the slightly flaky
green paint would open just wide enough for him to slip out,
and Rolo would only wait long enough to see Rolando recede
in the distance. Then he would enter quickly and take Clotilde
by force. She'd have no way to defend herself.

That wasn't how it happened at all, of course. Clotilde saw
him, called to him, and he surrendered as meekly as a puppy.
It was Clotilde who guided his hands along the trail of his
father's hands.

'He asked me to swear not to say anything to you, and I swore
and asked him to go on kissing me... As if I cared ...'

Rolando laughed a cold, empty laugh, but Clotilde went on
chattering. When she tried to cuddle up against his body,
however, the muscles of his back arched one by one, and he
leaped up, smashing his fist on the night table. A little while
later, though, he sauntered into the bathroom as if nothing had
happened. He came back looking calm and lay down beside
her, but then doubt assailed him again and he shook Clotilde
violently, shouting, 'I'm better than the kid, right? Tell me I'm
better than the kid!'

'Yes, yes.' she said, and she thought of the boy who had never dared to sigh, and she felt tender toward him.

The following afternoon, Rolando told his wife that he was going out to get some cigarettes, and she seemed to believe him.

Rolo, however, couldn't say, 'I'm going out to get some cigarettes,' because he wasn't allowed to smoke. But he was allowed to come and go as he pleased, so he didn't have to make up excuses in order to visit Clotilde and engage in something far more serious than smoking.

As soon as his father left, Rolo, as usual, ran upstairs to spy on him from the attic window. The scene was always the same: Rolando, hurrying, furtive, ran into her open arms, and he, Rolo, felt happy because he would soon be on the path his father had paved for him, thus proving that he was no less a man.

But any man is a man, given certain attributes. In a sense, Clotilde was as much a man as either of them: she manipulated them as she pleased, frustrating them, pitting one against the other, favouring one over the other. She was the real man there, and she knew it. She reaffirmed it every night in the bed that often bore the weight and heat of one of them before the weight and heat of the other had faded. Clotilde. She would look at herself in the mirror, caressing her full breasts, smiling and showing her teeth, white, even, indifferent. Thinking was a tremendous effort for her: she simply felt happy and at times nostalgic. She also enjoyed tantalizing those who had the good fortune to touch her. And she felt no remorse about it.

In the big house on the other side of the dense acacias and the soft rosy mattress of pine needles, Estela, Rolo's mother and Rolando's wife, was also in the habit of looking at herself in the bathroom mirror. Her image emerged from the cloud of foam she used to clean the mirror. She ran the rag back and forth furiously, sometimes allowing only her eyes to appear, sometimes an ear or a corner of her mouth that revealed a hurt expression. She would have loved to rub that image out altogether, but there it was, facing her, inexorable, and all she could do was wash the mirror and hope a little of the cleanliness would rub off on her soul.

She knew it: her two men were gone forever, gone to the other woman because Estela was soft and easy, not hard and strong like the other one.

Rolo crouched behind the thick maze of acacias. He knew that the door would open at any moment, and he curled up even more in his hiding place. But it was a false alarm, or, more accurately, a false hope. His father was lingering longer than usual on Clotilde's body; it wasn't fair; Rolo was restless. What if she was detaining him? Could she have asked his father not to leave her? Still, the one time he had asked her how Rolando caressed her, she had answered, 'Not exactly out of this world . . .'

'Please tell me what he does with you. I don't want to be less of a man.'

'No, I like the differences. He's a brute. He beats me. Sometimes he slaps me across the face and shouts while he's making love to me.'

She had turned toward him and put his uncombed head on her belly. 'But you are soft, almost like a girl. I like to stroke your face, your shoulders, your back.'

'Have you ever done it with a woman?'

'Hmm,' she had answered vaguely. Sometimes he interpreted the *hmm* as yes, sometimes as no, depending on his mood.

He had been hiding behind the acacias for over two hours. Soon his mother would wake up from her siesta; he was furious. Clotilde knew very well that he was there, but there wasn't even a sign from her. That whore. She was worse, devouring anything that came her way – men, women, old people, children; a sexual ostrich.

To calm himself, Rolo walked behind the cottage. Hidden behind the shutters, the father watched his son's every move.

He doesn't know yet Clotilde isn't here. What the hell, let him suffer. I'm suffering too, Rolando kept repeating to himself.

Rolo stopped abruptly. Behind the climbing jasmines, in

front of the bedroom window, there was a mound of cigar butts, some crushed, some smoked down to a nub, some only half smoked, all with a cork tip. His father had been there many times, probably hoping his son would leave Clotilde's bed once and for all so he, Rolando, could go back to her and have the last laugh.

Rolando knew his secret, he knew his son had also been there, just as he had been before him, just as he would be again. Always Rolando had to have the last word, the last loud laugh, the last act of love. His father always bested him, always flattened him out. It was Clotilde's fault this time for telling him everything, for not keeping her mouth shut. Whore.

Behind the shutters, Rolando felt jealous of his son and happy to see him standing there confused. Clotilde had left him a note saying she would be gone until evening. She must be avoiding him; she knew he would be coming that afternoon. And that poor boy, standing there disconsolate, believing his father was performing Heaven knows what feats, not realizing that those feats are usually a young man's prerogative.

On either side of the closed shutters, father and son stood overcome, defeated. He'll stay in there all afternoon, Rolo thought, all night, forcing her to forget about me. Finally Rolo decided to leave. He walked slowly down the path, kicking pebbles and telling himself that, after all, Clotilde must prefer women anyway, the struggle wasn't worth it.

Rolando watched Rolo move in the distance. He may be too thin, thought Rolando, and his back may curve, but still and all, Rolo is young and strong and intense in the way women like.

Neither of them could guess that Clotilde was fed up with the whole affair, with Rolo hiding in the garden while Rolando was with her, and then Rolando pacing back and forth in the garden like a caged lion, although he could never admit it. As if she didn't know that they were searching for each other through her.

That night, Rolo helped his mother wash the dishes, a thing he seldom did.

'Mama,' he said after a long silence, 'do you know the woman who rents the cottage in the back?'

'No.'

There was an uncomfortable pause.

'You should get to know her. Make friends with her. She's very nice.'

'I don't need friends. Not the likes of her, anyway.'

'Why not make friends with her, Mama? After all, she's our tenant.' It was a bold statement to make to a mother who must have known quite well what was going on. 'You could go see her tomorrow and bring her a piece of that delicious cake you make. . . '

His mother wiped the burners of the stove furiously, then took off her apron and went into the bedroom.

Rolando was in bed. He had not gone for a walk in the woods, he was not reading in the living room. He was simply there, installed in bed as if he'd been waiting for her.

She spent a long time in the bathroom and came back into the bedroom in her nightgown.

'Estela,' Rolando said, 'Estela, you've been alone so much, too much lately. If we're going to stay here another two months, why not get to know people?'

'My friends are coming after Epiphany . . .'

'That's a month away, Estela. Meanwhile what? Stay shut up in this house? The weather's nice now for the beach. You ought to have a friend to go with you.'

'You have someone in mind?'

'In mind, no . . . the tenant, maybe. She seems pleasant enough.'

It must be a conspiracy, she thought. They must be making fun of me. She was sick and tired of being treated like an idiot for trying to keep peace in the family. They wanted to see her act, well, she would act. The fight's on, she thought. Let's see who wins. An inspection of the enemy camp can't hurt; that will give me an equal chance.

'Fine,' she said, gently as usual. 'If tomorrow's all right with you, I'll go visit her and bring some cake for tea.'

Rolando was astonished at the ease with which he had convinced her.

The men in the family are sadder than ever. While they were enjoying themselves they could afford to overlook her pain. It had been a clean fight between men, altogether understandable. They had eaten with gusto, shown their happiness in an effort to make each other suffer. They had paid no attention to the woman who sat in front of them, doing her best not to burst into tears.

Now the situation is very different. Estela is exultant, she has turned into an eloquent conversationalist. She has acquired a new grandeur. She, Estela, now occupies an ample and warm place where the two men had once fit. Now Estela is alone and triumphant in Clotilde's bosom.

Listless, they never look at her or at each other. They only walk back and forth in the house that is no longer a home because Estela has neglected the floor, the meals. And she no longer bothers to put flowers on the table. She has other interests. From the last bite of lunch until sunset, she spends the day in Clotilde's cottage. A lightning friendship, one might say, blissful love at first sight, the reunion of queen bees, with the drones buzzing around like lost souls. Sometimes they circle around Estela, trying to get her back; at other times they attempt to get back to Clotilde. They haven't succeeded with either – no bread and no cake.

Finally, they are ready for a confrontation. But what can those two dispossessed beings say to each other, those two males who have learned that the only way they can reach each other is through silent competition?

The days go on until Rolo can stand it no longer. He walks over to his old hiding place to spy on the cottage. He has hoped to set his mother against his father, but the wind had blown another way: goodbye, Clotilde; goodbye, love; goodbye. Estela now takes up all her time, all her gestures, all her words. She had shown herself to be the most astute: she has conquered Clotilde effortlessly. 'You have a formidable mother,' Clotilde had said to him the one time he saw her alone. And she hadn't said another word – no apologies, no gratitude for what went on before. About-face, march, and once again she was inside her cottage with the door firmly closed.

Huddled behind the acacias, Rolo is remembering the past with Clotilde. He knows that a few feet away, Rolando is taking his customary walk behind the climbing jasmines. Both are caught in the same trap, spying on the women who are devoted to one another and have no intention of parting.

Neither knows what he is waiting for, and each ignores the other's presence. They ignore everything except the world from which they have been excluded forever. They listen, and each in his hiding place receives on his face the lash of a kind of laugh, a submissive laugh, somewhat ashamed, that rises suddenly to cover up something and then lowers in tone, changing into a whisper that filters into the bones. Rolo leaps up and runs toward the bedroom window and, unexpectedly, collides with his father, who has also left his hiding place on hearing that laugh that threatens not to end. They look at each other accusingly, but neithers says a word. They are both outside forever, and it is only because they had had the idea of putting Estela inside the cottage. Now Estela was never going to leave, for she had awakened Clotilde's laugh.

It is a well-tuned murmuring, like the pines, caressing, loving. Suddenly it begins to rain, softly at first, then with some fury. They remain in the garden, drenched, waiting until night falls.

Inside the cottage, Estela doesn't feel the cold, the rain, the night. She smiles with beatific happiness because her plan has succeeded. She makes Clotilde repeat once again the Act of Contrition and the Prayer to the Virgin. 'Hail Mary, full of grace . . .' The prayer returns and undulates like a laugh that leaves Clotilde's contrite lips. And Estela, who doesn't really care about Clotilde's contrition, smiles because she knows that she has won back her men.

translated by Hortense Carpentier and J. Jorger Castello

Luisa Valenzuela was born in Argentina in 1938 and now lives in New York. English translations of her work include *Strange Things Happen Here*, *The Open Door* and also *The Lizard's Tail*, published by Serpent's Tail in 1987.

GIRLS OF THE SIXTIES

Janice Eidus

The interviewer had placed an ad in the classified section of
The Village Voice:

> **PhD in sociology doing research
> for a book on the sex lives
> of women who were involved in
> the sixties' drop out/hippie/freak movement**

The paper had come out only yesterday, and already five
women had called. And this was going to be his first interview.

The woman was sitting across from him in the corner booth
in this dimly lit Italian café on MacDougal Street. He'd
chosen the booth because it was in the back and private.
And he'd chosen this café because it was usually fairly empty
in the late afternoon.

The woman was thirty-seven, she told him in answer to his
first question. Ten years older than he was, but he wouldn't
let her know that. Because he was balding, he looked older,
and he was proud of it.

Her hair was short and wavy, and she wore no make-
up, and a loose-fitting turtleneck sweater, tan, wide-waled
corduroy trousers, and brown shoes with round toes and

springy soles. He'd memorized all of these details even before
she'd sat down, before he turned on the tape recorder. And
she was dressed exactly as he'd expected, in a sexless style
that bordered on the mannish, yet wasn't even emphatic
enough for that. She could have been attractive. He had
nothing against older women. But, no matter what their
age, the women he found most appealing wore eyeshadow
and lipstick, and gold hearts on slender chains around their
tanned necks, and clothes that revealed the shapes of their
bodies.

'You want my . . . interpretation of "the sexuality of the sixties"?' Leaning forward, she tentatively repeated his question
back to him, as though he'd spoken some foreign words that
she didn't understand.

He nodded.

'Well,' she smiled, 'that's sort of a funny phrase – "the
sexuality of the sixties". Don't you think it's a funny phrase?'

He tried to keep his expression neutral. He suspected that
he'd get her to open up more if he appeared to be the
non-judgmental, quiet type.

'Okay,' she said, staring directly into his eyes, and leaning
back against the leather cushion of the booth, 'if we're going to
use that term, then, for me, "the sexuality of the sixties" meant
that a lot of beautiful, sexy, long-haired boys shared my bed
during those years. Maybe, in a way, too many long-haired
boys. Still,' she laughed airily, 'the truth is that I don't regret
having been with any of those long-haired boys. Not a one of
them.' She shrugged her shoulders. 'I really don't. After all, I
was just a long-haired girl myself.'

The waitress came over to take their order, and he noticed,
as she leaned over the table to place down some silverware,
that she didn't shave under her arms, and that the hair there
was thick and dark. He tried not to look at it, and he ordered a
cannoli and a cup of espresso. He'd never understood women
who, like this plump waitress in her sleeveless dress, didn't
shave their arms or their legs, who seemed to delight in
showing the world the hair which most women knew enough
to get rid of, or, at least, to hide.

'Just a decaffeinated cappuccino for me,' the woman smiled at the waitress.

When the waitress left, the woman turned her smile on him. 'God, I'd love a *cannoli*,' she said, 'but I'm watching my weight.'

He didn't smile back. He didn't want to encourage her to start talking about how sick and tired she was of always having to watch her calories because of all the men out there who oppressed women like her into wanting to look like emaciated fashion models. He simply wasn't interested. And, besides, she was thirty-seven. Who cared if she put on some extra pounds? Clearly, despite the way she dressed, she was vain. Probably it was a vanity left over from her days as a hippie girl. 'So, anyway,' he said, clearing his throat, 'there were a lot of these "long-haired boys" of the sixties, as you put it, in and out of your bed. Why don't you tell me some of the worst horror stories of your sex life as a girl in the sixties?'

'Horror stories?' She stared for the first time at the tape recorder. 'What do you mean?'

Maybe he was going too fast. He took a deep breath. He even forced himself to smile slightly. Maybe, in fact, it would be better if he appeared friendly and sympathetic toward her. 'I mean, you grew tired of these boys. You felt abused. You felt exhausted. Used up, perhaps?' *Used up* – that really was the way she seemed. Tired. Worn out. From all the things she'd done back in the sixties.

'No, I don't think so.' The woman ran her hand through her hair, and he saw a plain gold band on her wedding-ring finger. He also saw that she bit her fingernails and didn't wear nailpolish. 'Not used up,' she said. 'There weren't any real horror stories. Unless you mean . . .'

He gave her another smile. 'Yes? Unless I mean?'

'Well . . . maybe you mean something like this? I was about eighteen, I was at a party in Haight-Ashbury in San Francisco, a really wild sixties-type party, psychedelic posters on the wall, strobe lights, lots of pot and hashish . . .'

The waitress came over with the *cannoli*. 'I'm sorry, but the coffees will be coming out in a minute, okay? The kitchen's a little slow today, okay?'

He nodded curtly at the waitress, annoyed by the interruption. Also, he really wanted the espresso. He loved the bitter taste. He and his former dissertation adviser, who was now a friend, spent many long nights in dark, inexpensive cafés like this one, drinking cup after cup of espresso, and discussing the sixties, and women, and the state of the world, and the way things had deteriorated. His best times lately revolved around espresso. And he hoped that this interview with this woman with her pale, tired-looking face and her baggy corduroy trousers and her springy-soled shoes would turn into one of his best times. It would, it most definitely would, if it would help him to begin the book, which he so much wanted to write. He took a bite of the *cannoli.*

'Go on,' he said, wiping some sweet cream off his lips.

'So,' the woman said easily, 'this guy at the party in Haight-Ashbury, he was probably twenty-three at most, the quintessential beautiful hippie youth, long blonde hair in a ponytail to his waist, no shirt, tight, faded bluejeans with a peace symbol patch sewn on each knee . . . he came over to me and said, in this really seductive voice, "You're so beautiful, let's ball."' She began to giggle. 'Isn't that a funny word, too, now that you think of it?'

Again, he was annoyed. 'Isn't what a funny word?' He hoped he wasn't showing his annoyance. He really did need her to feel comfortable talking to him. He took another bite of the *cannoli.*

'*Ball.*' She seemed surprised that he had to ask. 'Isn't "ball" a funny word to use to connote the sexual act?'

The waitress returned to their table with the two cups of coffee.

He welcomed the bitter espresso. Eagerly, he took a sip before answering the woman. 'I see . . . so you find "ball" a funny word for sex.' Without any emotion, he repeated her own words back to her, in the way that he imagined psychotherapists did with their patients. This woman probably liked shrinks. She probably felt comfortable pouring out her guilty secrets to them.

She nodded. 'Right. But, I suppose,' she said thoughtfully, blowing on her cappuccino, '"ball" can also be seen as a nice word, implying that sex was just so wonderful for us all back then during the sixties. Like we were all just having a sexual ball together! That's sort of a sweet way to look at it, isn't it?'

He forced himself to nod. 'So, you also find the word "ball" a nice word for sex,' he said, in the same shrink-like tone.

She frowned at him, and then took a sip of her cappuccino. 'Hot,' she said, blowing on it again. 'So, anyway,' she continued, 'whether it's funny or sweet, I was into this whole idea of being the ideal hippie girl who was free to make love to whomever she pleased, whenever she pleased, so I said yes to this guy at the party. I told him that it would be "far out",' she smiled, 'to ball him right away, right there and then, even though I'd never seen him before. I was thinking how wonderful it all was, to be so different than my uptight parents with their, you know, bourgeois, suburban mentality . . .' She smiled again. 'So then he and I went upstairs to an empty bedroom in the house where the party was taking place, and I immediately began removing all my clothes, my long Mexican dress, my sandals . . . I felt so free, so unrestrained, so beautiful . . . And then the guy absolutely freaked out on me. He began yelling at me, telling me that girls should wait for guys to undress them, that I'd ruined everything by being so impatient and aggressive, that I'd completely blown it, and that he wasn't "into balling me" any more.' She frowned again. 'I guess that was pretty horrible for me. Pretty confusing, to say the least. Still, as we've all figured out by now, the sexual revolution of the sixties wasn't the women's revolution. But – revolutions aside – I guess that's a real sixties' horror story for you to use in your book. What's the premise of your book, anyway?'

He didn't say anything. He had no intention of telling her yet about his idea for the book. Besides, it wasn't just an idea. It was a conviction. It was his guiding light, his philosophy, his credo. Sometimes, recently, especially when he was teaching, he felt lost. Distanced from his students, who didn't seem to care at all about his class, who didn't seem to care at all about anything, really, except the 'fun' classes, the ones in which the professors chattered on and on about television shows and science-fiction magazines. But once he began writing his book, he was sure, he'd feel better. Because he knew that the girls of the sixties had left the world a dark legacy, and he would find a way to write about it, to prove it, to change things. And he would save himself, in the process.

'So, okay,' she said, looking up at him, 'what's your next question?'

'I see by your ring finger,' he said, 'that you've gone ahead and gotten married.'

'*Gone ahead*?' she asked. 'Gone ahead and gotten married?' She stared at the tape recorder again. 'What is *gone ahead* supposed to imply, may I ask?'

She was such an irritating person. 'It's just an expression,' he said, taking a long sip of the bitter espresso, 'that's all. What I meant is that you're married now. Legally married? Or by some hippie guru? Or even more informally, just an agreement among friends?'

'Legally married,' she laughed. 'When I was twenty-nine. Alan and I wrote our own vows so they'd be more meaningful. I wore a Mexican wedding dress, and Alan wore white pants and an embroidered shirt, also from Mexico. In fact, we bought them down the block, right here on MacDougal Street. There used to be this wonderful Mexican boutique . . .'

He nearly shuddered, imagining the two of them, this plain, unadorned woman standing next to a skinny, bearded man in feminine-looking clothes, and their pretentious, romantic notions about the simplicity of Mexican peasants.

'Our honeymoon was short and sweet, nothing fancy,' she went on, sounding cheerful, 'a motel in Woodstock. Alan and I had both been there for the big festival, you know, and we thought it would be a funny thing to do. Don't you think that was a funny idea for a honeymoon? It was wonderful, actually.'

'Yes, but how does your husband – how does Alan – feel

about your having been with all of these characters during the sixties?'

'"Characters"?' she asked. 'That's a funny word, too. As though you see all of us as characters from some play. Is the premise of your book going to be that the sixties were basically just theater, not real life? Or something like that? That we never accomplished anything real, that we were just about image and superficiality? I've heard people say things like that before, you know. It's not exactly new.' Her voice was polite.

'I'm glad that you find my vocabulary so amusing,' he said. 'And no, I don't think that the sixties were "theater". Shakespeare is theater. And there was absolutely nothing Shakespearian about the chaos of the the sixties.' He paused, stopping himself before he revealed too much. It would destroy the interview, ruin her spontaneity, if he gave her more information. 'All that I mean by "characters",' he went on, deliberately keeping both his voice and his features as expressionless as possible, 'is . . .' he searched for the right word, '. . . just what you, yourself, said before. That there were a lot of long-haired boys around. So what I'm asking is this – how does your husband feel about your having been with all of those long-haired boys of the sixties?'

'Why in the world would Alan feel anything about them?' Again, she seemed genuinely surprised by his question.

The waitress returned. She removed his cup and his plate. It seemed to him, though, that she was looking with distaste at the thick, muddy deposit which had formed at the bottom of his cup. If he came back to this place again, he'd be sure to avoid this waitress, who, he now noticed, also had some dark hair above her upper lip. There was something unnatural about this waitress. Or, no, maybe it was exactly the opposite. Maybe she was *too* natural. Primitive, almost.

'Another espresso,' he said, not looking at her, 'and another *cannoli.*' Despite the unappetizing waitress, he felt extremely hungry, even though he'd had both a large breakfast and lunch.

'Nothing more for me, thanks,' the woman said.

'Well, don't you miss those days?' he tried again, after the waitress had gone. 'I mean, doesn't your husband lose some of his ... charm ... compared to your memories of the beautiful, long-haired boys of the sixties? Those youths must have been at their sexual peaks then ... You must compare him, sexually, in bed, to your memories of those boys. There must have been so many...'

'But I don't do that. Why would I? Alan is delightful. Alan is unique. Well, some of the long-haired, sixties' boys were delightful and unique, too. One who played a twelve-string guitar right after we made love. Another who read my Tarot cards to make sure we were compatible before we made love. That was so sweet, so innocent, so ... sixties, I guess. Don't you find that sweet and innocent? Maybe the sixties *were* just theater, in a way. Children's theater. Now, there's a great idea for a book – that the entire decade of the sixties was just a very long marionette show intended to bring smiles to the faces of small children! How about that? Now, you've got to agree that that's a great idea for a book!'

He refused even to acknowledge her silly idea. Instead, he drummed his fingers on the table, wishing that the waitress would hurry up with his second cup of espresso. 'Let's get back to my question, okay? How does your husband feel about that boy, the one with the twelve-string guitar? And how does he feel about the other one, the "sweet, innocent" boy with the Tarot cards.'

'*Feel* about them? Alan didn't even know them. I'd met those boys years before Alan and I even met. I was just a girl then. By the time I met Alan, I was a woman. How could he possibly feel anything about them?'

The waitress was back. He practically grabbed the cup from her. 'But, still,' he continued, washing down a bite of the *cannoli* with the bitter espresso, 'how could your husband ever hope to measure up to the wild memories you have? How could anyone ever measure up?' He was trying not to sound as irritated as he felt. This woman was impossible, deliberately provoking him by obsessing on the meanings of words and phrases from the sixties, and then coming up with her own ideas for books. It was crazy, but maybe she really *was* writing her own book. Some sort of *apologia* for what she'd done? No, she was just being difficult. She was the kind of woman who prided herself on being difficult.

'I'm sorry,' she said, looking at him oddly, 'but your vocabulary really does amuse me. "*Wild memories*." What a funny notion.'

Despite how difficult she was, he was still determined to make the interview work, to get something out of her that he could use. In fact, she could very well turn out to be the catalyst that would finally get him started on the book. 'Well, what about your guilt? Does that amuse you, too?' he asked.

'My guilt?'

'Yes, your guilt. Even now, you must wake up sweating, remembering a certain night from the sixties, a night about which you're now deeply ashamed. A night, let's say, when you danced naked in front of strangers at a wild party in an East Village loft! Or maybe it isn't that night that haunts you. Maybe it's the morning after that night, when you woke up next to a hippie boy with needle tracks along his arms whose name you didn't even know! You must have plenty of bad dreams about those nights and mornings, about those wild parties, about the long-haired boys, about the way you behaved back then in the sixties, dreams that scare you, dreams that make you feel guilty!'

She leaned over, speaking slowly and deliberately into the microphone of the tape recorder. 'Okay. I'll share my very worst dream with you . . . I'm a little girl and my mother and father go away on a business trip and never return. It's a dream I've been having since I was six. And my second worst dream is that someone is throwing pancakes at me, and I keep trying to run, but my feet get stuck in the maple syrup . . .'

'That's very amusing,' he said. He felt tempted to shut off the tape recorder, and to call the interview finished. He might as well just give up and admit that he was getting nowhere with her. It didn't seem to matter whether he was neutral, or friendly, or shrink-like, or irritable. She was just too difficult. Now that he thought about it, all of the women who answered the ad were bound to be this difficult and provocative. Maybe it wasn't worth it to go through with these interviews. No, too much was at stake for him with this book. Besides, if he stopped the interview now, she would feel victorious, he was sure of that. She would feel as though she'd won some unnamed battle between them. And he couldn't stand that. So he took a deep breath, and he smiled again. 'Well, then, what about drugs?' He took the last bite of the *cannoli.*

'Drugs?' She laughed softly. 'I did do some. We all did. The sixties and drugs,' she said, 'we were some combo, weren't we? It's amazing, really, to think about our willingness to ingest just about *anything* in order to elevate our spiritual planes, or whatever it was we hoped that we were doing. I mean, I was so naive then that I even believed that smoking bananas could get you high. . . You remember that, don't you, when we all went through that silly banana craze?'

'No, I don't remember,' he replied, evenly. 'I don't remember the bananas.' She actually seemed to believe that he'd been a wild teenager back then also, smoking pot and hashish and banana peels, removing his clothes at the drop of a hat, chattering away about astrology, holding up his fingers in the peace sign and flinging flowers in the faces of policemen.

'Let's forget about the bananas,' he said. 'I'm asking you about drugs. What about the drugs?'

'Okay, fine,' she said. 'You want a sixties' drug story for your book, I'll give you a sixties' drug story for your book. Whatever your book may be.'

He leaned back, feeling pleased that he hadn't given up and turned off the tape recorder. He'd get something out of her, yet. He was sure of it.

'One time when I was tripping on acid,' she said, 'I thought some guys in this apartment in Brooklyn Heights were going to rub butter in my eyes. It was terrifying. I got so paranoid.' She smiled. 'But I was wrong, of course. They were tripping, too, and they were really feeling very peaceful and loving. They didn't have the slightest desire to rub butter in my eyes. They were just trying to bake a cake, so they were getting butter all over the place. Another time on acid I saw blue everywhere. It was incredible. Blue on the ground, on my friends' faces, on the moon, on my own arms, my legs ... so absolutely beautiful. An entirely blue, sensual, sixties' world.'

'What about the long-term effects?' He felt his shoulders tense. 'Undoubtedly, your memory is impaired. Too often, you find yourself, all these years later, still craving those highs. Wouldn't it be easier for you to take care of your daily tasks stoned? Or maybe you *have* kept it up, maybe you can't stop smoking pot, even now? Still take a toke or two before grocery shopping? Makes it easier to read all those natural, organic ingredients on the labels, right? So you pop some downers, and you take a few uppers every now and then?'

'Oh, please,' she said, wiping her eyes. 'Your vocabulary. I'm sorry. Those words. "Uppers." "Downers." I'm sorry, it's so funny to me. I can't help it.' She shook her head. 'No. Seriously. I don't pop pills. Or smoke dope. I sculpt, actually. I've been part of two important group shows recently. Things look promising. I stay alert. I also play softball. And Alan and I are thinking of having a child soon, so I'm planning on staying healthy.'

He stared at her.

'You're sneering at me,' she said, sounding curious, but not upset. 'Actually sneering. What have I said? Did I contradict something in your book?'

'You want to have a child?' He was excited now, and, if he felt like sneering at her, he would. Because now he had her exactly where he wanted her, and he was free to do or say whatever he wanted. The interview had led, finally, to the place where he'd wanted it to go all along. The path had been circuitous and rocky, but he didn't care. It had been worth it. This washed-out looking woman had selfishly delayed motherhood for so long. And now, after all this time, and after all of the things she'd done, she wanted, on top of everything else, to have a child. She had the nerve to sit there and tell him calmly and smugly that she wanted it all. Marriage, a hot-shot career as a sculptor, and a child, to boot. But he had a surprise for her. She *couldn't* have it all. She was the last

person on earth who deserved it all. She would see. *If* she
were able to conceive – and from what he'd heard, the girls
of the sixties had an awfully hard time doing that when they
were finally ready to, because of all the drugs and promiscuity
of their youth – she'd be a miserable, unfit mother, raising
a miserable, unfit child. 'You want to have a child now?' he
repeated, fully aware that his voice was contemptuous. 'Don't
you think it's just a little bit late for you? And of course you
wouldn't dream of giving up your oh-so-important career of
sculpting for your child's sake, would you? Certainly not.
The world would be a lesser place, wouldn't it, without
your sculptures in it? I bet you wouldn't even give up your
softball, would you? I bet you wouldn't even miss going to
one precious softball game for the sake of your child, would
you?'

'I want to know why you're sneering at me like this, and
what's going on here,' she said, at last sounding angry. 'What
is your agenda?'

He shut off the tape recorder. There was no need to listen
to her any longer. He'd gotten her to say all that he'd ever
really wanted her to say. She'd admitted that she wouldn't
be a good mother. That she couldn't be. He didn't owe
her another word. He'd been right all along. The girls of
the sixties were absolutely doomed. 'I'm satisfied with this
interview,' he said. 'It's gone very well. I don't have any
more questions.' He gestured to the bushy-haired waitress
to bring him the check. There was no reason to remain in
this claustrophobic café another moment. He was feeling
very, very pleased. He would write his book, and he would
get it published, and he would probably be awarded ten-
ure, too, in the bargain, for whatever that was worth. Most
important of all, though, would be that what he had to say
– what he alone could say – about the dark and evil legacy
of the girls of the sixties, would make a difference. A big
difference. It would matter. It would help to change things,
to change them back to the way they must have been once.
Before the girls of the sixties had marched onto the scene
in their Mexican peasant dresses, with their long, shaggy

hair, their dazed, drugged-out eyes, and their bare, dirty feet.

'Listen,' she said, angrily, reaching into her big, bulky leather bag, the kind of bag the ageing girls of the sixties always carried, 'I'll pay for my own cappuccino. I answered your ad on a whim, simply because I was curious. I didn't know what to expect. But since I've answered all of your questions honestly, I'd like you to tell me something honestly, before I go. Tell me what it is that you're so set on trying to prove to the world in this book of yours. Tell me what it is that you have such a burning need to say about my sex life, about the sex lives of the girls of the sixties!'

He reached into his jacket and took out his wallet. He didn't care that she was getting angry. In fact, he was glad that he'd provoked her into anger. After all, she'd been deliberately provoking him all along, so it felt good to give her a taste of her own medicine. But it did annoy him that she appeared to want to make some sort of self-righteous statement about her independence by paying for her own cappuccino. 'No, no,' he said, placing a five-dollar bill on the table, 'I'll pay. I insist. It's my ad. My book. My interview. I'll pay.'

'Sure, okay, fine. You pay. I don't really care which of us pays for my damned cappuccino. You just tell me what point you're going to make in this book. That's all I want to know right now.'

'The sixties,' he began, softly. He was happy, finally, to be able to tell her exactly what it was that she had done. 'You and the others back then. You've ruined things for the rest of us. You were unhealthy, unnatural. You went against tradition, against nature. Against womanhood itself. You and your girlfriends with your ideas about freedom and orgasms ... it was you and your sexual promiscuity that's led us to what we've come to today, with disease and drug addiction running rampant, ruining and polluting things. Our students are taught garbage in the universities, by professors who don't even deserve the title, because of you, the girls of the sixties. And, yes, it's you – the girls – who are far more responsible than the long-haired boys. Oh, the boys are guilty, too, there's no doubt about it, but they're not as guilty as you. Because it's your children who turn to the streets, and the gutters, your children who become runaways and crack addicts and prostitutes and illiterates, because you can't even be a mother to them! The sixties made you all unfit to be mothers! You all thought you knew better than everyone else. They were the hawks, weren't they, the mean, old, ugly hawks. And you were the doves, the pretty little white doves. But take a close look at yourself now. Doves age, too, you know. It gets harder and harder to fly, the older the dove gets, doesn't it? And even so, even now, with what the world has become, with what you've turned it into, you still insist that you were right. Little doves,' the interviewer said, 'little sexed-up sixties' doves now with your crow's feet, and your cellulite, and your pale, washed-out faces, and your emasculated husbands, and your screwed-up little kids . . .'

She stood up. She stared down at him. 'Okay,' she said. Her voice was flat. 'You've made your point. I get it. I wish I didn't, but I do. So I'm leaving now. And let's just say that this has been . . . "real", as we used to say in the sixties. Very, very real. All too real. Much more real – and much more scarey – than any childhood nightmare could ever be.' She turned and walked quickly out of the café, without looking back.

And then, for some reason, he changed his mind about leaving the cafe. He suddenly craved another *cannoli*, another espresso. He turned the tape recorder back on. He pressed the rewind button. He wanted to hear the tape again, all the way through. He wanted to savour every single word. Maybe she'd even come back. And, if not, well, there would be the other interviews. He was looking forward to them.

Janice Eidus lives in New York City with her husband, and their cat, Antigone. She is the author of *Faithful Rebecca* as well as the collection of short stories, *Vito Loves Geraldine*, published by Serpent's Tail. Awards for her fiction include a B. Dalton Fellowship and a Redbook Young Writers Award. She is a member of The National Book Critics Circle.

BAG LADY

Bel Mooney

It was eight in the morning when he first saw her. Not that you would call something like that a *her* ... nobody would. It made a mockery.

The bus was crowded: people coughing, edging from each other's newspapers, resting sandwich boxes on knees, not talking much. Always the same, this vast, slow unwilling movement onwards, towards the day.

'Nice pair.' The boy across the aisle, who could not have been more than sixteen, shuffled his boots and slapped the back of his hand down on the newspaper, so that the image of a naked girl crackled and withdrew, her breasts folding in on themselves. 'Uh.' The other boy whose hands, large and calloused and whitened with plaster, rested loosely on his knees, kept his eyes fixed on the window. His companion was staring avidly at the picture, smoothed out now. 'Could do some damage there, mate,' he said, with a short laugh.

Nobby Price barely noticed these things. He was rising, stretching for the strap as the bus lurched around a corner. His corner: the little line of shops – the Star Café, the small supermarket with a grille on its window, the Indian takeaway promising 'Real fish and chips', the Rave Cave boutique with the word 'Seperates' misspelt on its faded awning and the small sweetshop and tobacconist – leading up to the ornately etched glass windows of the Prince Albert on the corner itself, saloon bar entrance on Princes Street, lounge bar on Elton Road. And in the middle, between the takeaway and the Rave Cave, his own shop, there for ten years now. A grille over his small window too, but it appeared to protect nothing more than a dusty brown blind.

Nobby frowned as the bus juddered to a halt just a hundred yards down Elton Road. Someone waiting outside his shop – but that was not it. The lettering. There was no doubt that he would have to have it re-done. ADULT MAGAZINES. The sign was indistinct. He turned the corner.

Nobby took a pride in his shop. Now he understood more about things, he was proud he took after his grandmother. 'You have to keep up appearances, Malcolm,' Nan used to say, as she scoured the doorstep, her massive rear vibrating with the force of her attack on its perfectly clean surface. Doilies on the plates, and slippers by the door – and still she would breathe, 'Just look at the state of the place,' bending with difficulty to pick an imaginary speck of dusk from the threadbare rug, then poking the little fire with such vigour that the back boiler roared. Always, when she went to the shops, she wore a hat and gloves, her coat buttoned firmly even in warm weather. 'Neat and clean, Malcolm, that's my motto.'

He saw that the figure outside his shop was far from neat and clean. A bundle of rags, grey-brown like the street, lurked half in his doorway, half out, with a large bulging plastic bag beside it. *It*. Not a person, a thing. Nobby felt a second's uneasiness, as if the grimy walls of the street shrank for an instant in fear. But, 'Oi, you . . . !' he shouted, 'Git out of it!'

The effect was immediate. The bundle of rags gathered itself together, somehow absorbed the plastic bag into its mass, and lurched away up the street with surprising speed. Briefly, it glanced over its shoulder and Nobby glimpsed a face grey with dirt, and a mouth gaping black like a cave, as if laughing silently. Long grey hair hung down its back in greasy strands.

'Bleeding bag ladies,' he mumbled, searching for his keys.

Inside the shop he switched on the fluorescent light, its bright cool blueness making him blink after the soft mono-chrome of the street. He looked around with satisfaction. Once this had been a small grocer's. He had retained the old polished counter, and kept it mirror-like with spray polish. 'I love to see things all clean and shiny,' Nan used to say, as she ground the duster into a tin of lavender wax and attacked the furniture. And little Malcolm, plump even then, and dressed in old-fashioned clothes which drew mockery at school, would walk round after her, watching and asking, 'But *why*, Nan?'

'Why what, love?'

'*Why* did me Mam leave me? Didn't she want a baby?'

The lips would press tightly together, and the duster perform its circles with vigour. 'Malcolm Price! No good ever came. . .' She never said anything, not ever, and Nobby would sneak into her bedroom to take the single photograph from the bottom drawer, and stare at the pretty woman with a smile so wide you might drown in it, and whose hair curled in a roll right round her head – wondering.

Now he ran a hand over the counter, and stood, looking at the small shop. Twice a week he mopped the black-and-white tiled floor, panting with the effort and paying special attention to the corners. Behind him, in the wooden drawers where the grocer had kept dry goods, was the unusual material, brought out for certain regulars with particular tastes. And all round the shop, in neat wooden racks was the usual stuff, most of it shrink wrapped, but some of it, the harmless magazines, dog-eared beneath his stenciled notice advising clients of the shop's cut-price swap service. Nobby had bought a child's alphabet stencil, and done the notice carefully in red biro, covering his work with transparent stick-on plastic.

He put the kettle on, in the tiny galley behind the shop, next to the store room, and waited.

Once a journalist had come from London to write an article, one of those women who sparkle at people, dazzling them, and something in her face had reminded him faintly, disturbingly, of that photograph in the drawer. He had let her spend the day in the shop, even though at least six clients took one look and retreated, seeing a woman at the counter. 'You're driving them away, Sara,' he joked, making more tea.

'What made you start?' she asked.

'Start what?'

She waved a hand around. 'This. Selling this ... er ... stuff.'

'You think it's terrible don't you, love? Well, shall I tell you something? This is a service I'm giving here. If it wasn't for me, these blokes, they'd have nothing.'

'Well, they've got nothing now – really,' she said, smiling at him, so widely and brightly that he had to turn away, and busy himself tidying the racks.

'Yes, they have,' he said, 'they've got me.'

'But *how* ... I mean, why this?'

Nobby shrugged. 'I dunno ... I spent my life ducking and diving, a bit of this and a bit of that, and I ended up here. I always wanted my own shop ... and that's about it.'

'But *this* ...'

'Just something people need to buy. Like sliced bread,' he laughed.

That day one or two young men came in, looking for the stuff showing breasts so big they seemed deformed, but that was it. By afternoon he could see the journalist was bored. So he made up a few stories of police raids, closed up the shop and took her on a walk through the neighbourhood. She brightened as a couple of the girls chatted to him on a corner ('Wanna free go, Nobby?' – laughing loudly), and Tony, who owned the massage parlour told his usual jokes, and the CID man, Andy, in his leather and jeans, promised Nobby that he'd turn a blind eye if he slipped a couple of mags in the window. 'Gotta watch the law though,' he said, without smiling. 'We're bound to get some old bag complaining.' Then he grinned at Sara, fancying her.

It all went into her notebook, surreptitiously, and then she had gone, flashing her smile in farewell. Nobby waited eagerly for the magazine. He didn't read much, and it took him a long time to finish the columns of print. When he had finished, he walked into the back and looked into the old spotted mirror that hung in the toilet. He knew what he would see, having no illusions – but you stop *looking* at your own face, as you get older. Nan used to stand him by the mirror, and spatter him with water as she dragged a wet comb through his hair. His face was pink then, scrubbed with a coarse flannel. Now . . . he saw it fleshy, almost fat, with the straight fringe he had cut across his forehead, combing the hair straight from the back to cover the thinning patch.

'A small stout middle-aged man, almost revelling in his own ugliness,' she wrote, *'whose days are spent in mind-numbing monotony, shrivelling the spirit.'*

But he *liked* his days. Besides, he thought, contemplating the glass, his face was not that bad. He had seen worse. Old Mr Evans, who kept a blow-up dolly in his bedsit, came in every Wednesday at nine in the morning, on his way home from his night watchman's job, to buy a new magazine. He never returned them, and sometimes Nobby thought of the piles of magazines growing taller and taller, until Mr Evans ate off them, and sat on them, and slept on them. Paper furniture in full colour. But *his* face . . . there had been a fire once, and so half his skull was prawn-pink and taut, the features stretched tight, like a mask, whilst the other side of his face hung in wrinkly jowels. Nobby joked to another customer, one day, when old Evans had shuffled out with his new purchase inside his overcoat, that no wonder he was a good night watchman, because he would terrify any intruder.

'And at night Nobby goes home to his small bedsit, where he keeps a photograph of his grandmother on the mantelpiece, and tattered pornographic stock under his bed, and listens to the clock ticking, wondering why he is alone. He never asks questions about what he does . . .'

She made it sound so sad, so hopeless – the life of a small plump no-hoper trading in dirty books, instead of a perfectly happy shopkeeper giving a service, quite happy to put his feet up at night and watch the TV. He could not recall telling her about his Nan's picture, but what was wrong with having it on the mantelpiece? Thank goodness he did not forget himself (that smiling face, dazzling, inviting confidences) and tell her that tucked behind it was the other picture, of the pretty woman with the hair-halo. She would have made that sound even sadder. As for the questions . . . 'No good ever came of asking questions, Malcolm.'

After about twenty minutes the first customer came in, quickly followed by two more. He had seen them all before, and nodded greeting. They all began by browsing in the unwrapped stock, then moved to flick through the shrink-wrapped covers, sometimes stopping to stare at a particular cover, all pink flesh and strategically placed stickers. 'Nice day now,' said one man to Nobby, as he passed cash across the counter.

Nobby followed him to the door to look out. The rain had stopped; a watery sun lit the city street, streaking puddles with silver blue. As the customer murmured goodbye and turned to walk away, Nobby noticed *her* again. The bag lady was standing motionless across the road, staring at the shop. There was something deliberate, almost expectant about her stillness – as someone will freeze, waiting for the shutter to click.

Nobby opened his mouth to shout, then closed it again. He had no right; she was not standing on his doorstep; it was a matter for the police if she was causing an obstruction – not for him. Yet that did not calm his sudden rage. He did not want her there, that was all. 'Bad for business,' he muttered to himself.

He slammed the door, making its metal grille rattle. Seeing they were alone the man left in the shop sidled up to Nobby, whispering, 'I'm looking for y'know, something, a bit . . . a bit more . . .'

'You want the hard stuff, mate. Any particular bag?'

The man's eyes flickered. He was about fifty, quite well dressed, and had been in the shop once before. Usually Nobby could remember when customers asked for something special, but this one defeated him. Sometimes he would try to guess: something about the mouth of some men showed their secret desire to see girls tied tightly, heads pulled back by their hair, limbs twisted into submission – see them punished. Nobby sometimes entertained himself by placing mental bets, as he watched customers finger though his wares. What about this one? Little boys perhaps . . .

The man looked around again, and whispered hoarsely,

even though there was no one to hear, 'I'm an ... er ... animal lover, if you see what I mean?'

Nobby turned to the drawer.

'Here,' he said, dumping a small pile of magazines on the counter. 'Some good stuff in there. Not cheap mind, and I'm not unwrapping any of it.'

It pleased him that they went away with what they wanted. Personally, he once said to Andy, over a pint, he wouldn't give tuppence for any of it, not even the normal stuff. 'I don't know why they do it, these birds, that's for sure.' Andy laughed and emptied his glass. 'You're not normal, Nobby, that's your trouble. The only man I know who works in a sweet shop and spits out chocolate! Turns *me* on all right ... Anyway, you know as well as I do why they do it. They do it 'cos they want the money and they're little slags. Now, if you'll excuse me, I got to go and meet this bloke – my new grass, and he's a right bastard ...'

At 12.30 prompt as usual, Nobby locked up and went to the Star Café for dinner. Sitting down with his plate of sausage, egg and chips, he saw her again, in the corner, her back to the room. Again the wave of irritation washed over him, and he waved a hand at Avril. She stood by his table, wiping her hands on her apron.

'What's up, Nobby, sausages not done right for you?'

'Why'd you let that dirty old woman in here?' he asked abruptly.

Avril glanced across to where the bag lady sat, or rather squatted, at the red formica table, her back hunched.

'Her? Oh, she's not doing any harm. As long as she can pay for her cuppa ...'

'Seen her before, have you?'

She shook her head and shrugged. 'They pass through, sometimes, these crazy old girls.'

'She's been hanging round my shop,' he hissed.

Avril laughed. 'Maybe she wants to be a model in a dirty magazine, Nobs.'

'Well, I want her out of here while I'm eating me meal,' he said, with such vehemence the girl looked astonished. 'I come here every day, Avril, and I don't want the place . . . con . . . *contaminated* by whatever germs she's carrying.'

A few minutes later he heard a short laugh, more a cackle, which stopped as abruptly as it began, almost as if a throat had been squeezed. Then a movement, a rising of rags and tatters; and in sudden dread he averted his eyes, and stared fixedly at the tomato ketchup bottle, as the old woman shambled out of the door, leaving a sour smell in the air behind her.

When Nobby came out of the café and turned towards his shop, she was there, squatting in the gutter outside, looking up at his sign. Then – he stopped and stared in disbelief. She hitched up her rags, and he caught a glimpse of skinny shanks, the pinkish-grey flesh of slack buttocks, as the stream of urine spattered into the rainwater that ran down towards the drain.

'Oh Jesus,' he said aloud, feeling nausea rise in his throat, as the familiar street bucked and curved around him.

('You're a dirty, *dirty* little boy,' his Nan screamed, thrashing him with her belt, as he cried and wriggled, and his wet trousers chafed his thighs. He could smell his own pee still, soaked into cotton knit and grey flannel, which were picked up between finger and thumb as she sobbed with weariness and rage, 'It's me who has to wash and iron, and no thanks for it, no thanks from you, and not a word from *her* all these years. Dirty little cow, and you take after her, you hear me? You take after her!')

A passing van driver catcalled the bag lady from his window. Nobby rested his hand on the wall for a second and closed his eyes, waiting for the dizziness to pass, as the distant roar of traffic echoed strangely. When he looked again, she was crossing the road. A car swerved and the driver yelled abuse from his window. The old woman lurched on, dragging her bulging bag, stationed herself on the corner pavement opposite his shop, and sat down. Was she waiting for someone? But who? No – Nobby knew that she was there for one purpose: to torment *him*.

His hand shook as he dialled the number. All the boys at the station knew him. It was easy. He made a joke and heard laughter down the line. All he had to do now was wait. He walked slowly around the shop, tidying the rows of magazines so that they overlapped at precise intervals, showing half of each wrapped cover: the overall impression was of serried pink flesh bisected – one jutting buttock, one breast, all topped by half a head, half a smile . . .

On impulse he plucked one of the magazines from the stand, and slid his nail around the wrapping, letting it drift to the floor. It was years, probably, since he had actually looked at much of his stock. Run-of-the mill bondage this one was, with most of the women posing, usually with a group of men, shaved, and dressed to look like little girls. Nobby flicked the pages over dispassionately. Funny what people liked, he thought, uneasy as he contemplated faces mimicking tears, fear, pain, grief . . . Or was it real? You couldn't tell.

It was like your own, he thought. You looked back at things in your life, trying to remember how it felt, reading in a posh magazine of your own ugliness and seeking deliberately to recapture that momentary lurch in the stomach and rush of tears of self-pity, rage and betrayal . . . but nothing came. Nothing. It had all gone, somehow.

Even that other time was distant, viewed down the wrong end of a telescope, so that he was indeed very, very small, but so were the others, the three of them, older boys at school, who finally told him the truth.

'You know who your mother is Pricey? She's a slag, that's what.'

'She's been on the game for years, over in Moss Side, me brother says,' crowed the other.

'What's it like to be a slag's lad, then? Slag's lad, slag, slag, SLAG!'

You couldn't fight if you were small; there was no point. Pointless too the direct question a few says later, 'I want to *know* about me Mam, Nan. Where is she now?'

'She's dead, Malcolm, and that's all you need to know. And I want you to make a promise. I want you to promise me never to ask me any more questions, not ever.'

It was easy to keep that promise to the old lady, Nobby thought, for even when he heard the soil rattle down on wood, a few years later, and looked down on her cheap coffin, returning to the little clean rented house for the last time to pack his things – even then, he did not really want to know at all. There was no point.

He heard the police car pull up, and went to the door. She was standing outside the shop now, her face about a foot from the door, looking in. Her sudden nearness made him recoil. As he stared, her withered lips curved back in an enormous parody of a smile, black and wide and empty, reminding him of something he could not identify. He shivered, and felt tears prick behind his eyes. 'Take her away, oh please God, take it away,' he whispered. Then the uniformed constable was at her shoulder, laying a hand gingerly on her filthy ragged coat.

'Come on, mother,' he said in a loud voice, 'let's be going . . .' And with one last backwards glance at Nobby, her shoulders shaking in that crazy, silent laughter, she was led to the car.

Nobby bent and picked up the filmy plastic wrapper that lay on the floor, rolling it up and depositing it in the waste bin he emptied every day. Then he took out the spray polish and intensified the mirror finish on his counter, until at last, through the mechanical motion, his hands stopped shaking. All afternoon he stood there, as the trickle of customers came and went, talking even less than usual, staring fixedly at the patch of light behind the grille, the space where her face had been. Now it was there no longer, he needed somehow to picture it, as if summoning up that hideously familiar image would give him the answer to something he had long wanted to know. But there was nothing beyond the grille, nothing out there except the scrap of grey sky above buildings, the perpetual presence of the street. Still he stared, in a daze, fancying suddenly that were he to walk across his tiled floor to that door, it would not open, never again, leaving him locked in with all his stock, behind that grille forever.

He closed up early, and walked along to the café, feeling hungry, as if he had been emptied out. Avril leaned on the counter, smoking another cigarette in her chain, and talking to a young woman Nobby had never seen before. He didn't like the look of her, pert and over made up, with a too-short skirt.

'Nobby, this is me cousin June. She's come here to work.'

'Doing what?' he asked.

The girl giggled, and drew deeply on her cigarette.

'Dancing,' she said, 'Go-go type of thing. In Chenies Club.'

'Bit of a dump, isn't it?' he said, and the girl looked downcast, then shrugged. 'It's a job,' she said. 'You take what you can get.'

'Do you just?' he said, with an attempt at jocularity. But the girl heard the coldness in his voice, and bridled.

'Yeah,' she said, 'don't *you*?'

'Nobby's real local,' Avril explained trying to make something right that wasn't, without knowing why. 'He owns the sex shop just along the road.'

June raised her eyebrows suggestively, 'Oooh, really!'

'It's not a *sex shop*, love,' said Nobby patiently, flattered that Avril's cousin was looking at him at last as though ... well, as if he was a man to reckon with. 'ADULT MAGAZINES – that's what it says on the sign, and that's all it is.'

And at the annoying memory of that sign he frowned for a moment. The letters were so faded now, the T, the M and the S barely legible, so that in some lights it might be taken for an Asian name, or something equally daft. '*A shabby little shop in a grimy street*' – that was what the woman from London had written. It wouldn't do at all, Nobby thought. No – now he would spend money on a proper new sign, a big one in red perspex with the lettering in yellow, bright and clean. You've got to keep up appearances.

Bel Mooney is a writer, broadcaster and critic, who has written three novels, *The Windsurf Boy*, *The Anderson Question* and *The Fourth of July*. She has also published five children's books;

a satire on Thatcherism (with Gerald Scarfe); a book about Somerset; an anthology, *From This Day Forward*; and a collection of journalism, *Differences of Opinion*. She lives in London and is working on her fourth novel.

TAKING THE CAVE MAN SERIOUSLY

Steve Katz

'So there they are, in that well-known zone, and all of them are floating on lines.'

'You talk like hockey.'

'It's no game, man. It's someone's life.'

'Sounds just as primitive.'

'Listen to me, man. I'm talking magenta. I'm talking from day before dowdy to suddenly electric blue eyeshadow.'

A white limo pulls up in front of the club and three men step out. The most elegant is a woman dressed like a man. Her name is Myrtle, a name she hates. She hates her parents who named her Myrtle, and thinks it must have been out of spite because they wanted a boy. Though she is dressed now as a man she nonetheless insists they all call her Myrtle. Him Myrtle. She likes Him as a name. Horace admonishes them not to register revulsion or astonishment once they get inside. Horace is a name one can resent as well, though he never thinks about it. That's his name.

'How big?'

'I'm talkin' great big. I mean the woman fills the whole entrance. I'm talkin' ample.'

'Now you're getting real descriptive.'

'Really. But you should get the whole picture, man. Him

too, moving like a mink, banging away. All of them floating on lines.'

They press the bell and wait. Claude gazes at Myrtle. He has difficulty seeing her as a man, though she is all spit and polish. He can't call her Him, because he sees her only as the woman he loves. Thus can love penetrate the most wilful disguise. Him is the woman he continually undresses with his eyes. Horace explains that once they get inside they will see people in bizarre situations, ordinary people doing things strange. It is incumbent on them, Horace admonishes, to be nonchalant, keep their cools, to avoid a twitch.

'Flabbiness, I mean gross. At one point she rolls out her tongue and licks all the interior; I mean, grundgy. I mean this is your average contented homemaker on the rampage.'

'Why should I be interested in this? I watch a lot of sports. I'm not that kind of person. I use my time with absolute precision.'

'A big fat tub of warts slides across the floor on her tongue. You'll change your mind. I've seen it before.'

'I think you hate women. You always have to remember your mother is a woman. Why can't you talk about ordinary people?'

'My mother is not an ordinary person. These people are. It's the men too. No one is exempt from the little secret stuff closeted away here and there. That's why this is so great here, and when all of them are banging on lines, floating in that well-known zone . . .'

'What well-known zone? Sometimes you talk like a million-aire.'

'Sometimes I feel like a millionaire, buster.'

They ring again and once more. The wait makes Him (Myrtle) even more nervous about passing. Only Horace of the three of course has come here before. Claude came along of course just to be with Myrtle (Him). Him (Myrtle) is on the verge of suggesting they forget it and leave, when the security window opens and she is hit by a puff of air that smells of something oozing up for millenniums to reach the surface of the earth. A face with the complexion of a smashed goldfish appears in the square aperture.

'Well I have to admit that once I met a person, a woman like that, who did something like that. A nice woman, of superior intelligence. I liked her.'

'I'll bet you did.'

'Her first boyfriend was the worst. Before they did anything he liked to burn garbage in front of the TV. And she was right there too. Right in that zone.'

'Which zone?'

'You know. Same zone. Banging on lines. Floating. But then she married a guy who applied his computer knowledge to making pasta. Now he rivals Buitoni.'

The door opens for Horace, Him (Myrtle), and Claude. Horace steps over the threshold. Myrtle (Him) and Claude hesitate. They have never smelled an interior so absolutely musty, and for one insecure moment Him (Myrtle) takes Claude's hand and squeezes it. When she lets go she feels a bang of courage and steps over the threshold into the well-known zone. Following Myrtle (Him), Claude floats on a line of inexplicable joy.

Steve Katz lives in Boulder, Colorado, New York City, and Cape Breton, Nova Scotia. Previous books include *The Exaggerations of Peter Prince, Creamy and Delicious, Moving Parts, Stolen Stories, Wier & Pouce* and also *Florry of Washington Heights*, published by Serpent's Tail. 'Taking the Cave Man Seriously' first appeared in *American Made*, an anthology edited by Mark Leyner and Curtis White.

MINITEL 3615

Leslie Dick

It was a love affair by electronics, a love affair by MINITEL, the Paris computer system that offers interactive communication between users, who type texts onto their computer screens, these texts transmitted instantly from monitor to monitor, through the telephone lines of the city. An abstract, immaterial love affair, therefore, a literary love affair, epistolary without the literal object, no pen, ink, or paper, only an ephemeral alphabet written in white light against a plain grey screen. The MINITEL system is low tech: you can book theatre tickets, or find out railway timetables, you can check your bank balance and then, you can give in, accept the invitation posed by incessant, all-pervasive advertising, and dial 3615, the number that lets you into the network of lovers, those who pursue sexual gratification through the exchange of texts, only. No kiss, no touch; no object: no letter, or scrap of silk; no image, no voice, even; no trace of the body. The body vanishes, leaving a flickering screen, rows of words inscribed in fugitive white light.

C: Hello. Edward?
E: You speak English? – or write English?
C: That's right.
E: Good. We can do it in English, then.
C: Excellent.

E: Begin
C: How?
E: Any way you please.

C: Do you know the 3615 poster, the big one at the corner of rue Malher and rue St Antoine? The one of the very young girl, the girl with dark hair?
E: The one that's repeated all along the tunnels at the Bastille?
C: Yes. That's me. Catherine.
E: That's how I imagine you. A libertine child, the child who read James Bond at the age of seven, Fanny Hill at nine, and was deep in Philosophy in the Bedroom and Henry Miller at eleven.
C: But of course!
E: The intellectual, precocious, clever child, the voracious reader, sneaking these forbidden books off her parents' shelves. Your parents are absent, uninterested, preoccupied, and would possibly be amused, if they knew – until they dicovered the extent of your depravity, how every afternoon after school you lounge, like those girls in Balthus paintings, your skirt falling back over your skinny thigh, book in hand, eyes racing, racing over the page, and then moving more slowly, desultory. Eleven years old, lying on the sofa – and already too old, corrupt, fascinated. Hooked. That's how I picture you, Catherine.
C: Yes.
E: The apartment was rather large; long rooms with windows opening onto narrow balconies, thin white light reflecting off pale stone, Paris light, reflecting back on the white walls of these rooms. There were paintings on these walls, and the parquet creaked in places. You remember – a specific set of sounds, the familiar sounds of different people moving through this space, these rooms and corridors. The woman who cooked and cleaned and kept an eye on you. Your mother with her luncheon appointments, her shopping, her endless telephoning. Your father so beautiful, with his dark hair falling across his forehead. Every day he shut himself into his study;

he would eat his lunch off a tray that was left outside his room, in the corridor, and invariably he would walk for an hour after lunch, to clear his head, he said. You remember, perhaps, one afternoon when you got up from your nap, and walked down the corridor. You could hear Ariette singing quietly to herself, working in the kitchen. You wanted to ask your father the meaning of a word in a book you were reading. He was not in his study. You went to the bedroom, your parents' room. You looked through the keyhole, your dress falling forward as you bent down to look. Your legs were bare, and they began to shake slightly, as your heart pounded, watching your father fucking your mother. She was pale, naked, absolutely passive, flat – her arms were stretched wide, he held them out, flat, as his body moved over her. You saw, you understood, you wanted that – that precisely, to become him, to become her – to lie on a bed in the afternoon, the shutters drawn across the windows, a sense of the busy city traffic below, the white reflected light of Paris outside, autumn, and you, and Ariette, carrying on your normal afternoon, and here, in this shadowed room, this excess of passion enacting itself. As you watched, your mother didn't move, it was as if she were dead, but her mouth was open, a series of little 'Oh!s' came out of this mouth, and you felt your vagina flicker. This was what you wanted, precisely this.

C: Perhaps. Go on.

E: The next afternoon, you were alone, reading, as always. Your parents had gone to the country, to stay with friends, without you. Ariette was asleep, sound asleep, in her room. Taking a glass of apricot juice from the fridge, you'd looked in and seen her sleeping there. You were reading, and as you read you rocked back and forth gently in your chair, as was your habit. You sat with one pale, bare leg folded under you, your foot tucked under you, and rocked gently. Now you associate the flood of words in your mind, reading, that pressing flow, moving onward, reading this, now, with the rising pleasure, as you gently rocked back and forth. But the book was surprising: suddenly it described a scene of petticoats, white thighs, a thin leather riding whip across those thighs. Your fingers longed to touch yourself, you remember your mother lying flat, so thin and pale, her arms held outstretched, held down by the man with the beautiful body. She could not touch herself. You can. Reading the scene over and over, picturing the woman's pale legs, her skirts pulled up, the fine whip coming down, you put your hand under your skirt, down into your knickers, and slip your middle finger easily between those lips. With your other hand you stroke your mouth, leaning forward over the book, which lies flat on the table. You come. You think, as the rush recedes, you think, that is what I want. To be the thighs, the whip, the eyes, watching, the woman leaning over, who cannot see. The hand that holds the whip, the thighs that feel it. That is what I want.

C:

E: I'm still here.

C: Do you want to make a date?

E: Do you mean here, on the machine? Or in real life?

C: The machine is better than real life, don't you think? We could arrange the time, and meet.

E: Yes.

C: Every afternoon at half past five, perhaps, a conversation in writing. An exchange, of some sort.

E: Not at the weekends.

C: All right.

E: I'm afraid I can't make it tomorrow. Wednesday.

C: Till then.

C: Edward?

E: Catherine.

C: Lassitude.

E: My theme for the day?

C: There should be a symbol on this thing for laughter, asterisks or something. Or maybe I should write it out, as they do in novels: she laughed.

E: There should be symbols for all the different bodily responses. A sharp intake of breath. Heart beating faster. Biting the lower lip. Eyes closing.

C: She blushed. She began to shake.

E: You are lying in a pool of shadows, lying flat on your wide, low bed. There is yellowing sunlight outside, the curtains blow in the mild wind, shadows moving in irregular patterns across your body, over the bed. It is late afternoon. You know you will have to get up soon, to put your dress over your head, pull on stockings and slip your narrow bony feet into high heels, put on your make up and go out – to stand like a tower, swaying slightly, holding the cold wet long glass of vodka and tonic. Yes?

C: Isn't this getting a little too Martini-ad-esque?

E: Is it the condensation on the drink you object to? Too slippery?

C: This is supposed to be Lassitude.

E: O.K. You are lying naked, flat on your bed, knowing that soon you will be standing upright, swaying slightly, in your high heels, your lipstick marking the edge of your glass. The transformation, from your present position, prone, seems unbelievable, beyond your power. Yet you know, magically, it will take place. Your hand gently slides over your naked thigh.

C: My hand gently slides over the soft inner skin of my naked thigh.

E: You hear a sound in the flat, you know there are other people nearby, they could call out to you, disturb you. It's nearly time to get up, get dressed, but you lie there, in the evening light, stilled, suddenly, listening – one hand on your thigh, one fingering your nipple absently – listening to see if someone is approaching.

C: I don't want anyone to interrupt me, to interrupt my pleasure, my lassitude.

E: Your hand moves, and your fingers slip perfectly along your cunt. Your cunt is wet, there isn't enough time. You must come straight away.

C: I must come quickly, knowing –

E: Knowing they are watching?

C: They are watching me.

E: I am watching you.

C: Yes.

E: I raise my hand and I bring it down with a great slap on your white arse. You are lying on your front now, your fingers moving, arse high, and I hit you over and over, your white skin turns red.

C: I'm coming now, as you hit me, watching me come, hitting me.

E: Good.

C: Thank you.

E: Tell me what you're thinking.

C: I'm thinking about obsession and writing. Pornography, or written sex, sex writing, seems to be made up of a series of clichés, endlessly banal. What we agree to do here, our implicit contract, is to submit to the clichés of the other. I give in to you, I accept whatever you designate as sexy – or erotic – or whatever you want to call it. These elegant little cuts and blows.

E: Yet no marks remain, no bruises, or scars.

C: True. I suspect my pleasure lies in the knowledge that we are invisible to each other; it amuses me, the endless permutations of this relation. A woman possibly, or an old man, you can write to me as if you were a desperate teenager, maybe, or an eleven-year-old girl.

E: Or none of these.

C: The public images sustain us, in the background – more clichés of pleasure. As we walk down the street, on everyday errands, we can't not take in the erotic billboards and posters that the phone company so thoughtfully provides, enticing us back to the machine.

E: I see you every day, Catherine, in the metro – your gigantic shoulder, your flawless skin, seduce me.

C: We can pretend whatever we like, flawless skin, unlimited wealth – huge flats with creaking parquet, mottled mirrors over the marble fireplace, some image of Paris derived from a grotesque hybrid of 60s movies and Atget photographs – when in truth (maybe) we can't pay the fucking phone bill, with this terrible MINITEL amount stuck on the end. I've stopped going out, lately, making some crazed economy that an evening at the MINITEL monitor is cheaper than an evening out. Compulsion?

E: Obsession. I find that I've begun to like writing, for the first time. The writing disappears. There is no copy, no original. This writing (like no other) is pure gift.

C: For me everyday life has become charged with sexual possibility: the young man in the butcher's, the fishmonger, the woman behind the bar, the man taking tickets – I've made it with any one of them, or none, or all. Who knows? No one knows. I think we'll have to stop, soon.

E: Why?

C: This could get dodgy, don't you think?

E: What?

C: All this reading and writing.

E: I've been reading this book about Greek lyric poetry, Sappho, which claims there's a connection between desire – or the possibility of writing about desire – and the invention of the Greek alphabet. Because apparently the Greek alphabet was the first to have consonants, and this is crucial because consonants are abstract – they cannot be spoken without a vowel, like T is spoken 'tea', etc, etc. Which means that writing T itself, alone, is a radical break with the previous, oral culture.

C: Oh.

E: Shall I go on?

C: Don't stop.

E: Consonants mark the edge of a sound, or a word. And since desire is all about representing what's absent – since desire is about edges, because the child discovers the difference between itself and the world by encountering edges that it wishes didn't exist – so consonants are crucial to the writing of desire. So Sappho is possible, supposedly.

C: I always think consonants are penises and vowels are vaginas. And a comma is like a clitoris, and a dash is like a prick.

E: I want to meet you, Catherine.

C: Never. Over and out.

C: Begin, Edward. We'll take turns, today.

E: She knelt down to suck his prick.

C: They were travelling on a train.

E: The floor was dirty; the train rocked as dull green fields rolled by: England.

C: She undid his flies, and looked at his prick, poking out; the naked skin, a sudden contrast against the woollen fabric of his trousers, the coarse material of the railway seats.

E: The inside lining of his overcoat was shiny pale grey satin; she rubbed this against his prick.

C: Her knees were beginning to hurt; she stood up and raised her skirt, slightly.

E: He put his hand under her skirt, he felt the silk of her slip smooth against her legs, he felt the edge of her stocking, the tight elastic garter, he felt her naked wet cunt.

C: His hand touched her clitoris, and moved back to find the opening of her vagina.

E: She raised her right leg, placing her foot on the seat beside him, and moved closer, lowering herself over his prick.

C: His hand was holding her pale arse, under her skirts, guiding her onto his prick, while with the other he fingered and pinched her small breast through the thin fabric of her dress.

E: Kicking off her black high heels, she clambered over him, her arms around his neck, beginning to fuck him.

C: As she moved slowly up and down, her tight wet cunt sucking his prick, her clitoris brushed against his trousers, touched the cold metal of his belt buckle.

E: He looked out of the window, amazed at the oblivious world passing by. It crossed his mind the train might arrive at a station, someone could get in.

C: Holding his head in her hands, she bit his lip, looking into his eyes. She said, I want you to come.

E: I want you to come.

C: Come now, she said, moving faster, the buckle clicking against her clitoris, hard prick inside her, coming.

E: Now.

C: Yes.

E: Now.

C: Yes.

E: Now.

E: Tell me about sex in cars.

C: I don't think I'm in the mood.

E: Mood?

C: Moving cars or parked cars?

E: As you like.

C: We met in the street. We were very young – city hippies. People always think of that time as all about geodesic domes in Arizona and health food, nature, you know, but really hippies were street people, city streets, hanging out, smoking, doing drugs, passing the time. Anyway we met on the street – he was leaning against a car, smoking a joint, and he smiled and offered it to me. So I leaned up against this car beside him, very cool, and we talked, obliquely, easily. He was giving me the eye, he had a wild, sexy look, crazy smile – classic ex-junkie's bad teeth – and you know, I was happy, I was laughing with him, it was fine. Very quickly it became clear what we wanted. It was maybe nine at night; the sky was dark but the streets were wild, a hot night on the North Side, lots of people on the street, cars slowly moving by. We got into that car and started to make out. In retrospect it strikes me that maybe he could have driven me somewhere, if it was his car, but probably I've forgotten, maybe he was waiting for somebody, his friend ... I don't know. What I remember, what I remember is pulling my tampax out, opening the car door and dropping it there in the gutter, so that we could fuck. That's sex in parked cars.

E: I have to admit I didn't find that account very erotic. More of sociological interest.

C: I'm struck by the amazing urgency of it, we had to have it, had to do it. Sexual momentum. And of course the extraordinary discomfort of fucking in that car, our physical contortions to get his prick into my vagina – and then the secondary, peripheral sense of people passing by on the street, the lights, cars... It was dark in the back seat, and hot, the car windows were half open, we were trying not to make too much noise. We were all breathless and laughing when we were through, and I remember pulling myself together, finding my underpants and pulling them up, and stepping out of the car, onto the busy sidewalk again, my body flushed with excitement. We never saw each other again.

E: It sounds like an inversion of Baudelaire – instead of the flâneur who sees the woman of his dreams and loses her forever, walking through the crowded city streets, you find each other, fuck, and say goodbye.

C: That's right. Immediate gratification, simply. Not like this.

E: How's it going?

C: There's something so strange about sitting down to this little monitor, little monster, text producer, this machine. It's like an altar in my house – it reminds me of a Nichiren Buddhist altar; my friend used to chant before hers, every day. And every day now I come to my little MINITEL altar, every day at the same time, I kneel down, to read your written words, to direct my pleasure.

E: To submit.

C: It seems so exposed – are others listening in, despite these closed lines, closed doors. . . What about the technicians, the phone company itself?

E: Others like us.

C: This weird combination of exhibitionism and anonymity. You can never find me.

E: Yet I know your secrets, I know what makes you come.

C: You know, and therefore everyone knows. Anyone.

E: You would like to be truly exposed, to an audience – to see yourself being seen.

C: No. That's what is so perfect about this machine. Alone, I can imagine your look, your knowing invasion of my control, my privacy, my autonomy – I can give in to it, ashamed of myself, this shuddering exposure. Your look turns my careful world inside out, peels away my skin. My cunt flowers, reaching out. I crouch here in the darkness, these winter afternoons, scanning your words, entirely alone, invisible, and yet entirely exposed – to you, dear reader.

E: Dear?

C: Dear stranger. You have become dear to me, since you get it right.

E: And the others?

C: Others?

E: Who get it right, or wrong.

C: You imagine me glued to this magic box all day? All night?

E: No.

C: Sometimes late at night when I'm alone I wake up and listen in, play the field. I take my chances, as they say, and once in a while I come across congenial types. Other times I am bored, simply, and continue only out of politeness. Occasionally I'll do a party but it always seems that everything's happening at once, it's hard to keep things focused.

E: You and I are good at taking turns.

C: Which do you like better, transmitting or receiving?

E: I like giving you pleasure. Your orgasm confirms my power, it is always infinitely surprising to me. The idea of your excitement makes me extremely excited.

C: Maybe it's the machine itself we like, really. Detachment.

E: Sometimes I like to listen in to an exchange, where the lines have been left open. I like to listen without making my presence known, like watching through a keyhole.

C: There, it's just power again. That's what you get off on.

E: Let's leave the lines open, and see how much you like the notion of a silent listener, or reader, I should say.

C: Someone watching me. Perhaps.

E: Yes, next time. I insist.

C: There are men on the scaffolding across the street, working. They look at me, they can see me, here.

E: The man sees you reading, reading with your hand between your legs, he knows you want him to watch. You pretend you don't know he is watching you. His hand touches his prick, hard in his loose trousers. You continue to move your fingers, sinking them into your wet swollen cunt.

C: I pretend someone is watching me. I pretend you are about to walk in, surprise me, punish me, fuck me.

E: I will fuck you until you cry out to stop. . .

C: Yes.

E: Now.

C: Yes. Stop.

C: This whole process is in some ways so reminiscent of the couch – with the difference that you respond, so to speak, while the analyst could not. I imagine that you know everything anyway, already. Possibly the analyst knew everything too, but couldn't show it, couldn't let himself show it off.

E: This is nothing but showing off, this machine, turning towards an imaginary audience. . .

C: I feel so completely vulnerable, now, suddenly, and you seem so impenetrable, opaque. A blank wall, one-way mirror, mechanical camera, hidden eye. . .

E: Click, click, click. It was the clicking of her clitoris, wasn't it?

C: That's right. I didn't know you knew about that.

E: No dirty stories today?

C: I want to give you a text I found, l like it very much. It's very amusing. It's from a book about Leopold von Sacher-Masoch. I'll type it in, tomorrow.

E: Like jazz, you can type in a text, and then we can play variations on it.

C: Or free associate off it.

E: The talking cure, or in this case, the typing cure.

C: In which case you're the analyst?

E: I'm the object of desire, sweetness, surely.

C: There's a line in Fanny Burney, my favourite: 'You have been, as you always are,' he said, twisting his whip with his fingers, 'all sweetness.'

E: Not bad. Naked on her hands and knees she whimpered with mingled pain and excitement, her mouth dry, as he slowly brought the leather riding whip across her pale thighs, making shocking pink lines across her white skin. She knew he would fuck her, she was waiting – wanting it to go on forever, time-less, this combination of bright pain and blissful anticipation. With his whip he gently touched her wet cunt. He held his prick in his hand. She was shuddering, wanting to touch him, to touch herself – he forbade her to move. He reached to pinch her nipple hard, and moving suddenly, he fucked her up her tight arse, his hand grabbing her cunt, reaching greedily inside her.

C: She cried out with acute pleasure.
E: Now.
C: Now.
E: Thank you.
C: À demain. Over and out.

C: It's a contract he drew up with his lover in 1869.
E: O.K.
C: One: Herr L. von Sacher-Masoch gives his word of honour to Frau Pistor to become her slave and to comply unreservedly for six months with every one of her desires and commands.

Two: For her part Frau Pistor is not to exact from him the performance of any action contrary to honour, i.e. which would dishonour him as a man or as a citizen. She is also to allow him to devote six hours a day to his professional work and agrees never to read either his correspondence or his literary compositions.

Three: The Mistress (Fanny Pistor) has the right to punish her Slave (L. von S-M) in any way she thinks fit for all errors, carelessness or crimes of lèse-majesté on his part.

Four: In short her subject, Gregor, must accord his mistress a wholly servile obedience and accept as an exquisite condescension any favourable treatment she may extend to him. He recognises that he has no claim upon her love and he renounces all rights whatsoever to a lover's privi-leges.

Five: Fanny Pistor, on her side, promises to wear furs as often as possible, especially when she is in a cruel mood.

Six: This period of servitude is to be considered at an end

after six months and no serious allusion to it will be permitted at the expiration of the period.

Seven: Everything which may have happened must be forgotten. The original love-relationship will then be resumed.

Eight: These six months need not run continuously. They may be interrupted for long periods, which will begin and end whenever the Mistress chooses. This pact is hereby put into force by the signatures of the contracting parties.

Commencing date 8 December 1869

Signed: Fanny Pistor Bogdanoff

Leopold, Chevalier von Sacher-Masoch.

E: It's wonderful. I love the way she's not allowed to read a word he writes.

C: It was all about her, his writing.

E: And furs.

C: Especially in a cruel mood.

E: Basically she agrees to abuse him, within strict limits, set by him.

C: Those limits are counterbalanced, almost, I think, by the fact that she's the one who decides when to play this game, and when to stop playing.

E: I also like the way they're never allowed to allude to the six months, seriously, once it's over – as if they were only allowed to make jokes about it?

C: I think Fanny managed to extend the contract over a period of two or three years.

E: Wow.

C: I'm going to stop this soon.

E: When?

C: Next week.

E: We should make a new contract, like this one you've seduced me with.

C: If I have nothing more to do with you, I can pretend it never happened.

E: And the machine?

C: Send it back!

E: I don't believe you. I think I'm falling in love with you.

C: You've got to be joking. Over and out.

E: Tell me a story, Catherine.

C: I'm bored with stories.

E: Bored with solitary sex, with the machine, or with me?

C: When you write lines like that, I lose enthusiasm for all three.

E: Let's begin again. Describe yourself to me.

C: Ah, the appeal to narcissism. I'll tell you the truth, perhaps, this time. I am five foot three, with very thin, almost transparent skin and dark hair. I am wearing a black slip, appropriately, and I am sitting at a rather primitive computer screen. I have always wanted to look like Louise Brooks, but in fact I tend to look more like Bette Davis. I have wide round eyes, a bit buggy, and a pointed chin. I would like to have long, narrow eyes. I would like to be at least three inches taller. Some days I would like to be a man. However, I am older, these days, than I was, and I am beginning to accept my height, my buggy eyes, my femininity, and even my obsessive, repetitive, compulsive and dubious attachment to electronic pornographic exchange.

E: Let me tell you what you like.

C: No, let me tell you. You like to think about children, you like to think of children being beaten and children doing sex alone, fearful of being caught, found out. For you the beatings and the secret sex are part of the same thing, they go together. You take up the position of spectator – punitive, controlling – in defence against your deeper identification with the punished child. You project all these elements on to me: the thrill of forbidden masturbation, the longing to be caught, seen, looked at, the combination of innocence and depravity, the pleasure in punishment itself. This allows you to simply look on, passive, while I . . .

E: While you come, my love, tied up, whipped, prick in your mouth, your cunt, your breasts bruised, deliberately, deliberately, I make you cry out to be allowed to come, to be released.

C: Yes.

E: Now, do it.

C: Now.

E: Now, I'm watching.
C: Yes.
E: Yes.
C: Goodbye, Edward.
E: Until Monday?
C: Monday, yes.

C: What I've come to understand is that this machine has provided a space where the ambivalence that tears me apart is almost tolerable, only just bearable, within this highly artificial, totally isolated space of writing.
E: But, it seems, only if you know I can never find you out.
C: You were the faceless voyeur, I was the one doing sex, no? I was the object of desire, not you.
E: I find your use of the past tense excruciatingly painful.
C: There has to be a limit to this.
E: I cannot force you, I can only invite you to submit. I know it will please you.
C: Tell me once again.
E: I can refuse you also.
C: Once again.
E: You are at home, alone. The man you live with is away for a few days. You don't want to see anyone; you've left the answering machine on. Let them think you've gone away too. The days stretching empty before you, you know you can do whatever you please, alone in your shadowy flat, sleep as long as you like, read novels all afternoon. You take a bath at nine o'clock at night, and then stay up, listening to jazz and looking through old papers. You find a bunch of letters from a woman you seldom think about. You remember what it was like, the first time, in bed with her. She had thick, heavy red hair, that fell around her narrow face, dead white, and the softest skin you ever touched. You remember the transformation, how complete it was, like magic. She was a friend, an acquaintance, years ago; you went round to see her, then, for tea; you smoked some dope, fell into her low bed. She became the most beautiful woman in the world. You remember how she put you down, how she told you she

really wasn't into going to bed with straight women – as you melted, dazed by the creamy softness of her long body. Her hand on your cunt, wet kisses so sweet, she made you come over and over again. Remembering, you sense again those soft long arms, long thighs circling yours, you see her neck thrown back as you bite her breast, fierce suddenly. She laughs. You want her to come too. You touch her there where you like to be touched, and eventually she comes. Now, your lips are wet, your hand moves to touch your mouth, remembering.

C: Yes.

E: You powder your face, dead white, standing in front of the mirror; you put on your black coat, and go out. It's late, dark streets wet with rain, and the smell of oil on the city street as you cross. There's not much traffic. You walk down the wide street, knowing you'll be taken for a prostitute, knowing you're wearing a slip and nothing else under your coat. In the all night coffee shop, there is a young woman sitting alone, reading the paper. You look at her, you ask if you can sit down. She nods briefly. You do not speak, but glance up, occasionally. Each catches the other looking, and you like her intelligent eyes, her blonde hair. At length you leave the café. She follows you. You wait in the dark street. She pauses, then she walks up to you. You are taller than her, you incline your head, slightly. You kiss her, on the lips, in the dark street.

C: And I take her home, into my bed, my soft sheets, I stroke her all over, I brush her hair, my sweet doll, my baby, my darling, I give her everything she wants, I never say a word.

E: No words.

C: That's what I want.

E: Let me be silent, then.

C: Goodbye, my dear.

E: Behind the figure of the punitive father, the man you imagine me to be, the man with the leather riding whip, lies the punitive mother, the woman who forbids, refuses. The man watching you, the man in control is a shadow figure. It is Mama who subdues, who gives and withholds your pleasure.

C: I know, I know all this, too well.

E: I will never hurt you, my love, I will only cause you the most pleasurable pain. I will give you everything you want.

C: Why do you say this? Why? I can't bear it.

E: You said you loved the idea that we both could be anyone we liked, the machine allowing infinite permutations of desire. I don't want to stop. I want to go on meeting you.

C: Desire is about the limits, the edges of things, endings of one kind or another. What's not there, what you can't have, haven't got. Obsession, this obsession is only a denial of those edges, endings, as repetition insists, persists, preventing possibilities of something else, something different. I want you to let go of me, stop looking at me, now.

E: Too many words. I've touched you. I want to go on and on, pleasing you.

C: I don't want to play any more, I've had enough. I want you too much, or this, and now it's become precisely what I want, I have no choice, I have to give you up. It.

E: You repudiate your own desire, you undo love.

C: This isn't love. This is a fantasy exchange. It can't go on, you know, it's too easy for me to see you as utterly undesirable, the sadistic man, cheating on everybody, endless lies, somehow manipulating my fantasies until they coincide, until they intersect with yours. It's like fucking in the back seat – prick into cunt, it's exciting, but it's so contorted, uncomfortable, it's not something you want to repeat, indefinitely. I'm uneasy. I've had enough of this. I don't want your stories any more.

E: Safe sex, darling, it's only words, writing. We cannot hurt each other, there's nothing there, no residue, it melts like snow, this writing.

C: No.

E: You can have whatever you want, no kiss, no touch, I will give you anything you want.

C: It's too dangerous, this, wanting this, and you know, for me, really, to tell the truth, it's not dangerous enough. I want more – or less, maybe, not this.

E: Then let's begin again. I will meet you tonight, Catherine, at that café, I will meet you at eleven tonight at that bar near the corner of the rue Malher and rue St Antoine. It's the one on the left, as you go up rue Malher, not very far, maybe one hundred metres, the little bar, on the left. Opposite the Hotel Carnavalet. There's a pinball machine in the window. You won't have any trouble. I'll meet you there at eleven, tonight.

C: How would you recognise me?

E: You'll have short blonde hair, a pale raincoat, black boots.

C: I don't know what you mean. Is this a date on the machine or in real life?

E: I will find you easily in the crowded, noisy bar. I can see you, sitting in the dark at the back, the glass you are holding gleams in the dim light; you are waiting.

C: Don't you see I can't look at you.

E: I will blindfold you, my love.

C:

E: Then you will be entirely naked, only the silk scarf tied over your eyes.

C: No. No more words. Over and out.

Leslie Dick is an American writer whose first novel *Without Falling* was published by Serpent's Tail. Born in 1954, she has lived in London since 1965.

THE SPRAY PAINT KING

Rita Dove

When did you first take to the streets? Bitch with pad and pencil, doodling cocks in the margin while digging at me with that cool soft voice. *What criteria determined your choice of buildings?* Blue eyes trained on some far-off point as if she were driving her BMW on the autobahn. *Why do you use black paint?* Blonde hair crimped like a statue's. A down home German girl.

I walk over to the window, casually, and stare down at the Rhine. I know she wonders just how black I am. She wonders how many sessions before she can ask me about my ancestry. *Ach Mädchen* – when I see you sitting on that straight-back chair, ankles crossed and pad balanced on those waffly thighs, I imagine you as my private stenographer. Taking down all my pearls.

If she would look a little further than my crinkly hair, if she would glance over my shoulder, I would point out the Cologne Cathedral, rising from the glass and steel *Hauptbahnhof* like a medieval missile launch; I would show her the three blackened arches of the Hohenzollern Bridge and, further to the right, upriver from Old St Alban's, the bare metal stripe that's the Köln-Deutz Autobridge, then the little tower at the tip of the harbor whose name I've forgotten and . . . there it is. Severin Bridge. Saint Severin of the eleventh century, whose bones lie boxed in gold in a church on the south side of the city.

I'll call her Severin, that bitch who calls herself my psychiatrist. Though her ID might show otherwise: Doctor Severin.

How do I feel about Diana, she asks. Why don't you guess for a while. Gives you something to do when you're lying alone between the frottee bedsheets, exhausted from your own pleasure but unable to sleep. (I've watched you squirm in that hard chair. I've seen you secretly sniffing your fingers as you put away pad and pencil in the desk drawer.) And if you still can't sleep, you can type up your notes. I see it now: Case History of the Spray Paint King.

Dr Severin has decided I should keep my journal private until I think I am finished. My first entry shocked her (did you cream in your panties, my bride, my Edeltraut? Did I catch you right?). *Seventeen and already asocial.* She thinks she can take the wind out of my sails. He will tire of these juvenile insults, she thinks, when no one is there to read them. She has provided me with a list of questions. Why did you drop out of high school? When did you join a motorcycle gang? How did you meet Diana? What satisfaction does defacing public buildings give you?

I am forced to do your bidding, but it is not easy. So many questions! I'll need an outline to answer them all:

I. Background
  A. Family
  B. Sexual experiences

II. Onset of Criminal/Artistic Activities
  A. My friends above the river
  B. Concrete vs stressed steel
  C. Flick of the wrist

This, then, Lady Bockwurst, is for you. Take it in memory of me and the deeds I have wrought upon this blighted city, scab on the banks of the Rhine.

When I was ten, my mother sent me to the cellar to haul coal. I was frightened, and the scuttle banged my knee several times in my haste to escape; but by the third trip, I gathered courage to linger. Under the flickering light of the naked bulb swinging, the coal gleamed dimly, like wax, in huge craggy mounds. All that coal dust I had inhaled every winter, all the tenements dulled with soot and the chilling rain and the sky like an iron glove, all that dusty and gingery despair settling on the skin like grit – blackness undiluted, one hundred per cent.

But years went by before I unzipped my pants for the first time. I didn't know what would come next – just that it felt good. I couldn't stop, even when my spine threatened to sink between my knees. Then something broke inside me and splattered against the wall of coal. Now I'm going to die, I thought, watching it grow translucent, darken to a gray jelly.

As such, Diana's nothing special. But the way she walks! – as if her head doesn't know what her body is doing . . . and what it does is sensational. Not that she's a knockout. Her breasts are average but she's so slim that they're . . . well, *there*. And legs like a young boy, legs that don't stop. And a round trim ass. She wears corduroy pants, tight, in orange and pink and lilac; she looks like a tree and the fruit on it.

Diana hung out at the Hi-Fly, our pennyarcade on the east bank. Everyone in the gang was afraid to touch her unless they were high – then sometimes they'd take her for a ride across the autobahn bridge. Every time she came back, she looked as if she were drowning.

But the oddest thing about Diana, what made me start paying attention to her, was that she read books. Philosophy, anthropology – follow things like that. She'd sit at a table, a flair pen between her lacquered fingernails, underlining. I watched her several nights before I went over. The guys liked to kid her, asking her if Sigmund Freud was her great-granddaddy, stuff like that. But when I sat with Diana, I didn't ask her anything. I didn't even talk. I just watched her read. I believe she understood what she read, because when she was reading was the only time her head and body seemed to come together.

It got so I'd sit there until the Hi-Fly closed, watching the flair pen move under her fingers. I drank one mango juice after another; watching pink ink move through the words. (You wouldn't understand, Dr Severin, how peaceful I felt.) Then one night – the sky was a deep, tricky blue – Diana finished a book. I had never seen her finish one before. I waited for her to fish the next one out of her handbag; but she clicked the pen shut and threw the paperback on the table. I stared at the cover, something about the phenomenology of space. The author had a French name.

'Let's go for a ride,' she said, standing up. I nodded and went for my bike.

We rode every bridge over the river that night, all eight of them. We roared around the square at Neumarkt four times. We teased the prostitutes on Weidengasse and the bums at the *Hauptbahnhof*. Somewhere in Ehrenfeld we got lost and wandered around through the deserted underpasses until we stumbled onto a familiar street and started back into town. Swinging past the radio station, we saw a man in a three-piece suit practicing turns on roller skates. His briefcase lay propped neatly against a balustrade.

'All the white buildings,' Diana whispered, and when I turned around she had that drowned look.

And finally the dingy spires of the cathedral, spotlit to remind us all where we were, the great *Köln am Rhein*, home of toilet water and pale bitter beer.

Anonymous benefactors send me sketch pads and charcoals. Yesterday a packet from Zurich – precision drafting pens and an arsenal of pastels. I distributed them among the guys on my corridor. As if, after painting the town, I would doodle on a slip of paper.

The only decent gift came from a Martin Tauber, DPhil., Free University of Berlin. 'You keep good company,' he wrote inside the front cover. Lithographs by Picasso. I'm not sure what he meant, DPhil. Tauber – I'm not academic. But the book's not bad. A series of sketches of a bull caught my eye. First Picasso draws a bull in every detail – cock, balls, muscles and all. In the next picture, the bull has lost his muscles, but he's still a damned fine beast. Next he loses his hooves and eyes and the tail's just a swooping line. Then he sports a branch with two leaves sticking to it instead of a cock. By the time Picasso's finished there's only two or three ink strokes on the page. But it's still a bull. Inside the front cover Dr Tauber had also pasted this newspaper clipping about my sprayings:

> **The young artist's style is reminiscent of Picasso in austerity of line, of Matisse in fantasy and social comment. The bitterness, however, the relentless scrutiny of what we so vainly call civilization, the hopelessness which pervades his work, without coquetry nor call for pathos – these qualities are all his own. He is, so to speak, his generation's appointed messenger.**

Bingo. The Big Time. Razzmatazz.

Certainly Dr Severin considers the possibility that I might, one day, pull her onto the shrink-couch: she considers the possibility with a mixture of thrilling curiosity and propitious dread.

There's a term for me – *quadroon*. Every time I say the word, I think of pale chewy cookies and laugh. I'm what girls call a treat – *ein Leckerbissen*. Gray eyes with a slight tilt. Flaring nostrils on a sharp nose. A large, clear brow. Women either shy from me on the street or linger, smiling. Men's eyes narrow.

The negro blood is more prominent in me, in fact, than in my mother. From a very light baby with a cheesy complexion, I darkened during kindergarten. It began at the ears and descended with frightening rapidity to the neck (pale coffee). Lines appeared in my palms like lemon juice scribblings held over a flame. The hair, so fine and wispy, crinkled. The pink cheeks of my classmates huffed and puffed: *Negerlein, Negerlein.*

My mother, conversely, lightened as she aged. When I was younger she reminded me of some magnificent bird of prey, tall and goldenskinned with an aquiline nose set into the flat strong bones of her face. Her plucked brows perch like talons above her eyes which are hazel and wide apart. She wears her thick hair tied back with a ribbon, like a girl.

But way back in Aachen, during the last snow-whipped days of 1945, my grandmother – when she studied the caramel-colored face of her new daughter – had been in despair. She had never set eyes on a black person before the soldier from the land of chewing gum and grapefruit spoke to her in his elastic voice. He gave her chocolate bars and promised to return. Then the British arrived, and she packed her things, walking eastward towards her hometown, Dresden, pleading aid from military convoys – the swarthy baby helped. By the time my mother learned to walk, they had gotten as far as the border of the Soviet Occupied Zone and were turned back, placed on a US Army truck headed west. A negro Military Policeman was loading the refugees; my mother began to cry when his hands reached for her; she did not stop until, smiling, he drew on white gloves.

My father works construction; his idea of recreation is to take a streetcar to an unfamiliar quarter of town and to walk his family through it, pointing out buildings which are in need of repair or soon to be torn down. Once, when I was eleven, we took the streetcar as far as Chlodwigplatz; we got out near St Severin's Gate with its little terracotta tower and strolled through the cobblestone streets. My parents held hands and laughed at my Lancelot-like attempts to spar with the neigh-borhood dogs. It was one of those September evenings when the sky is rinsed clean and hot, a light that makes you feel exhilarated and melancholic, in the same breath. To the right, between crenelated facades, the Rhine glittered like an alche-mist's greed; all the sparrows of late summer swooped to the lowest branches and blinked at the earthbound pityingly. We turned down Dreikönigsstrasse, towards the river, and when we could go no further, my father stopped and pointed a blunt finger at the pale green Severin Bridge.

'Like a bird's long dream,' he said, 'a tribute to modern

engineering.' And with a proud sigh: 'I helped build it . . . for three years of my life.'

The next day I looked it up in my *Kinderlexikon*. Span, 300 meters. Steel box girders braced by three sets of cables passed over the top of the A-shaped tower located near the east bank. I went to the public library to find out more details. *Köln – History of a Modern City*. Five men were buried in one of the cement pilings . . .

I ran to my mother and found her bent over the bathtub, rinsing sheets. 'How could they?' I asked.

'How could they what?' she countered.

'Leave those men to die!'

'Don't tell me,' she began, slapping sheets against the side of the tub, 'you've been reading those westerns again.' Then she saw the book clutched to my chest, and her hands ceased their convulsive wringing.

'Who are you talking about?' she asked.

'Josef Breit, Mathias Metzger, Winfried –'

'Not their names!' She caught herself shouting, spoke softer. 'I know.' The afternoon sun splashing through the blinds and across her face turned her eyes pale gold.

'They fell into a hole while pouring concrete. The others kept pouring . . . '

For a moment my mother hesitated, her hands quiet in the water. Then her face hardened. 'That's your father's territory,' she replied. 'Ask him.' Bending over, she attacked the laundry with renewed energy, wringing the sheets.

'What did you want us to do,' Dad said, leaning back in his armchair, 'stop production and dig them out?'

Yesterday the street cleaners, under orders from the city, prepared to erase one of my sprayings with XR-3, the chemical abrasive concocted to eliminate political graffiti left over from the student movement. The spraying in question, nicknamed 'Space Flower' by the press, blooms on the facade of a prominent bank; this plant with its dagger stamens and cone-shaped appendages arcs in perfect imitation of a statue poised beside it, a bronze replica of the bank's first president.

The street cleaners moved in early – around 6 am – hoping to avoid a confrontation. But news had leaked; already grouped around the statue, in a neat but impenetrable mass, were the apprentices from the art academy, many non-partisan radicals and some Young Socialists.

Supposedly no one said a word. A fine cold rain began. After a few minutes, the cleaners turned on their heels and drove away.

Diana comes to visit; she wears a blue dress and looks exhausted. I wonder what Dr Severin has been telling her.

'I knew it was you,' she blurts out. 'I knew as soon as I saw which buildings you picked. The newspapers. The radio station. The sides of tenements, concrete retaining walls. All white.'

Getting the spray cans, easy. The clerk at Hertie's department store couldn't take his eyes off Diana's butt. The youth centre ran out of black paint while decorating their float for the *Karneval* parade. But how to explain the drives at night, my bike lubed and polished for the trip? How explain the building calling with its face blank as snow awaiting defilement? Natural canvasses.

'It started that night, didn't it?'

We had stopped in the middle of the Severin Bridge; I cut the motor. The bridge was too high for us to hear the movement of the Rhine but the wind hummed through the cables; it was almost like listening to the water. Five men are buried in this stanchion, I told her, staring into the glittering lights. I recited their names, I repeated what my mother and father had said. She listened, and when I turned around her eyes were gliding from one side of my face to the other as if I were one of her books. She took my head in her hands; her palms burned but her fingertips were like ice. She kissed me. I was twisted half-backwards on my motorcycle – an awkward position – but we did not get off.

Today Diana looks straight into my eyes. The room is brightly lit, and the greenish wallpaper makes me shiver, despite the overheated iron radiators underneath the barred windows. Rush hour traffic roars outside of this 'detention home for youthful offenders'.

'Why did you paint the Madonna?'

Can I explain what itch built up inside me, how I tried to ignore it at first and *act responsibly*, then learned to welcome its presence and nurture it, prime it, hone the vague desires to a single, jubilant swoop, one vibrant gesture?

'I didn't paint her,' I replied. 'She painted herself'.

The Madonna. When I had finished I just stood there, looking at her – I would have stood there all night, the stars shone so soft and cool. I didn't give a shit about anything, except for that picture. I didn't budge, even when a pair of young lovers strolled around the corner. For a moment we stood quietly and gazed at her. Then the woman pointed: 'The police!' – and I bolted.

'I always thought . . .' Why does Diana look down at her lap, Diana whose eyes were reputed to batter the most lascivious suitor to a bale of twigs? 'I always figured . . .' – a coy swoop of eyelashes – 'you drew her after me. You know – tits and ass.' She laughs disparagingly.

That's why the dress. Blue, too. Ah, Diana – again you are right, but it means so little. The Madonna is my masterpiece. The councillor in charge of education (a member of the Christian Democratic Party) has called her 'the product of a sick and filthy mind'. What do you think, Diana? Am I sick or are you just beautiful?

My mother comes every day and cries. She says it's all her fault. She says she knows how it feels to be always stared at and never loved, how one is never comfortable except in the smallest of spaces, at the stove or bent over a tub of suds. She raves. When it gets too much I play out the fantasy I had as a child; I am sent down to the cellar for coal. While I am filling the scuttle, the Americans drop the Big Bomb. When I come upstairs again, I am the only German left in the whole country – all because I have to haul coal when other little boys are outside playing.

Dr Severin will read this and say: 'The coal saves you –

your black blood.' And when I paint I'm spraying blood on the walls or semen, a fascinating example of reverse projection. She wants to ease me back into society; she will tell me I have a talent I mustn't squander.

First there is the blue of the air as they fall, open-mouthed, open-eyed, toward a deeper blue. Then the red of impact, the stunned blow as their mouths fill and capillaries pop. And then, for the longest kind of time, the black before death and then the black of dying, the black of metal before it is painted sea green and the black of sea green metal against the sun, an unfinished web. But when most people have forgotten, when those men become no more than a macabre joke at a party, or the niggling conscience of an engineer as he drives to work, they will float up out of the stanchion and through the rain-slick streets of Cologne, looking for a place to tell their story. The newspapers will scoff; the radio station will shrug. Their walls are clean.

The city stands in concrete snow and even the cathedral's turned white overnight. Oh citizens who have forgotten, I was there to remind you, I put the stain back on the wall – no outraged slogan, no incoherent declaration of love, but a gesture both graceful and treacherous, a free fall ending in disaster – among the urgent scrawls of history, a mere flick of the wrist.

Rita Dove, was born in 1952 in Akron, Ohio. She received the 1987 Pulitzer Prize in Poetry for her book *Thomas and Beulah*. She has published three other poetry books, most recently *Grace Notes*, as well as a collection of short stories. Currently she is a professor of English at the University of Virginia and is working on a novel. 'The Spray Paint King' first appeared in *Fifth Sunday, 1985*.

THE CHAIRMAN

Andy Robson

'Nick, old thing, where the hell are you taking me?'

Clean and confident as a spaceship, Eve shone in the dark. She could still hear the theatre people, see the theatre lights as her stilettos stumbled for purchase on the concrete steppings.

'This is the England no Baedeker will ever show you, Eve, deeper and darker than plummet ever sounded . . . '

'You're a schmuck, Nick.'

Ahead was only silence.

'Yeh, you heard.'

Anyway, why the fuck was she following some half-crazed Brit down to some inglorious, God-forsaken pit? Where did her brother find these guys? Business partner or not, back in the Big Apple she'd personally arrange the public garotting of her ever-loving sib.

She stole a glance behind. But already the irresistible inward downward turning of the concrete spiral took from view the theatre with its warmth and light and easeful company. Was falling from an ocean liner like this? Sucked down for the third time in your personalized vortex, cold and alone, would you glimpse – just – the liner lights thrown in a spangle against the night, hear a laugh, a bubble of conversation, the clink of cocktails in the cool?

'Well, what do you think?' Nicholas, somewhere ahead, plunged on down.

Although Eve aerobicized regularly, she still felt a tightness
in her calf as her legs stretched to find the earth falling away
beneath her.

'I think your National Theatre has professional if not
provocative productions that possibly cater too much for
American tourists. Its restaurant is overpriced but has the
virtue of being empty. Excellent battered mushrooms in garlic
butter and the New Zealand waitresses are charming. Your
licensing hours are dumb. I think we are in rats' alley.'

She stuttered to a halt and tore a nail as the floor found a
level of sorts. Around her dull light lay like a stain on the green
damp walls. Nicholas was the darker gloom ahead, his cloak,
like some shadow casually picked up along the way, disguising
any solidity he might have.

'The very bowels of the South Bank complex,' intoned Nick.
The anal complexes of the English schoolboy, thought Eve.

Who was this guy anyway? Jee-sus, he really did wear a
cloak. Is your life insurance paid up brother? Do you hear?

But you could hear the silence after the theatre's crack of
leather and rustle of silk. Only now and then came the clack
of the clean air system, a cicada clattering its legs together.
Then the whoosh of desert hot air through secret flues to the
theatre stacked above.

'Nick, dearheart, just what's this to do with a Song ceramic,
– a pair of Han wrestlers?'

'Everything, but everything. Don't you see?'

Eve did not. She was ever so slightly weary. She could feel
the claret and gateau, the steak and mushrooms curdle and
coalesce inside her.

'Eve, you and your brother deal in "exotic" antiques, yes?
You wouldn't dream of closing a deal in Japan without going
through a tea ceremony. Okay, we're not so elegant here. We
wine, dine and watch *King Lear*. It might just as well be
sushi and Noh. Either way, we must go through these ritual
introductions, one nation, one culture to another.'

'Hey, Nick, I'll pay well for your oriental connection. But
the lecture I don't need.'

'Come on, Eve. I'm a doormat. Walk all over me to the

last knockings of Empire. It's through me to Hong Kong and then mainland China. You shipped out Britain's treasure by the boat load – now the yellows are in peril.'

Eve pushed a crushed Coke can with her toe. Her brother told wild tales of hairy deals sealed in Penang's midnight heat, a knife drawn in Rangoon back streets. She gets a lulu in Ye Olde Londone Towne.

'Nick, I believe our package refers to substantial K?'

'Peanuts to you – or any decent pimp. And what's that make me? Oriental studies PhD with all the contacts of a pauperized colonial family – two a penny these days. With me as middle man you get a thousand years of art and elegance and China gets Madonna and McDonald's.'

The political awareness of a brick, thought Eve.

'Nick, unlike your forbears, we have no intention of invading China.'

'No. Just buying it.'

Nick's shadow continued to back off. The air system clattered. Eve shivered.

'Nick, darling, you're a sensitive soul, I know . . . '

'What price the head of a Quin warrior, Eve – a million, two million – dollars, pounds?'

And then he was gone, dissolved to black. Eve wished she'd had more brandy. Or less.

'Terribly sorry. Bit squiffy.' Nick suddenly swung round a pillar and stuck his big moon face white as a clown straight into Eve's.

'The aristocratic disaffection for trade, you know.' Tobacco smells spilled out as his mouth opened and shut like a fish.

'No way to treat a guest. Sorry. Terribly.' He hid a small belch behind his hand. 'Mind, you're lucky. When Hans Andersen used to pop over for a bit of cultural exchange with Charles Dickens, young Chas's idea of a wing ding was to take the poor bugger for a quick spin round the city morgues. But I want to show you the living, not the dead.'

She glanced at her Corum. Nearly 1 am. She liked the firmness of her forearm since her new weights regime.

'You're quaint, Nick, but maybe we shouldn't rush this . . . sleep on it, OK?'

'Don't misunderstand. I want to be rich. Filthy, stinking, coming-out-of-me-ears rich, but you must understand . . . '

She looked behind, trying to see the path back through the dark to the spiral of the steps and the light. And then he gripped her wrist. He wasn't strong, but his fingers were long and seemed to double, redouble, tight mistletoe binding oak.

'You see, it's not just me you'll have a contract with – it's a whole country.' Tight like a tourniquet he tugged her deeper into the dark.

'Meet my fine philosopher.'

As a child she'd seen a hedgehog in a spinney. Its little legs waved. Deceived, she ran to pick it up, but as she clutched it, boneless, soft, she saw through transparent skin a million maggots writhe, working the hog's limb like mad puppeteers. Now, as then, a thing of definition misled. The wall ahead wombed suddenly about and above, rounded into flesh. She trod on something soft. With a twist it grabbed her ankle, then recoiled in terror.

'Bugger off, you buggerin' buggerin' bastards. Bugger off out of it.'

'Hush, Cal, hush – it's only me,' soothed Nick.

Cal was a man of many parts. Arms and legs grew from the walls and floors all over. First here, then there, bits of lightlessness sleeved in flesh. It took Eve a moment to realize that Cal was not a many-armed Shiva, but that many Cals were waking and watching. There was an underworld to the nation's theatre in the city's south, and it was a peopled world.

'Sweet Jee-sus peace – just leave us in peace, can't yer?!'

'It's me, Nick.'

'I know who the fuck it is, yer tormenting bastard.'

'I've brought you a guest.'

A torchlight flicked on. In the shock of its beam Cal rose like a breaching whale smashing up through layers of rotting cardboard sending bow waves of fresh piss smells before him. Blackness swept up Eve. She gagged, lungs corrupted. Cal's brow swilled sweat into crevices of his heavy jowl. He rested a second on the palms of his hands, a pigeon-toed bulldog, great barrel of a chest, blubber of gut swagging above narrow hips pinched tight as an ant's abdomen. All ant, dog and whale, he hung for a moment then urged his legs from under him. They flopped from the ledge that was his home and swung, little and useless, like Punch's swing from a beachside booth.

'You poor man.' As the words escaped Eve, coruscating ammonia rushed the vacuum, eating the pipes and wiring of the perfect machine of her body. A lowing came from Cal as the man inside struggled to wake, to shake the shag of dark from his shoulders. As he swayed to a kind of balance, she instinctively moved to hold him, but again saw her hedgehog beckon. A strength went out of her.

'Take me away, Nick. Straight away. This is a stupid joke.'

'But Eve, this is the Englishman in his castle.'

'Forgive – please – I'm sorry – forgive us, love. We get so many people down 'ere, come to bring us grief.'

The words seemed to come singly, in no rhythm of speech Eve recognized. She did not understand.

'Cal, I'd like you to meet Eve.'

The formality almost brought Eve to hysterics. But quite serious, Cal took away a propping arm. Eve took his hand as much because she feared that, imbalanced, he'd topple from his perch. His palm lay in hers inert and damp as a cod straight from the marble.

'Calum Bannon.'

'Eve Ash.'

More ammonia, acerbic.

'American, I guess. I have many cousins across the water.'

'Indeed, Mr Bannon.'

'Oh, Calum, please. This young devil,' Calum swung a wet punch at the side of Nick's head like the playful slap of a fluke which scatters a school of seals, 'presumes an intimacy with his abbreviation, just 'cos I've chosen to chew the cud with him on occasion. I hope he's not filled your head with rubbish.'

'He seems to think we ought to meet, Mr . . . Calum.'

Cal swayed back in a huge laugh.

'Shut the fuck up,' came a thin voice from the dark. But Cal's laugh swept at the voice and danced it away, down the dank pillars of concrete. Lank straggles of hair clung to Cal's head like wave-tugged weed on bare rock.

'There's good crack to be had in this, Nick. Is it a tourist attraction we are now – poor naked wretches in the auditorium, and the real thing for a few pence extra. Do I get a cut, Nick? Are we a partnership now?'

'I just think Eve ought to know that we English – British – aren't all David Nivens living in rose-covered cottages.'

'Jeez, Nick. I'm sure Miss Ash has seen enough bowery bums, crossed the street from crack dealers on East Side without us adding to her troubles. Can't we do better than a freak show?'

'You don't believe that of yourself.'

'Don't I?'

'It was you first called me – told me to tell the world what happened here.'

'Perhaps it was. My little messenger to the nether world, eh?'

Cal had now blinked awake. Eyes, slow and wet and brown slurried first to Eve, then to Nick and back again.

'But you looked so sad and lonely, Nick – needing someone to talk to.'

Aftershocks still juddered through Eve. Beyond Bannon she sensed other creatures, other eyes.

'How many productions did you just gawp and stare at us for? Two *Antonies*? One *Pravda*, and I think it was your third *Enemy of the People* before you screwed your courage to the sticking place and came over, wasn't it? We'd seen yer, though, peeking round the stair like a snotty kid who sneaks down at midnight to see what grown-ups do.'

'I just wanted to help . . . to know.'

'To help! Why thank you – is it Mr Gladstone I see before me, night-wandering midst the fallen ladies, or perhaps the good Dr Barnado himself, after his little boys?'

From the hugeness of Cal's bulk came the giggle of a child.

'I couldn't believe how much, up there – and down here, such . . .'

'Yeh, what? We have the riches of Croesus.'

Flashes of torchlight hit chromium, broke, and bounced back at Eve in shards. Cal was dragging something in front of him. He rested on it, a weary knight on the pommel of his horse.

'What's that?' Eve wanted to bite back the words. Dumb to ask questions, dumber to ask such stupid ones.

'This – is my symbol of office. What else would a Chairman have?'

With the aplomb of a magician, Cal jagged a lever, the glitterings coalesced and a wheelchair unfolded before Eve.

'Chairman?'

Eve heard the question hang in the dark. Couldn't she just pluck it from the air, stuff it in her clutch and go home?

'Cal's the chosen one hereabouts. He's their spokesperson, leader . . . '

'No, not that – voice. What else is left but words?'

Cal trailed his hand across the wire fan of spokes. His wheels. A music rose.

'Come, Eve, rest.'

Conjuring, Cal waved his other hand above the chair. Eve felt cables slack at the back of her knees. Just a moment's ease, to rest her piston-rigid spine. The chair sparkled. But a coldness inside her warned that she might not raise herself so readily as she might sink.

'No, we've disturbed you enough, Mr Bannon. It's cruel to wake a man from his dream.'

Like a rocket ready for launch, she felt the power burn up inside her. Wraiths of dry ice seemed to pour from the various valves and exits about her body. It was only water vapour condensing in the night chill.

'Ring me, Nick. If you don't want to close this deal then I can always find other contacts.'

All the lugs and restraints that kept her earth-stuck started to withdraw. Then Cal's voice dropped a tone.

'But Eve. Why stop at smashing up my slumber? Nick, for

all his gentle breeding, knows no such reticence. Nothing he likes better than to sniff through the rotting. He'd make a good bagwoman, rucking through the trash for a tasty morsel.'

'Come – come now, Nick. He'll suck you down.'

All inside her doors locked, hatches sealed. No return.

'Here, here's one – Sweet Beth ...' Cal's torch wand flashed across space. A cubicle of concrete suddenly bright lit and a small huddled mass edged into a corner, knocking down neat cardboard castellations. '... a hero of the Blitz, our Beth, a firefighter 'til the men came back all crippled from the war and threw her out. Or take Don and Ellie, down from Droitwich, quite the honeymoon couple.'

Another quarter burst alight, full of the twining of hands and legs. A single rose lolled in a sawn-off Squeezy bottle.

'No more jobs here than there of course, but at least they're together, whilst poor Tom's all alone ...' Again the torch soared through the dark like an Aldis from ship to ship on a dark seascape. It lit a tattoo made flesh with matted Medusa hair. '... since Mack was locked away. Still at least he can't kick ten kinds of shit out of yer now, eh, Tom? Leave that to the queer-bashers, yeh?'

Dead-eyed Tom stared straight into the beam, the unfinished Crucial crooked in his palm. The column of fire rose in Eve. She clenched her fists and raised them above her head, ready to crash them down on the soft brown egg of Cal's head.

And then he was gone, like a broken wave. 'Find your own freedom, Nick ... I release you,' he hissed, and slid beneath the cardboard covers. The torch glowed a moment, diffuse beneath the cake of rot, a golden carp bottoming a pond. Then that too was gone. Only the chair's skeletal outline remained, approximate. Eve's fists stayed up, as though about to chop a wet log. Nick gawped.

Nick sat cramped in the corner of the cab. Passing streetlamps, like searchlights, probing, lit Eve's legs, long beneath the silk wrap of skirt. Her calf was snug and round and brown like the butt of a rifle.

At his flat the deal was done. Retainers from his father's

diplomatic days could smuggle out selected prized ceramics. Furniture was more tricky. But that was for the future. A palm greased, an appeal to old loyalties, a promise of haven for when the communists eventually came; the treasure would soon be in New York. All parties would be satisfied. The package was mutually beneficial.

And then Eve was quaintly charmed, refreshed even – it had been so long – when he took her missionary fashion. But she wanted a little something for herself this night. He looked a trifle surprised when she smashed the china whiteness of his shoulder bone against the brass hardness of the bed head. And she thought the juices of his eyeball would pop all over when she stuck her fingers so far up she could practically tickle his prostate. Then the black came, and she slept, – yeh, okay.

A little sun leaked in and yellowed the soles of Nick's feet. At least she guessed they were his. Peeking from the bed end, they looked queerly at odds, as if dismembered from the paleness of the rest of him. Proportions were all wrong. She felt she should remember something. But he looked happy enough. A smile played at the corner of his open mouth – didn't any Englishman sleep with his mouth shut? – and his nose puckered prettily.

She slipped from the bed. Cracker crumbs wedged between her toes. Last night they'd listened to Fauré and nibbled cheese. She remembered. She remembered the flat had the colour co-ordination of a caravan site. A morning chill touched her.

She stumbled for something to wear and fetched up against a cricket jumper slung across a chair. The rough wool stroked down across her breasts like the calloused hands of a stranger, she thought. A little rankness of sweat came to her. Then something did stride across her memory. Cal was there. He stood for a moment, bold, in front of her – then his legs went from under him. He sagged like a bag of meal. His arms reached out. Her hand went to her mouth, spew to the back of her throat.

Annoyed, mainly at herself, she walked with big strides to where she thought she remembered the bathroom to be. She forced back down the bitter taste. She looked in the mirror, wished she hadn't and out of habit checked her weight.

It was a male's bathroom. Eve bent to lower the toilet seat and smells of Nick's acrid inaccuracies on drunken Friday nights rolled up to her. And with the piss smells came Cal. The shower curtain billowed like a sail, and as the shroud takes the corpse's form, the curtain swelled to Cal's relief. She tore it, leaving slashes like weals across a cheek. Shrapnel of splintered crimson nail ricocheted round the bathroom. Through the torn veil she saw Cal swing sheet white naked. He swept along the shower rail with a series of dipping chin-ups, lugged about by forearms long as asses' jawbones. And all the time the child's giggle.

'You're not here! Not here!'

'Why not? Who says so?'

His puppet legs whirled like a flail. She ripped at him, the legs gyred – between them they smashed Nick's few cosmetics. The mirror sank to the floor and crazed with a single crack.

'Haunt him, you bastard! Your friend, brother, country-man!'

'Isn't he dead already? Leastways, he will be if he don't wake soon. The brothers and sisters, halt and lame, might cast aside the Chair, smash down his door and smash in his skull.'

Eve lashed and gouged.

'You're not real – you can't always be with us!'

'Heh, if you can smash in our sleep, who's to stop us waltzing in at your precious moment or peaceful time, the warmest hour, the second of intimacy. We'll bang on in, sever the arteries of calm. Don't worry. You won't have to look for us. We're looking out for you.'

Still Cal's legs carouselled. A loo roll streamed across the room. A cheap deodorant careered over tiling.

'Why me? Why me? I don't want to care!' Eve screamed.

'Isn't it those that have to?'

Cal rocked gentle now, like a great spinnaker slaps the boom with the big wind gone out of it.

Glazed by sleep, mildly curious as to the noise, Nick wandered to the bathroom. He was long and white and naked.

Eve sprung at him. Their eyes met unpremeditated. His pupils dilated black and Eve saw for the first time something good and warm, safe and soft. Slow, a smile came to lip and eye.

'Fuck you and fuck your stupid country,' Eve spat. 'It stinks.'

Down that long decline of the tunnel to the tube she saw the handsome boy play the trumpet with thalidomide flippers. Eve was the horniest thing he'd seen that morning. He played a little brighter. The heavy purse she slung fetched him a sharp blow behind the ear. The day could only look up, he mused, and stretched to pick up the purse.

Andy Robson, born 1955, lives in London and works in desktop publishing.

A MODERN GOTHIC MORALITY TALE

Kate Pullinger

Mina lives with Vladimir in the docklands of London. Vladimir bought an enormous flat there when the area was first being redeveloped. He likes to be by the river; it reminds him of his voyaging days. The flat takes up an entire floor of one of the old warehouses. They have a lot of room all to themselves. Vladimir likes it that way, he says he is a modern man and modern men need to stretch out and be expansive.

The flat, however, is the only thing about Vladimir that is expansive. He lives a closely guarded and careful life. He has to stay out of sunshine and prefers to function at night. During the London summer this limits his lifestyle because in June the sun does not go down much before half past ten and then comes back up again extremely early. In the summer Vladimir and Mina go on holiday to the dark places of the southern hemisphere.

In the winter London is a night city and Vladimir is content and busy, rising as soon as the sun goes down. In December he is up as early as half past three. His work in the City is independent enough to allow him to define his own working hours. Vladimir is a rich and successful businessman. He makes his living bleeding money and power away from other businessmen.

Mina works with handicapped children in an impoverished area in the east end of London. She has always considered herself left-wing and feminist and before she met Vladimir was involved in many different valuable political struggles. She has spent years campaigning for the rights of the handicapped as well as the rights of the poor, the homeless, the powerless, and the various victims of British imperialism. Mina's grandmother was a Victorian lady who devoted her life to charity. Mina is proud of her heritage.

Vladimir claims that his ancestors were British aristocrats with vague Russian connections, hence his name and his impeccable upper-class accent. The night they met he told Mina he was the only child of long-dead parents who left him a vast fortune which he had since made vaster.

The fact that Vladimir was an orphan drew Mina towards him; it made the man seem vulnerable. Never one to ignore an opportunity to comfort the bereaved, Mina insisted that Vladimir tell her his lonely life story. The tale was a bit thin on details but, despite that, Mina was charmed.

'This is the only photograph I have of her,' Vladimir said, producing from his breast pocket a sepia-tinted picture of a tall, slim and high-cheekboned woman dressed in a marvellous bead shift from the 1920s. 'She was young in this photo. It was taken years before she had me.' Mina could have kissed the picture and wept but instead she kissed Vladimir. His lips were very cool as was his skin but Mina assumed that was because of his class.

The next day Mina spoke to one of her co-workers. 'You know that friend I have who works in the City?'

'You mean the one with the incredible car and the enormous salary?' the co-worker replied. 'I bet I know who she votes for.'

'Yes, well, I went to a party at her house last night and I met the most extraordinary man. I spent the whole evening talking to him then he drove me home. Or rather, his chauffeur did. He didn't make a pass at me though, he showed me a photograph of his mother.'

'Sounds weird to me. Never trust a man who shows you a photo of his mum the first time you meet, that's what I always say.'

'He has black hair and long fingers and a very seductive smile. He is incredibly posh. I've never met anyone so posh.'

'Oh yeah, what's his name?'

'Vladimir.'

'Vladimir? That sounds foreign. Where does he come from?'

'Well, he is English . . .' Mina and her co-worker continued discussing the previous evening. The other woman was not sure what to think; the whole episode was very unlike Mina who was usually prone to having affairs with homeless immigrants and refugees who offered themselves to her like political sacrifices, sent from heaven to gratify Mina's vast curiosity about the barbaric world outside the east end of London.

That night when Mina finished work she pushed open the door of the building and, just as she was turning her collar against the wind, noticed the long black car. The passenger door opened and Vladimir stepped out. He waved at Mina and, after letting a car pass, walked across the street to her.

'Would you have dinner with me this evening?' he asked, his face pale under the streetlamp. Mina was flattered. She was unaccustomed to such flamboyant elegance and the attention of a rich man. She said yes and followed Vladimir back to his car, immediately worried about what she was wearing.

'I am not dressed for anywhere smart,' she said covering her embarrassment with a laugh.

'You look wonderful,' he replied. 'I love a woman who has just been working.' Mina felt even more embarrassed then. What an odd thing to say, she thought. The car glided off through the night to a small Italian trattoria somewhere in an area of north London unknown to Mina. They sat at a table in a dark corner and drank large glasses of full-bodied red wine. When the food arrived Mina noticed that Vladimir did not eat but she was so enthralled with the telling of her own life history that she did not think it worth interrupting. Usually men wanted to talk about themselves.

After the meal was finished, Vladimir smiled his handsome smile and said, in a low voice, 'Would you like to come and have coffee at my hotel?'

'Your hotel?' asked Mina, flustered. 'I thought you said you lived in London.'

'I'm looking for somewhere to buy.'

Mina smiled. By now she felt quite drunk. Vladimir's careful questions had made her feel clever and active, as if all things she did were fascinating. Earlier she had tried to discover what exactly his business was. Vague and dismissive about his work, he said only that he took good care of his money.

They left the restaurant and got back into the car which had waited outside while they ate. On the wide black leather seat Vladimir pulled Mina's body close to his. She felt warm and excited and her mouth was dry with nervousness and anticipation. Vladimir kissed her on the neck. His cool lips felt unbearably soft and Mina let her body relax.

In his fifth-floor suite overlooking Hyde Park, Vladimir poured Mina another glass of wine and, as she raised it to her lips, unbuttoned her shirt. She put the glass back on the drinks table and let herself be undressed. He led her into the bedroom and laid her down on the bed. After taking off his own clothes he stretched out beside her, kissing her hair and her face. His lips travelled down her body and when he reached Mina's abdomen she tensed and said, 'I am bleeding.'

'I know,' he replied. Mina sank back into the pillows.

Not long after that Vladimir bought the flat in the docklands and Mina moved in with him.

At night while Vladimir is away working Mina sits up and looks out their windows at the Thames which quietly slaps the concrete embankment below. The old refurbished warehouses seem empty and lonely even though Mina knows all the flats have been bought by people like herself and Vladimir. Sometimes when the wind blows it is almost as if the area is derelict again, lifeless and without industry, the canals and wharves corrupt with rot.

Vladimir's money buys Mina all sorts of things that she never knew she needed. It brings her warmth, freedom from bother, security and lots of space to be liberal in. Vladimir treats Mina well. He is faithful and amorous, especially when she bleeds. Things have always come easily to Vladimir. Mina thinks she might love him. He is tortured and sad, and her heart bleeds for him.

Kate Pullinger was born in Canada in 1961 and has lived in London since 1982. She has published a collection of short stories called *Tiny Lies* and a novel, *When the Monster Dies*.

ON THE DOG

Zolan Quobble

The dog you know is a disguise.

It whimpers to be let out.

Let it out is good advice because even the best trained dog opens its mouth, its throat, its lungs and its diaphragm to call the shadow.

The shadow that stalks canine dreams for the timeless existence of all dreams begs to take shape and take the eye-white from the moon.

Your dog feels the pathos of the vision. It barks frustration at the mysterious dog's mysterious form.

Dogs hear things humans don't. Dogs have a communication system which the police cannot monitor. Dogs are telepathic.

Telepathy is extremely complex. You learn it with mother's milk and it helps if your whole body is specialised for communication like a dog's.

Telepathy is their parliament – a network of boundary piercing calls – a collective unconscious – the full potential of all dogs – a symbol system that relates stars to lamp-posts and turds to their owners.

At the full moon, dogs howl.

It has been a long sleep since the dog went free.

The real dog is an animal of unknown dimensions, neither fox, nor wolf, nor in-between. The dog is hiding in the domestic animal, hiding the original shape of dog in bizarre mutations.

At an ice age zenith humans stole the dog's freedom with fire.

Dogs resent this. In particular they resent the forced in-breeding, the supposed pedigrees and the fatuous tasks.

Barks, gruffs, growls and howls, a shepherd is a dog.

Dogs have talked on telepathy and made plans with the resource of an infinitely sophisticated organic machine.

Dogs use this system by linking together, nose to tail, to make a transmitter.

One dog begins with the note of the message. It emanates from the diaphragm and pulses in every direction. Other animals echo this.

The telepathy field has electromagnetic symptoms, eddy currents which charge the animal's transmitter batteries.

They use a wet tongue to make a better connection.

It is more and more common to see whole chains of dogs transmitting telepathically in this way. The pulses of messages and echoes growing quicker and more quick till they become indistinguishable one from another.

When dogs form a long chain, the organic state connection which they make with the telepath system becomes so strong that they can never be domestic again.

They live on the fringes, mongrels one step closer to the original dog, the dog that roamed free in its own shape, the dog that passed on the gift of telepathy.

Fringe dogs pioneer original dog behaviour experienced during plug-in time with the living library sessions of connected dogs.

Dogs have lost their hierarchical organisation. Instead of pissing in the same place, time after time, dog after dog, to claim and reclaim one individual dog's territory, each dog is so lustful for the one true dog's lineaments, that no dog pisses in the same place as another, and the dog territory expands and eats the land.

Here is liberation. Every adult dog swears by the face of the moon, now the moon's face is full, to devote all its energy to as much copulation as possible, to encourage all mating, to produce as many generations as possible as quickly as possible and so find the original heart-broken dog before that dog pretended that the dog's heart was broken.

I was brave. I opened my heart to the Dog God and I was told.

The dogs stand on kennels, on fences, on walls, on balconies. They occupy the highest points and howl, just howl. Ninety-five billion dogs wake up and howl and begin to search for their ancestor.

Packs of dogs threaten security firms to make them unchain the starved and tormented.

Packs of dogs break into butchers and steal so much meat that there are gorging hours and slow, belly-carrying days.

All dogs are free.

Some telephones are liberated from British Telecom. It looks like a side effect, like an excess of enthusiasm, an act of ecstatic blindness.

Packs of dogs with undefeatable teeth work on the tyres of strategic vehicles and vehicles parked in strategic places.

A rank of dogs spills round a corner in assorted sizes and colours. They play leap the lamp-post and race each other to the next lamp-post. The winner pisses on it while the rest race for the next.

At any time in any rank, if both dogs are willing, one dog may jump on another.

One dog mounted on another dog is like a ringing phone. The other dogs form a loose circle, a spinning spiral, nose to tail, and lay themselves open to the power of the telepathy complex. The vision vividness is enhanced. The dog motives are cleansed. The source dog is brought a little closer.

Another rank of dogs tumbles round the corner – ranks because of the non-military smell, feral dog, dogs close to their roots. This rank of dogs is playing leap the paving slab, a game with a lot less pace but a double volume of rules, and each rule is open-ended and subject to change. Now three dogs, a dalmatian, a red setter corgi cross and a bullnose terrier roll an oaf-faced boxer along the ground. The boxer is laughing all the time with little gruff barks and the rest of the gang are pissing themselves as well as the slabs. There are two teams, the dog rollers and the pissers. The dog rollers have to cover one dog in dog shit before the pissers run out of piss.

This game is quickly overtaken by the car-tyre pissing group, who in turn are passed by the gate-post pissing gang, who move so fast through the street you cannot distinguish individuals. For this rank speed is the thing a real dog loves, travelling fast tipping over prams playing with babies, tipping over shopping trollies eating food, building enough momentum to leap and clear a riot shield.

There are no gate-posts in this street.

After rank upon rank, of running, walking, rolling, zigzagging, snarling, salivating, snuffling, pissing, shitting, barking, howling, copulating, freely expressing dog has passed down the street, the street is the dogs'. They lose it to a huge municipal team trained especially to reconsecrate dog turd streets for human use with tons of disinfectant, tankers full of boiling water, mechanical, stiff brooms, mechanical, soft brooms and mechanical fingers. The workers are covered from head to foot in plastic to keep the germs off. They look suited to another planet.

The dogs don't mind losing a street. It gives even an unplugged dog the same illusion of limitless territory.

Dogs are supremely confident, not because they have the sixth and seventh senses or because they are capable of complete silence while communicating globally, they know the pitches to hit with a howl to jam every possible radio transmission.

The dogs talk about the party. They never talk about anything else.

The dogs rehearse for the quickest complete round of copulation.

The dog party is underground debating with sheer dog sensuality sheer dog sensuality party policy.

Cats remain aloof even in this story.

The dogs howl. Countless dogs give voice to countless,

suffering generations, howl willingness to participate in the one dog regeneration, scratch to give direction, whirl round in a confined space demonstrating pent-up energy, demonstrating destruction, vases shatter, mirrors break, food scatters and windows spray in the revolutionary dog leap.

Magma curdles.

The dogs have woken and shake off their insult like so much moulting hair.

Dogs roll in muddy puddles, run up to friends and enemies and spray it all about.

The orchestrated, dustbin-lid climax, the end-game coda, the gruff tone poem is countless dogs bundling as they follow the moon around the earth.

My mouth is full of dog hairs, and my nostrils full of a dog's rich odour. My ear itches to be scratched by my paw. My face is dripping with dog lick. There is a disturbing realignment taking place in my loins and my legs twitch for a good long run. I have to go now. Message received.

For Hector and Victor

Zolan Quobble, also known as Christopher Cardale, born in 1951, is a member of the South East London Music Collective. Assistant muralist and mosaicist, bodhran player, and member of performance poetry groups, his poetry has appeared in *The Angels of Fire* and *Apples and Snakes* anthologies.

SERIOUS KISSING

Carole Morin

November 1989

After I met this man I couldn't eat. I tried but I couldn't. He would sit and look at me and say, 'You'd better eat something. You have to eat.'

Of course he is a rich man. He's also black. I had never slept with a non-white before. A real jungle bunny. The kind my friends make fun of. He's hairy as well and has great lips and the best voice you ever heard.

His attitude to money's impressive. He just deals and accumulates and invests and hardly notices. Once you've been seriously poor you're always aware of money no matter how much you get. Jones said that.

The black man went back to London and I went back as well. He sat in the first-class smoking section. I locked myself in the toilet and thought about Jones who looks a bit like Hitler: cute haircut, sharp cheekbones, eccentric hands. History labours round the clock to discredit him. He survives. He becomes more dangerous. Because Adolf, like Jones, is immortal. There's only one of him per bunker. And we secretly want to be him. He's a bit sexy, dresses Northern hemisphere military, has a machine gun.

People didn't look at us funny on that plane because a lot of overweight black men travel with thin white girls. It's the sort of thing you only notice once you've done it yourself. Like buying a brown car then realizing everyone has one.

This black man is called Boy. I like him. He sat with me for twenty minutes while the guy in the next seat to me was throwing up in the toilet. While Boy was sitting there he asked if I was nervous. Then he went back to the smoking section, and then the sick guy came back and I took his place in the toilet.

I don't mind Boy asking me questions like that. I was nervous. And he isn't the sort of black guy who expects an answer to a daft question.

What he does enjoy is oral sex, in the morning especially. I don't have to. He has his pride. But he likes this one thing. Some mornings I can hardly get my mouth open. Jones used to say it was psychosomatic insurance against eating breakfast. But how could I have known, when my mouth started sticking, that almost a year later a black man would want his black penis down my throat regularly at 7am (sometimes even earlier).

But it's comfortable living with this man. I like him. He doesn't have AIDS. His colour's his only indulgence.

Of course I can't explain how it became a mess. We rented an apartment on Queensway. We had our own rooms. The morning ritual was less of a habit. He went about his business every day, and sometimes at night also. I never asked a thing. I wasn't interested.

Sometimes we'd sit together in the evening. I told him about my grandfather's fridge. My cousin Wendy used to get left with us each Wednesday afternoon. Her mother was worried about Granddaddy's money. She felt me living with him was an unfair advantage. He didn't have any money left but no one discovered that until he died. So Wendy's greedy bastard of a mother brought Wendy every week and went out to the shops herself after saying, 'No fighting now,' in this big fake voice before she left.

I hated Wendy. So did Granddaddy. At fifteen she was diagnosed backward. At this stage she was five, I was seven. I didn't fight, I organized the house. I told Wendy to defrost the fridge and locked her in the kitchen.

By the time her mother got back Wendy was red in the face attacking the ice with a hacksaw.

As I was discussing trivia like this with Boy I sometimes felt like sitting closer to him. But he didn't allow himself to look keen, so sitting closer to his chair was too decadent.

Being rich and black and crippled has its advantages. Exceptions are made for the token nigger, to prove the point, excuse the rule, patronize the critics.

Some evenings Boy and I went out together. He could afford it. One night we went to Raymond's Revue. That was the same night Boy made friends with a policeman and both of us (me and Tommy, the policeman) found out about Boy's white leg. You'd think I'd have noticed it before, but I don't like looking at him.

Boy was driving fast around Soho, desperate for a parking space because we had tickets for the slow show starting at midnight. Boy hates to miss the beginning.

We couldn't find a parking space. Boy's agitation was increasing. Irritation makes the sides of his face wobble and his moist lips go maniacally in and out, similar to how they move during a really energetic kiss.

He drove in the wrong direction down a one-way street then parked in the pedestrian section of Berwick Street. This policeman (the one Boy made friends with), I'm sure his name must have been Tommy, pounced on us as we climbed out of the car saying, 'You can't park here . . . sir.'

Boy said, 'Yes I can . . . officer.'

Tom took out his notebook and took down the number of Boy's big car. He was about to say something when Boy pointed out the disabled sticker on his windscreen.

Tom snorted. 'There's no one disabled in this car.'

Boy doesn't look like a legless cunt. He has good balance. But he confirmed his disability by removing his left leg – which is made out of white plastic – and waving it at Tom. Boy confessed to me later that he enjoys being part white.

When I realized I loved him I felt pathetic. Sometimes I shook when he came into the room. And couldn't talk in case my voice was stupid. It's so degrading, I thought, pacing around during the day. How can I get out of it? I could leave. But then I'd be poor. I'm not brave enough to be poor again and selling drugs is just as embarrassing as being in love.

I was sick of being in love as soon as it started, but there was nothing to be done. It dragged on. There is no solution. Even if I leave, that doesn't guarantee I'll forget. Even if he decided to love me eventually one of us would get fed up. It always happens. We'd grow old then die.

It's bad enough loving someone. But if they ever find out. Boy started to suspect after about a month. He'd just sit and look at me, saying nothing, absolutely not a word, an odd expression on his chocolate face.

Once he touched me. He put his hand on my arm as I was climbing out of his big white car. I thought I was going to die. It's because I wasn't expecting it. If we're in public or even in front of a taxi driver I know he might help me out of the car. But when we're alone he never does. That move was a surprise. I said nothing for the rest of the evening. Neither did Boy.

Trying to figure out why I decided to love him I put forward all sorts of reasons. Maybe I'm trying to act aesthetically perverse to shock everyone? But he isn't that ugly. Some days quite handsome, in a way. I'd start thinking that then get a shock next time I looked at him.

Eventually I decided the reasons aren't important, the mess is what's relevant. I concocted solutions. I considered confessing. The humiliation might work up a rage and then maybe I could run away.

I walked across Hyde Park in the middle of the night saying I hate him I hate him I hate him into myself.

I knew I would feel better if I cried, but I couldn't cry. There isn't any point. Because feeling better is only temporary. You may as well conquer the worst, just get it over with.

Living with the knowledge that everything was spoiled I longed for the old carefree days when he'd insisted on plonker kissing before breakfast. When we'd slept in the same hotel bed, when I hadn't known I loved him but just got on with it with Jones as my dream.

With Jones I had very short hair and the air was damp. We walked uphill for a quarter of a mile then he said I like you. I said it to him. We walked further. It wasn't planned.

One day last summer, when I was ugly and unhappy, I did something. But that's not how I remembered Jones. It's always raining when I think of him, even in summer. Summers aren't for cities or poor people, he told me. Sunshine is dirty in the city.

There are people (I know there are) who will say: She didn't have to do *that*. She could have done *this*, or gone *there*, or any number of endless possibilities. They will find evidence of a dress I bought instead of food. Or they'll blame it all on Jones, it's his fault, he should have known – helped her, saved her, done something.

The first time we touched he promised it couldn't last or ever be perfect again but I felt safe, the way everything is safe at three o'clock when Granddaddy's poured his fourth whisky and is warm in his chair, and it's never threatening to be in our room overlooking the gardens, thinking of Jones. I always knew him.

The Lord Giveth and The Lord Taketh Away. When I was ten I loved phrases like that. I moved from the kitchen to the front room in a straight line at my Grandfather's house chanting: Vengeance is mine saith the Lord, the power, the glory, the glory, the power. Children called me from outside where they had skipping ropes and footballs. I never took much exercise but read a lot of books about kids who enjoyed all sorts of adventures.

Before I was ten I was six and then seven. When recollecting my childhood I usually include the phrase 'when I was seven' somewhere in the story, but most of it happened when I was six.

Angela was out a lot, and her husband drank and gave us fifty-pence pieces which seemed like a good bribe at the time. My brother loved football and girls during the summer, and I had friends, but at lunchtime we separated at the bottom of our drive and I climbed in the window and cooked a tin of chicken soup.

One day my Grandfather came. He rang the bell three times,

our family code, but I checked by standing on Angela's most expensive chair and looking from behind the turquoise velvet curtain in case it was a trick.

He told me not to be silly when I said I was in alone, but after he'd been in every room, and called out relentlessly for Angie, he finally admitted that I was right.

He sat there all afternoon. He was still there when I came back from school so I didn't have to climb in but did. Angela eventually came home and I was put to bed far too early and heard from the top of the stairs her saying things like, 'Daddy it's the seventies, there are no servants anymore. Anyway we can't afford that sort of thing.' There was a lot of silence then somebody said I was impertinent and after that I went to live with Granddaddy.

We kept ourselves to ourselves. He had never approved of work. He was not a lazy man, he had just never done it. He spent his life 'enjoying himself' and didn't believe in forcing people to do things they don't like. But on those days I didn't go to school he insisted on teaching me something himself in the afternoon. There was usually some weak sunshine causing dust in the first floor sitting room where we sat by the fire, me with an Enid Blyton face down on the carpet, him with a whisky. He got an opportunity to make me wise that did not come up with my brother who was sent abroad the year I went to Grandfather's, where he later became a fairly successful gigolo in the continental style. How can you be a gigolo with round shoulders, Jones asked. How can you be anything?

Granddaddy never felt guilty about enjoying himself. And if he was insecure about dying he never mentioned it. He wasn't the sort of man who talked about his dreams or fuck fantasies either. But every day he gave me chocolate that didn't make me fat, but established a lifetime's habit. He told me about the Book of Fate, and how if your name appears in it destiny can't be evaded. Jones liked that.

Jones listened to Hoagy Carmichael and Richard Wagner while everyone else in Glasgow was still going to see Simple Minds and jealously wondering whether or not Endgames would ever have a hit. He had an automatic razor when the others were still using hammers, and his haircut emphasized his bonestructure. He has a perfect face, but never allows his photograph to be taken.

The first time I saw him I didn't look, I couldn't. I had just finished school and decided to become decadent before it was too late forever and went to a club with a girl who didn't suit it. Jones didn't speak to me, his friend did, a bleached boy with strange ears who invited me to his party. I went because of Jones. It wasn't his thrilling composure or his resemblance to Hitler that first attracted me, it was his refusal to look interested when approached by the best dancer there (who turned out to be one of his sisters).

There was never any nonsense between us. He liked me and was silent about it but I knew. We didn't speak the first night.

His friend called me up. My band are playing on Sunday do you want to come I'll get you on the guest list you don't have to pay you can bring somebody if you like but it's best to come alone.

I went alone avoiding the funny-eared boy who had unsuccessful surgery later and wasn't really a friend of Jones. I stood next to Jones at a wall outside where he was breathing in silhouette. We didn't watch the band. I was wearing white. I was sure he was thinking about something significant, and knew he was sincere when he complimented my nose. I decided to like it myself.

Attracted by my nose and very straight shoulders we went on seeing each other all summer, but never alone. Until Jones started to paint me the boy with the ears or some other chaperone was always present.

Jones paints all day, but rarely sells anything. He pretends that no one is interested but really he can't bear to part with his masterpieces.

In Glasgow he made a living selling fashion shirts and designed me a grey spider shirt which I never wore after what happened.

But that autumn he said things like, 'I wasn't born with the idea of happiness,' making me laugh and laugh, happier and happier. The first night we touched he promised it couldn't last.

Scarlett O'Hara lived across the square from us, an eighties' version with red lips (you'll long to kiss). I first noticed her because of her husband, Willoughby, a man of about ninety dressed fashionably and known as the only millionaire in town (his boast). He had a yacht and a Mercedes and bowel trouble and was always taking girls to Barbados to fuck their brains out, as if he couldn't do it in Glasgow.

He bought a shop for his wife and Carlan filled it with clothes her own size which fitted me as well. My association with Jones seduced her to favour me and she gave me the pick of the shop to wear 'as advertising'. She suggested we sell her husband a Jones original.

'Does he like New Northern Expressionism?'

Carlan shrugged.

'He may not want a painting.'

'I'm sure he does,' she said lazily.

Willoughby agreed to see me in one of his restaurants where a man was trying to sell him a hundred French chairs to match the cuisine. I told him they weren't French and immediately won his favour. My decision was taken to annoy the salesman, but Willoughby didn't know that. The salesman was fat.

Of course Willoughby bought the watercolour, a sunset unworthy of Jones, but he had to do it badly to bear parting with it to a man like that. Willoughby commissioned a painting of his house, and at the same time Jones did a portrait of me for Granddaddy who removed Angela from a heavy black frame and put me in.

Willoughby convinced himself Jones had talent and arranged an exhibition for him at the opening of his new restaurant. Jones insisted on displaying nurses with sliced throats and big brutal men like the working-class fruits in Earls Court garotting each other. We'd soon have enough money to leave town. We wanted to escape.

In Glasgow your friends take it as a personal insult if

you succeed. And everyone always talked of Jones's success, imagining it was real. By success they mean money, but we didn't have money we wanted it.

Jones met a man at the Sub Club who offered him a free flat in Earls Court 'to paint in'. It wasn't empty yet because the current lease didn't expire for two months, when Malcolm Brown (who was nearing the end of a mixed anglophile experience) was going back to Boston.

We arranged to move in as soon as Malcolm moved out but couldn't spend the intervening month in Glasgow. We went on a boat to Paris, because it's more romantic by water, and no one would know us there. I stood on deck thinking, 'Nothing can threaten me,' wondering if I should jump? I wasn't afraid to sleep at night or get out of bed in the morning or meet someone I didn't want to talk to. He convinced me we were perfect by consistently denying it.

Magnificently cold, November, all French winter sun and insecurely sophisticated people and neither of us had been before. I couldn't love a man who'd loved someone else already or a city he saw first without me.

Happiness is an insecure thing and yet we don't reject it, we allow it to overwhelm us, to confuse; to convince us, as we stop in the Louvre at the Seven Sacraments smiling at each other's reflection in the glass.

Holding hands the whole time, walking to the edge of the river, terrified.

Jones smiling protectively as I was stared at in the all-night store on rue Rambuteau.

'Are you French?' the Arab asks intently.

'No.'

'Are you sure?'

On our last morning Jones looked seriously at me and said, 'You know your bottom could be thinner.'

I was desolate.

'Everyone needs to lose ten pounds – everyone thin – everyone else should starve.'

To have a physical deformity is bad enough. But for him

to have seen it, close-up, naked, daylight coming through the drapes the way we left them intentionally last night.

I punched it for weeks, and almost gave up chocolate, hating myself until he said, quite unexpectedly: 'Your bum's reduced.'

Earls Court

We arrived in London the week before Malcolm Brown went back to Boston. Jones had his head shaved for a part in a movie that never transpired and I was left with my long hair in a cheap hotel while he camped in Hyde Park.

The plan was for me to shower and make up and wear clean clothes and make lots of money as a model or an actress or something respectable but lucrative. I stuck it for a day, having my photograph taken by a neurotic who pretends his name's Rogier who tried to pick Jones up in Leicester Square.

The next day I went to Soho and had my head shaved. I kept my hair, gathering it up off the unbrushed floor afraid I'd mingle it with strands of somebody else's – forced to treasure theirs forever as well as my own. Jones didn't suspect.

I liked living in the Park. I read by crewlight before falling into that abandoned sort of sleep only an exhausted person is brave enough to allow.

In the morning we smartened ourselves with mirrors and booked into a hotel. We always picked a good one, with a receptionist snobbish enough to be impressed with my stolen credit cards. We lay in the bath until lunch, chattering about fame and fortune and the desert. We were great friends.

I called Granddaddy, but he never sounded enthusiastic. I thought he was sulking with me, jealous of Jones. And though I never admitted it or even thought about it, I was angry he hadn't offered us money. Jones wasn't.

'It's our responsibility,' he said. I agreed but he meant it.

I didn't call again but sent a regular stream of uninformative postcards. Asking for help is impossible, accepting it is easy.

Malcolm Brown went home and we moved into his free flat in Earls Court Square but pretended it was somewhere else because I felt like one of the undead walking along Earls Court Road and I wished the IRA would blow it up.

Jones searched the flat for bugs and hidden cameras in case the landlord's a voyeur. He's the sort of anonymous type that could be anything, and he obviously has a motive. Free flats are not often offered. We couldn't be bothered worrying about it.

Apart from being free the flat was clean and white, which surprised us. We blacked the windows in with crêpe and kept the music on. The day after we moved in the call came. It was Carlan.

She said: 'Your grandfather's dead.' She didn't stay on the line long. I sat in a corner on the floor facing the wall. Jones left me crying for a while then told me to stop it.

'You knew he was going to die', he said.

'What! How could . . .'

'He was an old man. The oldest man in the world.'

'Shut up.' I picked up as much as I could from my corner flinging it everywhere and screaming more, blinded. Jones put on his coat.

'I'm not indestructible.'

'You are you are don't ever say that ever. You are or I hate you.'

While he was out I cleared up and it wasn't mentioned again.

April 1989

We didn't answer the phone so the landlord sent us a letter. *Your rent has stopped. You must leave the flat.* Jones went to see him. The worst part had been finding out at the funeral Granddaddy was having our rent paid all along. He'd wanted to get away.

We have to leave at the end of the month. Jones will be back before then. He's away painting. He hasn't told me where.

I don't know what I am going to do at the end of this month. Where are we going to go? (I know already Jones is going to go off alone, to a field or someplace he won't even tell me about.) It's me, without Jones, anyone. No money. That's the worst part. With money it's camouflaged a bit.

I feel dirtily warm like a ragged nail no one's cut off. Alone with my mistakes. Sometimes sleep around sunrise, certain the inside of my stomach is erupting in boils that will eventually be labelled a new disease.

I intend to eat two cartons of Chinese scampi and go to a very long movie. Naturally I feel a fool breaking my heart over a man in 1989 and don't intend to ever tell anyone.

The sun outside is on the snow. I can see it from bed. I know now I cannot mean anything proper to Jones, he's too closely associated with himself. It can't be snow it's April.

My hair's scraped back in a covered elastic. If I'd really broken off all relations with society I would have used any elastic band that came to hand. But of course in the back of my mind I'm still trying to grow my hair long, unsplit. I'm still sitting with my face in one of those non-committal poses that discourage wrinkles. I'm still thinking: Jones.

An obvious obsession would have been easier. To talk about him ceaselessly while alone and introduce him into every conversation. But thinking about him is even too dangerous. Sleep in the ordinary way impossible because he intrudes.

Baldness and fleshlessness would be peace. An ultimate perfection I can't explain. But I'm fat. Not the deliberate kind a dietician would take seriously. But it's discreetly there at its worst in the full length. My recognition is despicable. I am the worst thing imaginable: a middle-aged woman's idea of thin.

The night before Jones returned I was in a dream that encouraged me not to think about things for a while. We went to Russia, Jones and I, on a long slow train, and it was never called the Soviet Union, but I wore my revolutionary clothes and Jones covered his baldness with a hat, and people announced what they were to say before saying it: 'I have a piece of news' and then . . .

When I woke up it was cold and soon I was too. Feeling hungry, I ate some cereal with a little milk. Not too much milk because I don't like the taste. I sat down on a hard chair and read a bit of a dull book and wondered if I had enough courage to put earphones on. There's more light than yesterday, I notice, while deciding not to, it isn't safe until later.

Tonight I'm going to be ugly, my looks are unreliable like that. Music isn't safe later either, I could be attacked any time, unless Jones is look-out sitting on the floor with an army issue spade by his side. He isn't coming back.

Jones tell me it'll be all right and I'll believe you and come to wherever you are now it doesn't matter nothing matters but my soul is yours whatever that is do you believe in souls I do if you do Jones Jones Jones.

June 1989

A boy appears on screen in the Greek stance with toes like nails. Jones sits watching, a spade in his hand.

Prosper from downstairs came up to watch Jones watch television. He says to me: 'It's a sure sign of poverty, sharing a flat.'

Prosper is a male tart. Every time I go down there he's in the shower rinsing the secretions off between clients.

He's embarrassed when there's a client in. Jones says no wonder, I should call first. Silly when he's right below. Jones respects privacy. But I know he took medical advice to see if I was in danger of anything from talking to a fruit.

'Have you been mugged yet?' Prosper is impatient with our silence again. He expects something from these quick visits to the heteros. He's also secretly in love with Jones but took the trouble to tell me, 'If I was a man I'd fancy you.'

'Of course not. I'm not the type.'

Prosper laughed. Jones continued to stare at the television.

When Prosper went back downstairs Jones still didn't look at me. Maybe we would have more chance alone. I'll not be one of those women who cries about the death of love until she's too tired.

More than anything I want his attention. I crept up behind his shoulder spraying his eyes with the last of my mace.

But the next day he gave me the Blackglama, I loved him again, every young capitalist should have one, I always love him, even though it's useless until winter and he explained Southwark during my glee. He's taking me to dinner with a family I can stay with when he goes to paint in a small caravan, big enough for one (and canvases and oils and a sleeping bag).

But Jones is like my past. Whatever happens now, it will always have happened. Jones is always there. Like air and chocolate and excrement but mainly chocolate and always that first autumn in Paris. Perfection cannot be replaced. It's pathetic forever trying to reinstate it.

Jones moved to his caravan at Brimsdown behind iron gates that clatter loudest when climbed at night. It is small without electricity or wheels or water. He paints there.

I went to stay with the family in Southwark. I came out the exit at Elephant station after climbing the spiral and temporarily losing my sun hat. The road didn't look the same as when Jones brought me to dinner last week to see if I could face living with them.

Tonight it's sunny with hay fever and staring niggers. Three bald children on a doorstep in a simulated poverty pose.

People want you to have nothing. I bathe every morning and take my dresses to the dry cleaners and keep the scissors sharp for Jones to trim my hair and they think, 'She doesn't look hungry.' They want me to be tired and unhappy like them. I'd rather be thin. Eating is undignified. It spoils lipstick.

My make-up case isn't heavy. Heavier than the plastic bag with my change of clothes, but not heavy. But heavy for me, in the sun. I'm hungry and don't know what to say when I arrive. They are not expecting me tonight. They don't know me. Jones did the talking that night they fed us tough chops and beans I couldn't look at.

Their children do not realize yet. Perhaps the eldest boy (still under ten) knows. He is sullen. Maybe he knows he has nothing.

'Mum,' a blonde child shouts, running ahead of me into the house. She is wearing pink and has her hair in a long bob. 'Mum it's her, it's that woman.'

'Hello, Jones said . . . '

'Come in, come in!' she said christianly.

She offers me a bath and a pie. She is my age. A working-class feminist, I'm not sure whether Liberal or Labour. I admire her energy, but wish she'd remove the moustache, and stop saying 'It was really nice' in a sincere south London accent.

They give me the blonde's bed, she shared with her brother in the same room. The sullen one is in with us too. He wets the bed. I can smell it. His apology in the morning is rebuffed.

There's a prayer on the coffee table. 'Thank God for the people of Southwark, we share your grief that a rich society has exploited us and made us all violent unemployed drug addicts with no power.' She intends to read it out loud in church on Sunday.

I lie flat on the bed. I must be dead by Sunday. Or gone. Please God don't let me be ugly. There's a window behind my head. Someone will smash it in the night. That's OK. I'll be dead or ruined without an escape route with an imperfect face. It's been ransacked by the burglar. An ice-man. He wants Revenge instead of videos and loose cash.

In the morning there's a note in the kitchen advising Help Yourself. The house smells of last night. Do not open the window, there is crime, whatever happens keep all the windows *shut*. But the smell, surely during the day, when I'm in? *Do not open it. Don't answer the door. It is not safe.*

The floor makes my feet gritty. I want to do the dishes for her while she is at work expending more energy on *other people*. But the water is lukewarm, I can't touch the wipe, there are no rubber gloves. My nails scrape at the stuck food for a few minutes then give up. Guilt is a waste of time.

The bath, scrub it first. East End water makes my skin itch. A large grey scum always on top at the end. It is not the same as Kensington. You can pretend a glam bathroom makes it seem better, but I know it isn't the same stuff. Drink it here and you'll get gastro-enteritis.

Go out and buy some Coke. All the stomachs stick out. In Kensington they belt their tummies tightly, making a roll of fat above and below the Lagerfeld buckle. Whether this is an attempted disguise or vain defiance I don't know.

My brother says when I die and they cut me open to find out how I was murdered my insides will be an ugly dark brown from all that Coke. 'It hasn't made my teeth brown.' It will.

'Don't be ridiculous.' He's one of those people who thinks living deteriorates you. I know it doesn't, if you retain your will. Jones says it's the only thing worth keeping. Just to have it is enough.

A glass of flat Coke, pour it quickly then let it stand on the salty table long enough to lose its fizz. I'd like to wipe that table one day. The patronizing advice of my hostess last night.

'You can always find a place to live.' (It's your own fault.)

'What about a hostel?' (Have you tried compromise.)

The hostel. Rubber sweat, catarrhal breaths, in the morning everyone's hay fever starts at once. They all know each other. In the breakfast room I can't eat and think of the wasted £1.40 (it could have been McDonald's) and the plate of blood in the fridge here, tonight's dinner.

I went out. I went to a chocolate shop. I saw a woman in gloves lifting a silver box. I decided I want to look like her. Not to have her face, to have my face, but that expression. For a few moments each hour, maybe, and to be able to afford that box. Of course it's silver-plated, and well designed. I could fill it with diamonds after, I said to Jones. I always talk to him. I know when I feel sentimental about which tin of Coke to buy and worried about the ones left behind (though I never confess this to the person with me) that it's time to see Jones. His bone structure makes me ruthless. A determination to be as perfect as him. The ultimate dream is for him to love me and me to be strong enough to reject him. And be happy alone, it's a trick otherwise.

I had the ideal opportunity to harm him the night we were sitting diagonally opposite Waterloo Bridge after dark. A stripey woman with bleached hair interrupted. She must have felt sick and had to leave the theatre. Or wanted to be alone, mentally. Doubtless made a fool of herself somewhere.

Before she appeared I could easily have struck him unobserved as he was leaning too far over the rail to impress me. Engrossed in the water, it would have been easy to sever a finger with my French flickie then push him into the Thames. After the sky Jones loves water best.

But of course he can swim. The river would like him, It would be a pleasant experience. It would alert him. He would ask more regularly *Are you all right* and watch my face when he thought it unguarded. Of course the perfect time is when he's asleep, next time we share a hotel. I could inject him with something then spend hours hacking off a limb. But that's weak. There has to be an element of risk, a chance for him to save himself.

In the meantime I went back to Southwark on a bus and took one of my hostess's painkillers. As soon as the family got home I went out for a walk and had an attack on a park bench.

A smooth skin is an act of will, acne an obscenity. Acne and obesity are cheap publicity. I saw a flaked cheek in the mirror and the beginnings of a line beside my nose. I check my face every couple of hours. Maybe it will be gone next time I look?

It's cooler here. There is no one in the park. Legs splodged onto the wooden seat. Fatness is a continuous state. One cannot be sometimes fat. In a particular outfit, a certain light. Being thin: always thin. It is no use otherwise. It is just as well I cannot eat.

The wooden slats chew my legs. Economizing in heat must be impossible. Living in heat only barely possible. Heat and poverty. The summer is not for cities or poor people.

Maybe I should leave Jones as he is? His perfection is a comfort. Don't be a fool.

This is what it feels like when there's no one. The decision is mine. I suspected it was a superior thrilling feeling, being alone. It isn't in Southwark with a migraine and an overdrawn cashpoint card.

I must get out of the sun. You would think it would be gone by now. Jones says illness is the worst thing. The most difficult to accept. I would have argued, if it wasn't for the migraine.

But poverty, anyone who says No is a liar or a fool. No it doesn't matter, it doesn't bother me, I don't care, what do I need money for anyway. Poverty is impossible. And knowing it's all going to happen again tomorrow.

The sort of person people look at on the train and think

It's OK for her. Easily impressed with the classic profile. But it all happens again tomorrow, or next month, or sometime inescapable.

When it gets dark I will have to move from this bench. But when it's dark the children go to bed and there's only her to listen to, her husband is out. She tries coffee and enthusiastic chat.

In the hot sun of the next afternoon (the hottest day yet for the purposes of sanity) I went out with a new migraine having previously decided not to return to Southwark.

This is it, the day to get Jones.

Dust and industry led the way to his caravan. The pounding road, the smell of burning flesh, the men shouting things. The whole experience would have upset and fatigued me if I wasn't about to do something very important: change my future.

But Jones didn't come that day. I thought he had disappeared. I always think that.

A sense of absurdity, a feeling I can't really be unhappy if I acknowledge it now as I sit here on the ground waiting to commit sacrilege. Suddenly a sense of wellbeing will come – I know it will – I'll be tricked again.

On Friday I am stronger than Monday. Accept no one can help. (Knew on Monday.) My energy must not drain. People call it luck but it is will.

Breeze pleasant. The sort of thing only notice when desperate. The breeze a bit too precise. Think about making a coin box call to someone who will change my mind. I can't. The leaves are blowing in my face. Sneezing. The patterns are created. I am not unhappy.

Next morning about eleven (before it was at its hottest) (in fact during a small patch of shade) he came towards me down the lane, face riddled with excitement. He didn't bother to ask what I was doing there. He did say, 'You're in this,' and pushed the summer issue of *Autre Monde* into my hand. 'Rogier sold them before he went mad.'

'But I don't want to be a model.'

'You're not. I've destroyed the negatives. And you don't have to go back to Southwark.'

'I wasn't going to anyway.'

He laughed. Everyone must help themselves. He's always telling me that.

'Let's get a hotel.'

'I'm going to hurt you sometime.'

'I know what you mean.'

'Take no thought for tomorrow.'

'Plan it meticulously.'

He smiles with negligible uncertainty. It's all I ever wanted. I am not unhappy.

'I cannot imagine you other than you are now.'

The hotel room was pleasant. Jones made the bath all foamy and climbed in. He twisted his neck to watch me approach. My face was calm. A smile would have been cheap and inappropriate.

I used his razor knowing it would be more of a shock that way. It's sharp and effective. His bath turned red. He stifled a cry then pushed me backwards.

After that incident Jones didn't want to see me again. And then I went to Morocco. And there I met this black man, Boy, the one with the big white car.

Carole Morin was born in Glasgow in 1964. She is a freelance journalist and lives in London. Her stories have appeared in *First Fictions: Introduction 10* and the *Red Hog of Colima*. She is currently finishing a novel, *Lampshades*. An earlier version of 'Serious Kissing' appeared in *Fiction Magazine*.

SODOMY

Gary Indiana

It was before the war. I used to meet Jack every Friday at the Oyster Bar in Grand Central. I was employed as a memory typist at a survey firm. Jack worked in publishing. He was my age, twenty-eight. He had the soft brown eyes of a southern boy, full lips and a strong chin. Jack worked out, he has an inspiring physique. His hair was the color of a motorcycle jacket. It looked very glamorous on him.

'Hiya, sweetheart,' was Jack's normal greeting. I arrived early, he arrived late. An inflexible pattern.

'Jack,' I'd say. 'My prince.'

He smiled a lot. Even his teeth were sexy. He liked my little romantic things. There was nothing binding in them.

'You look like a million dollars,' Jack would say, not just being flattering. Between Friday night and Saturday afternoon, Jack found me totally enthralling. We never had two consecutive nights together and I knew we never would. If I saw him on the street with somebody else it was always hello goodbye, no kiss, no handshake even. Fridays were different. Jack paid for everything, the oysters, dinner, endless gin and tonics, often a bottle of champagne at the end of the evening. We went to strip joints and discos and fist fuck bars on the West Side to dance and score poppers or a few hits of coke. At some hour we'd end at his place. He had a clean, dark apartment near Avenue A on East 13th. He shared this place with a former lover who was perpetually out of town, on nebulous business. Jack would put on some jazz and light candles, making an atmosphere. We'd smoke a joint, then Jack undressed me with an air of great confidence. One thing he liked, he'd spread honey and strawberry jam on his cock and balls, then kneel over me while I licked it off. The candles flickered big shadows on the wall. Jack eased my legs over his shoulders and drooled saliva across his fingertips, smearing it around my asshole and the head of his prick. He plunged in bluntly then froze with just the tip inside until my muscles relaxed around it, squeezing in deeper a half inch or so at a time. The shaft of Jack's penis was about ten inches long and almost two inches thick. Once he had it in all the way it felt like an iron pipe, but Jack knew how to make it nice, I'd tighten around it if he slid more than an inch of it out. I could twist over onto my stomach without losing any of it. Sometimes Jack carried me across the room, his arms wrapped around my thighs, fucking the whole time like an air hammer. In the mornings we fucked standing up in the shower, and usually once more on the carpeted floor in the living room, dog style, though this second fuck made both of us stoned and hazy for the rest of the day. I really had to struggle to get anything accomplished on Saturday afternoons the whole year and a half I was seeing Jack. But we were hungry for each other. To tell you the truth, Jack was about the only thing that made sense to me at the time.

As things go, it wasn't much. Jack couldn't make love cold sober on Friday, though he did fine on a Saturday morning hangover. The one time we skipped cocktails and the drugs, Jack barely could get it up and flung his wad in about two minutes. I wondered about that, after he apologized and fell asleep: did he invent his lust out of mere alcohol? Was it just convenient, after a hard week at the office, to fuck me instead of looking out for someone else? It's true we had sentiments about each other. But when we really scratched the surface of our real opinions and ideas, it was obvious Jack and I came from two distant planets. I wanted us to have more in common than we did, so I agreed a lot with Jack's dumb ideas; I'm sure he went along with mine, too.

In those last confused years before the war, it was possible for something like Jack's sexual organs to play a key role in my life, along fairly homely lines of supposedly vanquished stereotypes. He never let me fuck him, for example, pleading hemorrhoids. He went down on me from time to time, but mainly he played the man. It was fine for a while but it got boring. He could make me come with his dick, which isn't so common as people suppose; but I never came inside him, and I had the idea that this meant something important. Perhaps it didn't, looking back on 1978.

But there was this, too: I didn't love Jack, and Jack didn't love me. We liked each other's bodies, it went that far. The guy I did love didn't want anything to do with me, not physically anyway. Dean. Dean was an actor in off-Broadway, then. What attracted me to Dean was the certainty of rejection, added to a funny gambler's hope of somehow beating the house, seducing him through sheer will, making the unlikely blossom into heady passions like a million stale Hollywood endings. As a former resident of Nevada, I know perfectly well, and knew then, that no one ever beats the house. However, this never stopped anybody from dropping their mortgage payment on the table at Caesar's Palace and it didn't stop me from being in love with Dean.

Dean's appearance was nothing to write home about, so I figured I loved him for who he really was. He was tall and gangly and his face was full of odd scooped out angles and flatnesses. It had a certain grace, though. People sometimes said he was so ugly he was almost beautiful. Even if they never left out 'almost', he was beautiful to me. He was a person for whom I'd gladly have given up my will, if you see what I mean. Anyway, Dean was my comet passing once, and strictly poison. Unattainable people usually turn out weak and ridiculous once your feelings for them go; that happened to me once with a junkie landscape gardener, and another time with an opera queen who had astigmatism. But a certain few prove strong and dangerous: that was Dean, all in all. My wanting him stirred up a deep-buried stratum of nastiness in Dean, as excessive viciousness that sprang from some copious childhood reserve. Some people run away from unsolicited attention, it's the usual thing to do. Others channel these surprising energies and put them to work, the way voodoo doctors set zombies out in the fields to plant cane.

I didn't see Dean so very often at first, because this type of relationship doesn't exactly improve your mental health, even if it does give you something to think about most of the time. We went to dinner occasionally, flirting desultorily and keeping the muck underneath at arm's length. Later, though, there were several periods of intense, daily contact. Dean wasn't a big talker but he had an eloquent physical vocabulary. Silence can tell you a lot of things. Large tracts of emotional sewage passed between us in a wordless miasma. I wanted him desperately. Dean enjoyed this with indecent detachment. Something hideous generally occurred when we saw each other with any regularity. The more I saw him the less I liked him, but that didn't affect my desire for him even slightly. In fact, as I peeled the onion of his personality to its dark center and found more and more to despise, the stronger my need to possess him became. Dean revealed himself as a creature of masks, a manipulator of ambiguities spun in silences as deadening and calculated as surgical anesthesia. After knowing him a while I started tagging his masks and numbering them in my head. Whenever his blankness became too terrorizing for me to manage I'd do something spiteful to drive him off. Then I'd spend weeks rolling everything around in my head, finding obscure and noble motives for the rotten things he'd done, and in the end I'd miss him. There was something about Dean's physical aura that gave me a weird high. I always broke down and called him. And he always threw himself back onto my life with numbing, amnesiac enthusiasm.

We were in a Mexican restaurant once upon a time, and I, with great tequila courage, said: 'Dean, I can't see you any more.' I felt strong, too, because Jack had screwed me the previous evening. 'I'm in love with you, I want you, you know, physically, and if that isn't what you want it's masochism for me to be around you.'

Marimba music poured from two minispeakers near our table. Dean had heard all this before. It bored him. His long face took on a flinching, pained look that I'd recently decided to call Mask Number Three.

'I'm not ready for a physical relationship,' Dean said. 'I mean, we can be friends, and someday –'

'No, we can't. I can't just will my feelings away and act like they don't exist.'

'I'm not saying you have to, I'm just asking you to give me some time.'

'Time to do what, Dean? Excite yourself with my frustration?'

'Thanks.'

My thought was: if I were a decent human being, I'd accept this situation as it is and love him that much more. But I'm not a decent human being. Decent human beings live in India and perform blessed works among the dying.

'It's making me crazy to see you, Dean. I want you every second. When you aren't there I think about you. Constantly. It's idiotic. You don't love me, I don't even understand what you find tolerable about being with me.'

'I do love you, I've told you before, I'm too fucked up right now to get involved with anybody in a, a sexual relationship.'

The sense in which we were already involved in a, a sexual relationship was one that didn't elude Dean, exactly. Looking at it now, I think he always had half his mind on what things looked like to other people, and how far he could go without becoming involved in his own actions. In the material sense of sticking parts of his body into holes in other people's. The mind, whatever its penetrative capacity, is, after all, photographically invisible.

'Then we should go away from each other,' I told him, not very firmly. 'It can only make me bitter against you to want you when you don't want me.'

'If you love me the way you claim you do, you wouldn't insist on that physical thing, there are other ways to love people.'

I considered these other ways while Mask Number Two, an expression of incipient and sensitively withheld lust, began working itself through the skin of Mask Number Three. Dean was never as convincing onstage as he was across a restaurant table. But we'd done this number so many times that I simply watched the morphology shifting, as if witnessing some geological process beyond my influence. I'd known him for seven months, and registered every nuance of his voice, his eyes, his fingernails. Nothing he did would ever surprise me again. When I tried to break it off, he turned seductive and coy, opened his legs a certain way in a chair, brought his body closer to mine in a room, lit my cigarettes, kissed my neck when my head was turned to the clock on the wall or the exit sign in a cinema; when I responded, he withdrew with a fluttering of petty details, an abrupt assertion of surface. Mask Number One was a glossy, impervious fish face that all desire bounced off more like a superball, and its appearance was inevitable. When Dean needed an emotion he pulled the appropriate face out and held it up until the crisis passed.

'Relax,' he said at last. Marimbas jingled in stereo as we laughed off another horrid moment. When I think about Dean today, there are always waiters on the periphery of my mental picture, flashing cocktail trays and setting down silverware. And unpleasant music playing, through high distortion speakers.

I never told Dean about Jack, but he must have known a Jack existed somewhere: when I felt contented, and acted emotionally detached, Dean switched on the full voltage of his charm, became proprietary, gave notice to my person. He knew, he must have known, must have studied the problem carefully: if he'd fucked me in the first place he'd have lost all power over me. That wasn't what I wanted from him. It was the tangible aspect of what I wanted him to be for me – my lover, the person whose flesh was his bed. I wanted him beyond any simple craving, as a metaphysical principle: not to fuck him, but to disappear inside him.

This business of being in love, it's nothing but a little dance around a straw puppet unless the other person plays. Everyone knows this. What confused me in those days before the war was that Dean did play, right up to the edge of carnal finality. And there he flew away, to the next branch, like some mating parrot in the Amazon. Without letting go of a thing, he kept himself the most important thing in my life.

This all had its effect on my Friday nights with Jack. My taste for disconnected sex was turning to nausea. His cock began to hurt, though it never had.

'I can't, Jack. It's too much.'

He pulled out instantly. 'It's okay, baby. Let's get some sleep.'

'In the morning, Jack.'

'Sssh. Shut your eyes. Have a pretty dream.'

I didn't even know I was crying. Jack wiped my face with the heel of his palm.

'You got hurt, baby,' he whispered. 'How did that happen?'

'I don't know,' I sniffled. Jack crinkled the cellophane on a new pack of Camels. 'Because . . . oh, Christ, Jack, because I'm such an asshole.'

A match lit up his face. He frowned, leaned over, and kissed my forehead the way you kiss a small child, holding his cigarette with thoughtful poise.

'We're all assholes,' Jack said, with gravity. There was a cheap alarm clock near the bed, its face glowing dimly with a pinkish, defective-looking light. It was new. That apartment had hardly any natural light, waking in it was like waking underwater. We had never known exactly what time it was, on any particular Saturday, for a year and a half: hours had gone past like minutes, minutes like hours. The afternoon sun had always been a stinging surprise.

'I've never been good to you,' Jack said, 'except in bed.'

'That's not true,' I said. I kissed the warm flesh of his back. 'You've been great. I'm just sorry I'm so fucked up.'

I grabbed his arm and pulled him down to me, wriggling free of the sheet, wrapping my legs around his waist. I felt the head of his penis glide through the opening under my spine and pushed myself over his stiffening organ, folding him into me with a kind of mad insistence, arching over him as he lowered his back to the mattress, his lower back crushing my feet. I forced him through me and felt my insides tearing apart, ramming myself down on the thick, stinging prick until I could feel his pubic hair sweating against my balls. I freed my legs and shifted my knees, sinking my weight down against his lower abdomen and then slowly rising until the rim of his dick lay just at the edge of my sphincter muscles, holding him there and then delicately sliding the curled lip of flesh in and out of the slackened opening; I could feel the blood flowing in the veins of Jack's cock, and slid greedily down the hard tube of flesh, rose up again, and now Jack's hips began pounding him into me and out again, I braced myself with my fists buried into the mattress around his hair. I felt my bowels loosening and everything inside pummelled into shit and blood and pure pain, and finally felt his sperm squirting through me like a random laser, rivers of it splashing across the walls of my intestines, the cock burning like coals as it shrank and very gradually slipped out of my ass and slapped against the sheet.

The bed felt wet and when Jack turned the light on we saw it was soaking with blood, both of us smeared with it, though it seemed to have stopped flowing out of me.

'Jesus,' Jack said, pulling the sheet from the bed. He guided me into the bathroom, where he washed me gingerly with a face cloth and wiped the blood off his cock. 'Wow, I'm really sorry.'

'It isn't your fault,' I said. 'Anyway, I'm still alive, Jack.'

We put a new sheet on the bed. Jack went into the kitchen and came back with a glass of orange juice.

'Have some juice,' he told me.

'Oh, Jack.'

We studied each other in the dim greenish light of the room. My brains felt scrambled, I could barely focus my eyes. Jack sucked on a Camel, looking bewildered and suddenly much older than himself. Neither of us wanted to say, but it was one of those strange moments when reality foams up around your ears unbidden, so to speak. I put down the juice glass and slid off the bed. Jack picked his underpants from the floor and pulled them on.

'Listen,' I told him when I had my clothes on, 'you've been great to me, Jack, don't ever think different.'

He put his chin on my shoulder and said, 'Someday we'll figure out that we really needed each other.'

'Uh-huh.'

When I thought about it later I realized it was the most upsetting thing anyone ever said to me. It was the last time I went to bed with Jack; a few days later I began taking a lot of speed and went through another strange time with Dean, the last one as it turned out. For some reason Dean was also taking a lot of speed, and since I had the better supply he began turning up at my apartment every morning to replenish himself. By this time I just thought of him as a jerk, and had difficulty finding my former interest in his awkward body and oblique manner. He had always been punitive towards me, but now he seemed coarse and brutal, too. The last day I saw him, Dean said something so badly insulting that it gave away his contempt for me more directly than he'd intended, and I walked out of the room. Dean followed me into the kitchen. I poured some black coffee into a mug, paying no attention to him.

'Philip, do me a favor.'

'What, Dean.'

'Don't put on that wounded bird look. It just pisses me off.'

'I'm not putting on any look. This happens to be the way my face is. I think I can look however I want in my own apartment, anyway.'

'Well, I don't like it.'

'I know you don't like it. You don't like it, you don't like it. Maybe you should go find something you do like and stop subjecting yourself to me.'

A provocative, familiar silence. Long enough for me to catch myself and apologize. Long enough to read the New York telephone directory aloud.

'If that's how you want it.'

'Dean?'

'What.'

'That is all just words, you know.'

'Meaning what?'

'Meaning that we never really discuss what's going on between us, and you like to think if we don't discuss it that it doesn't exist, which is nice and safe for you, but I'm . . .'

'Listen to yourself, will you?'

'Listen to you, listen to the tone of voice you're using right now.'

'You're crazy, Philip.'

'I know that. So what. Who isn't?'

'Yeah, but you're *really* crazy. Do you really want to destroy everything between us over nothing?'

'According to you there isn't anything between us. According to you I'm a nut case like that broad in *Play Misty for Me*, going bonkers because some guy won't fuck her. So why keep coming around, Dean? To cop amphetamine? Clint Eastwood wouldn't do shit like that.'

'I care about you, shithead.'

I realized we were on the verge of something really irrevocable and said it anyway: 'So prove it, Dean. Get out of my life.'

And he did. Slunk out, more or less, but with an atmosphere of great pride later on, as if it made any difference. So it ended with Jack and it ended with Dean, and I suppose something new might have started with other people, but then the war came, which ended a good deal one might have looked forward to. A few years later I ran into Dean in a back lot and we fucked on a mattress in a pile of rubbish, but I didn't realize until later that that was him, and I don't think he recognized me either.

Gary Indiana lives in New York City. He has published two collections of short fiction, *Scar Tissue* and *White Trash Boulevard*, and a novel, *Horse Crazy*. He is currently writing a new novel. 'Sodomy' first appeared in *Scar Tissue*.

THERE'S TRADITION FOR YOU

Alison Fell

Wanda eases herself invisibly under the skin, tense/release, tense/release, mainly the long muscles of your back and the fatty gluteus maximus and you think back to last Wednesday teabreak when you keeked at the paper and your old pal Lovat keeked right back at you, fatter now and most of his hair away but him and no mistake. Turns out some lassie's collapsed of an overdose two doors down from his flat, dancer it said, stripper it meant, Social Services at fault the headline said for the lassie's not eighteen and still in Care. 'I was shocked to discover the background to the case and will of course be pressing for an inquiry,' never set eyes on her in his life you thought to yoursel', aye that'll be right, well pull the other one mister Right Honourable randy Lovat. Gerald's got you posed with legs spread, one flat on the drapes, the other crooked up and the brocade's bumphling up under you – this idea of theirs that women lie around nude on old curtains gets on your wick but there's tradition for you. One arm's thrown back over your head – faces of course, don't interest them – at least back in the old days in the sculpture studio with its plaster casts of rude bits and Greek horses you'd hear all the wee ohs and ahs about the line of Wanda's thigh or Wanda's thorax, fucking fabulous, and if they didn't say it you'd see it in their eyes, Wanda, she's a humdinger. Planes and tones, Gerald keeps whispering, pencil angled in the air and chopping you up, planes and tones, and you smell the sweat of one armpit and wonder how a man like Lovat gets to be Undersecretary-for-whatever-it-is and what it was about him that got you anyway. That lick of colourless hair flopping down on you while he worked and worked for his thin wee fizzle, the light blue eyes rolling up, the chest hot and blotched with flat freckles. And him that first time squealing for your nails, Wanda, your fingernails, and you felt funny about it but you stuck them in all the same, try anything once; if it had stopped there, okay, but what didn't he need on top of that? Malt whisky, a finger up the gluteus maximus, Wordsworth and a clean hanky on the bedside table, and then in the bottom of the wardrobe the hat-box with the switch in it, ropes, the polaroid camera, you never knew whether he was going to read you poetry or tie you up or get you to leather his bum pink, maybe it was the surprises you went for, and that sexy voice he had, furry and English with rs in all the wrong places Americar amnesiar My Wife Cynthiar you never could resist foreign accents, look at Magnus and his Norwegian one, sly hand under the broom bushes making you wet that day up at Erskinehall where the boarding school was with the midges coming up and sniffing the pair of you but they liked foreign blood better so it was his bum they peppered, oh Magnus with his red cheeks and yellow hair you wanted to sail away to Norway and have his baby even tried to learn Norwegian from a library book Isla said you could always said you were clever and maybe you would have if Ray Beatty hadn't come along and that's another bloody story. Six weeks, they said, you've to keep the baby six weeks for the papers to come through so it wasn't worth giving him a real name when they'd only snatch it away and christen him Graeme or Neil or whatever, but there's bad luck long gone and Lovat taught you a thing or two, give him that, remember his red tongue that first time coming out like a snapdragon and slavering spittle round your nipples, no one else ever did that in broad daylight and made them stand up so straight you felt your whole womb tug when his finger slipped in and he's whispering all the time dirtiest stuff you ever heard then the rope goes round your wrists in a sheepshank good boy scout that he was hauling them above your head your ankles

too, tied apart to the bedend so wide you're scared nearly
seeing stars saying Christ Lovat, but he gets the camera out
and snaps away smiling and purring while you feel yourself
running wet and when he shows you the pictures one finger still
fiddling you, there you were black and hairy under the swell of
belly, pinkness keeking out and giving you a fright at first, like
something slipped inside out, like a glove taken off and angry
like piles or something, fancy that, you'd seen enough cows in
calf, even had a full-term bairn tearing its way out but it wasn't
you then looking at that inside red slithery flesh it was medics
in white masks don't know what you thought you had down
there; seeing again suddenly the wet flat hair on Fred's head,
like Maisie the cat you buried in the garden by the gladioli, a
slate for a gravestone and a sad ceremony until the rain came
and flushed the earth away and there was Maisie's thin skull
with the black hair wet and transparent and pink flesh showing
through and it's not right no it isn't, that poor lassie in a coma
and you up here spread out like a car crash or a murder chalk
marks and all; what a greeter you were in those days though,
crying for Lassie and calves stillborn and everybody's dead
second cousin, Heartbreak Hotel howling for Magnus long
gone, Stand By Me and Ben E. King soaking your hankies
for Ray Beatty, until Lovat showed you that folded hole and
somehow got you like red muck sucking at him with such a wet
noise that you thought of the folds the tractor blades turned
in the long furrows, colour of the earth dark purplish under
the green grass clods toppling over, rainbow sheen of worms
slipping back in for safety, and moles, too, sleeked and damp,
and dead field mice sliced up in the baler, and your legs went
up round Lovat's neck wanting him to plant you, you couldn't
help it for with your eyes shut he wasn't lean white and clever
any longer but a thick brown man hairy as a beast with a red
cock spirting his stuff into you and you were ashamed but what
the hell they took Fred away didn't they and a lassie's got a right
to enjoy her sex hasn't she. And damn it all clean sheets
steak au poivre made a nice change, remember speeding over
the Forth Bridge with the top down, Radio Luxemburg on,
he was no chicken then, must be fifty-five if he's a day but
God was he wild, shouting drunk over the scregh of the wind

about My Wife Cynthiar and the thirty-six teddy bears he never knew about till he married her thirty-six bloody teddies Wanda teddies on the bed teddies hanging off the mirror I shouldn't be telling you this Wanda, met her on Gleneagles golf course she'd an MA and bloody good legs and it was high time I settled down, never laid a finger on her until the nuptials as it were, some women don't like it you see, not like you Wanda not like you my lovely, swerving all over the shop while he gets his finger worked up under your suspenders, I can set you up Wanda a view on Kelvingrove a shower your own front doorkey why live in a pigsty say yes Wanda say yes my lovely, well what a lot of blethers I ask you. It'll be fair shares for his cronies and all you mark my words, said Isabella in the canteen that day but anyway he dropped the notion soon enough, not a peep out of the bugger that time you reckoned you were pregnant, I'm up to my ears in the by-election my dear so much for Wanda my lovely and I need you and the true blue confessions bit about My Wife Cynthiar. Aye you've had your problems Wanda hasn't everybody, look at the Glasgow models gone to pot already, Dorothy who used to be a lovely girl down to skin and bone in the brothel at Dundas Street and Isabella dead of drink at thirty, well, I've some information that might interest you Mister Maxwell, men like that'll always get away with it and there's a thought to get anybody off their arse and away down to Mayfair in the magnolia-smelling dark where street-lights kid on they're gaslamps and there are no dustbins alkies sweetiepapers or the like and then we'll see about amnesiar, could you picture his face if you stripped on his doorstep, very *déjeuner sur l'herbe*, absolutely fucking Manet wouldn't you say, you could get to be a right bitch Wanda if you wanted but never mind you needed the practice aye hell hath no fury but there's tradition for you

Alison Fell, novelist and poet, is the author of *The Grey Dancer*, *Every Move You Make*, *The Bad Box*; the poetry collections *Kisses for Mayakovsky* and *The Crystal Owl*; and she edited and contributed to *The Seven Deadly Sins*, published by Serpent's Tail. She is currently teaching writing workshops and working on another novel.

MODELS

Diane Rowe

All I had to do was to sit down and wait until I became famous. Hugo, who breakfasted in underpants only, was watching me breakfast.

'The news is good,' he said, 'they want the job.'

We could just see Selma's grave, ablaze with lilies and gladioli; her house was once the rectory, despite the absence of any village. Now shadows circled the empty valley where, above the garden, sunflowers shone.

My finger left off tracing – in mid-writhe – my dressing gown. 'It's beautiful silk.'

And Hugo said: 'Percy would have picked it up either in Paris or in Bath. In Bath, most probably; he couldn't get around much any more.'

So there was Percy shuffling in Bath, with attenuated Selma – all toque and matching Borzoi – trimming her stride to match his step. Percy had artificial calves which Hugo had found in a crate in the bathroom cupboard.

Percy's other remains were buried alongside Selma.

'Grief is necessary,' Mum had said. 'He will feel grief.'

I believed her. I've never been too proud to admit that my mother is my mentor. My mother's thesis took in Fairground Art: a carousel horse reared within our hall and hundreds more (in celluloid form) in albums. They all had distinctive names. Hugo seemed more attractive through having a name just like a roundabout horse; I wanted to write his name upon his neck and frame it in golden squirls. I think you look for that little bit of home, if obliquely, somewhat, within your boyfriend.

'I suppose we must begin,' said Hugo, staring through the window towards the billiard-room beneath.

'That's where Selma taught the Babies tap.' He had a distant look as twenty silver-spangled tots hoofed across his memory.

'She'll be having fun now, I'm sure,' I said.

'If there's life after death she'll be incredibly surprised.' As even my open dressing gown could not distract him. 'There's no point in thinking,' I told him. And I told him again; I said: 'Hugo, what's the point it doesn't get you anywhere. It doesn't get me anywhere.'

I had a big box of kiddies' crayons, the kind you lick to make them draw like paint, and was sharpening the red most slowly. The archlike mirror, which once had helped to teach the Babies tap, contained a girl who sharpened a red most slowly and behind her on a piano stool sat a young life-model man.

He said: 'I never guessed that boxer shorts must hold in so much heat. Can't I be done as an establishment figure with a sort of fig-leaf from an old school tie. I'm not so sure that I want to stand out,' Hugo told me, 'painted on the wall of some Women's Group in Beckenham.'

'It's no joke. Don't start whining about my job.'

'Tulip, you forget that most people, bar you and some pigeon-messed muses in a park, think Thank God for Clothes; I'd shit on Me if I happened to be a pigeon.'

So I posed and he posed and I drew him painting me and he painted me drawing him and we both stared at the mirror and got so cramped, until our very eyes ached, that I said: 'I'm not so sure that I want to do this, either. My drawing's so raw, Hugo, that I don't want them to stare at it in Beckenham, and it's not good and new and raw, it's just bad and raw – I know it is. I'd better face the fact that maybe I'd just better stick at sitting. I'm good at that and you've never looked like that.'

You see, an experiment should have been much easier than that. I fled the room and the smell of paint and the carpet we had rolled up. There was the black umbrella-ed hall with prints of hunts, and fading Clan Tobacco smells and long carpets – Turkey – very worn because of Percy's artificial calves so by the time I'd finished fleeing, I'd fled right across the house and up two flights of stairs, so at least the view was something – a flourish, huge, of hay-baled valley, goose-swept. I'd fled to Selma's bedroom with its closets ranked to accommodate tea-gowns. It smelt of powder and scent, like an old handbag. Sufficient dressing table to recline on, curved, with three monumental mirrors and then The Bed decked out in puffed blue satin. And all that for Selma's self, I thought, since Percy had kipped downstairs on a bachelor's narrow slab, to make it all seem forbidden-like and separate.

We'd been left to sort their things out, so we knew.

And that which Hugo mourned, I knew, was the Selma he'd only met since Selma's death. The Selma who scrawled notes and hid them away in drawers.

That's death all over, such a tease.

Since you look back, as a model, at your uncommissioned forebears who might have married, died, or come from some-where, but rarely all three to anybody's living knowledge. Somebody had burned them, sometime, like we could chuck out Selma.

So it's a long time that you must wait, I found, before becoming famous.

And by that time we'd run right out of coffee.

'You'll have to put up with herbal tea, or Horlicks, or a tin full of dusty tea with a dirty spoon.'

Hugo's in the minor league when it comes to the world's Promoters.

'You should be a great designer, she-tycoon,' they'd said.

'Can't you picture your dusky limousine, all bronze-screened, with those cushioned tyres with which to flatten your neighbour round bends or on the central reserva-tion?'

I said I'd think it over.

'But you can't just think about it,' Hugo said. 'It's either Horlicks, herbal or the dusty stuff.'

In London, I said to the girl who now lives and works in Beckenham, that I wanted to be a famous artist. I was worried that I didn't have it in me. Life never gave me a single chance. She perched in my room on the junk-shop silks – laddered pink, crumpled mauve, all fag-soaked, all coffee-stained – and she stared at the sketches of me – with nothing on, in poses curious – made by young people who are going to be famous and, like all great thinkers, she was a deep-down Puritan. She said she'd help me. She'd have promised anything, then, just to get herself out.

So I got my chance.

How I'll cope with that central panel, God only knows. I don't think that I'll manage it.

'We could try one of Selma; a double canvas of you and me, Selma, then your pin-up portrait.'

'They didn't want a pin-up.'

'Yes they did; they wanted Stereotypes and then Equality. And fair enough.'

'No wonder that I'm tired,' I said. 'I'm watered down. What with the transmutation of souls throughout the years my femininity's been half diverted into stockings and into sunbeds. I won't be shown like that: I never have. I think the whole idea's a bloody insult.'

'You're hardly entrepreneurial. You fiddle around upstairs and you won't even do the tea. You can't even choose if you want tea.'

'I think a lot,' I shouted.

'I might not contribute much but I've the right to be left alone. No one gives me a decent chance.'

You're treated like that if you don't have a big black car with its cocktail box of your gall-stones there en suite. They can't stand someone slipping past and getting in to watch life without paying.

I started laughing. I gather that being laughed at, in a manner long and unexplained, is really quite provoking.

'Guess what I found in Selma's bedroom?'

Such a wonderful woman, you tell me; Selma was independent before her time and Selma was a dancer.

And then she sat in her room with her cat and her solitary boiling egg in its solitary boiling pan and watched the clock drip out the afternoons behind a locked door. Outside she could hear a football game. She could hear, but not see, the children play and when she went outside and saw, she was afraid of them. Widower Percy was encountered at a funeral. Love at first sight, it was, athwart the floral tributes, sweet nothings over a lachrymose buffet.

Like hell it was.

'Here's a clue. What if she did regret. Having nowhere else to go was never enough excuse to marry Percy. Those who couldn't live alone should have stayed forever mistresses and then they could stay in bed.'

'You're being very crass.' He probed the remaining tea leaves down the sink.

'Sometimes I think you came out of the ark.'

'So did all the best people: the rest of them were drowned.'

Yet he'd sounded so disgusted.

The sun had moved. The heat was ebbing. I sat down on the rocking chair; very cold and silent it became, sitting there and drinking tea. The rocking chair ground as they do in films, with no one to rock them except some watchful spirit.

Of course I said: 'I wonder what did happen to Selma.'

'She died,' said Hugo. He said: 'She died without revealing the secrets of the perfect dry martini.'

It sounded (believe me), when he said it, so abominably immune, but then I'd surveyed his walls of Hugo long ago – how tall they were and opaque. He enjoyed the futile and bizarre; the sight of naked Marxist females engulfing minor royalty would please him.

He said: 'She knew what loneliness is like. When I was at school – I'm sure I've said – she'd write every other day. At half term I would see her; she'd get us really tight. By four o'clock we'd be laughing or we'd be crying over iced cakes from a bag. On the way to the train there'd be peppermints to clean our breath and always it was raining. That London grey and sluggish rain. But then it rained at school too, all the time, with the windows jammed; so you knew it was fresh out there, but inside it was ... not fresh, anyway. She must have saved for weeks to buy that drink; I supposed I never realized. I still thought grown-ups were all rolling in it, then.'

'I still do,' I said.

I continued rocking. I watched his back, stacked up beside the window with that determined (now unconscious) slouch designed to provoke rebuke; and Selma, of course, made him unfurl, made him to cry or smile (and intensify in general, his chance of facial wrinkles). She must have really felt it when he did that; when his walls were low enough to vault over. Now I have to get a trumpet to blare across them, sometimes; like 'Joshua fit the battle of Jericho'. Jericho.

'You think you had it wretched, what about me? Lots of spirituals I sang at school. Lots of singing at school altogether.'

'I know,' said Hugo, 'but I also drank.'

'Not at ten.'

'You'd be surprised,' said Hugo.

Oh Yes: at the age when most kids are still on brandied chocolates, you could tell an Ankle Trembler from a Long Sloe Comfortable Screw against the Wall. You even had the proper cocktail umbrellas, plastic mermaids and furry monkeys to ping up straws, but these had to be washed and recycled so as not to be extravagant. You cut up the lemon slices, the sting was supposed to stop you nail-biting long ago.

'She would never write once she had married. She was too soft, (no doubt thought Percy). Or too busy maybe. Anyway, some doctor opened me up and stole vast chunks; I'm sure there are still huge gaps inside. I can feel the draughts there sometimes.'

I cut strings of dolls from my picture – the kind that stretch out clasping toes and hands.

'I assume the Artist's Life is off,' said Hugo, outstretching the remains.

I said nothing.

'Weren't you pleased with what you did? I think I looked aptly ill-at-ease. Yes, I really think quite gruesome.'

'I wanted it natural.'

'What's that? Some hope. You caught my Painting face – I didn't pull a one-off face especially for you.'

I heard him. He went on and on.

I listened to his voice, not to what he said, it was better that way when all was said and done. And I interrupted yes, of course, yes. He asked me what I meant and he meant. I started laughing; since 'Yes' means anything both parties want it is, above all, privacy.

And if what I felt when I watched him sleep was a gift that I couldn't give, then what was the point, if good things still fade away?

Autumn nights came – the stars were falling – with riverside mist for the cows to wade in. The owls began crying at dusk and I watched the sky swell as darkness moved under the hedges.

I crouched outside decapitating roses, since Selma should have done them. Selma who, in the guise of an Arab Slave, had been so fêted, painted, photographed.

Percy's artificial calves stood out there, lined up with the empties.

'I've no reason to make life easier for him,' Hugo told me. 'He never made life easier for me.'

So rose leaves fell as dried up as charred paper. She loves him, she loves him not (you might say), and certainly I'd seen the light from Selma's bedroom and Hugo's shadow up there, searching. He'd wanted to read that she'd loved him, I knew that. So I went, once the dew had fallen, back into the dark, chipped staleness whose space and silences were lobbed far between the playing clocks.

Hugo had pulled the wardrobes open wide.

'It's all been changed. Some things have gone. Some lingerie stuff is missing.'

I said: 'I know.'

'What else have you done?'

'You wanted a pink silk calendar girl, you said.'

By now I was playing with my lighter. I'm sure when Pharaohs' masks were made they made the eyes of agate, something hard to make them shine. I didn't like him when he wasn't smiling.

I wanted him to smile at me, but his face went strange instead. He will feel grief, as my mother said to me. Through fear, things would be left, inevitably, unsaid and, maybe, lost.

I said: 'It was for the best.'

And he told me: 'Always people say that.'

I recall that, briefly, tears fell plop, against my ear. He held himself quite stiffly whilst I watched the moths drift in and burn.

'I've never even had a proper chance.'

Diane Rowe was born in Hertfordshire and now lives in Somerset. She was the winner of the Whitbread Short Story Award for Young Writers in 1985. Her stories have been broadcast on Radio 3.

WHOSE WAS THE CORKSCREW?

Mary Scott

After last night's bitterness, the peace between them was as fragile and as precious as the thin china cups from which they drank their breakfast coffee. But there was room for optimism. It promised to be a fine day for shopping, warm and dry so they would not have to wear coats which were always an encumbrance in centrally-heated stores.

Best to tackle Safeways first, before the rush. They put energy into consolidating their reconciliation, offering every purchase to each other as a gift.

She selected a glossy aubergine for a ratatouille she would prepare for him. He chose for her a new Sabatier knife.

'Would you like trout with almonds tonight?' asked Lucy, knowing he would.

'I could do that mousse you thought was delicious,' said Andrew.

Both realized with a delicate, fluttering pleasure that so far they were enjoying themselves together today. They bought cracked wheat for tabbouleh, Cos lettuce, garlic, macadamia nuts, buckwheat for pancakes, rubbish bags and frozen peas for convenience.

The trolley was full. At the checkout Lucy unloaded and paid for everything; Andrew packed it all into stiff, brown paper bags. He wheeled the trolley to the car park. They shared the task of stowing the load neatly in the Volvo's boot.

Each of them, individually, would now like to return, jointly, to the flowered sheets of their king-sized pine bed. But getting the week's perishables hardly amounted to so much as a prologue. There were one or two carefully considered additions to be made to each of their wardrobes, tiles to be bought for the bathroom, beading for shelves and, most important, there was the purchase of the cause of yesterday's dispute – a new cooker.

They walked back to Shopping City. Less discerning consumers could complete the entire week's purchases under the one roof of this vast, modern complex which housed retail outlets of most of the major chains and offered everything for the home and garden as well as clothes and books and records. Lucy and Andrew visited each brightly-lit floor in turn. She studied the stock in the Sock Shop for something to suit him. He popped into a florist for a bunch of flowers for her. Together they bought a number of minor items and made a preliminary examination of cookers in a ground-floor showroom, before setting off to compare prices along the High Street.

At least the choice of fuel – gas – had been made. Apart from that nothing was settled because the emotional events of last night had overtaken the original plan to agree on a list of preferred and essential features.

Outside Shopping City there was a wider range of both quality and cost and much more scope for uncovering real bargains. Lucy rummaged through remnants of furnishing fabric. Andrew tried on a pair of stone washed Levi's. The junk shop in Castle Lane was always worth a diversion. And then there was somewhere called The Cooker Centre which Lucy had found in the Yellow Pages. They didn't stop for lunch. They never did on Saturdays.

'This is the place.' Lucy paused in front of a plate-glass door.

'We are clear that we want a slot-in rather than a conventional free-standing model, aren't we?' Andrew asked as he opened the door.

Earlier in the week they had consulted articles in the

consumer magazines together, so they were aware that the most important decisions would be centred on choice of grill level, oven size and hob type.

'I don't like eye-level grills.' Lucy inspected one. 'The sausages could fall on you.'

'The low-level ones are difficult to see to clean.'

'It's me that always cleans the grill.'

'I was thinking of you.'

A salesman hurried towards them along the green carpet tiles between rows of appliances. He then led them to the area of the showroom containing those models whose basic specifications fitted the ones on which Lucy and Andrew seemed most likely to agree. They made good progress. The salesman abandoned less intent customers as he saw the choice perceptibly narrowing and only two cookers still in the running.

In the hope of clinching the deal he drew their attention to the superior design of one grill pan handle. So it was his fault when the welter of additional features came crowding in upon his customers: catalytic oven linings, autotimers, minute minders, rotisseries, flame failure devices, trivets, splashbacks, viewing panels and plate warmers all had to be considered. And should the oven door be drop-down or side-hinged?

'What does it matter,' said Lucy, 'whether the grill takes six slices of toast or three and three half slices if the rest of the cooker's all right? Anyway, you hardly ever have time for toast.'

'I'm not going to buy something you don't really want.'

Back at home it was poor consolation to expose the prizes from earlier in the day. Okay, so Lucy had secured a fawn cashmere sweater, Andrew a rare John Mayall album both at significant reductions. But they had not made the big buy. The £500 budgeted for its purchase persisted in their current account, uninvested except by the bank.

The meal they had planned was now inappropriate. Bags of food bulged on every surface in the kitchen; yet in spite of the volume of supplies there was nothing Lucy thought she could transform into an alternative dinner worthy of a Saturday night without more effort than she was prepared to make.

'Let's leave this for a bit,' she said, heading for the living room. 'Open one of the bottles of Cabernet Sauvignon. At least we did all right with that.'

'If we'd discussed it properly last night this would never have happened.' Andrew followed her.

'It's not much to ask.' She extracted the cork herself. 'Why do I have to do everything?'

'It's only sense to work out what we want in advance.' He pulled out one of the upright chairs and sat with his elbows on the dining table. 'Why do you turn it into something personal?'

'It is personal when you accuse me of being irrational. All I said was that white was the proper colour for a gas cooker. And this afternoon I made it quite clear that the Philips would do.'

'Since when did I spend my money on something that would do?' He reached across the table for the case of Cabernet.

'It's just as much my money as yours. Why are you opening another bottle?'

'Nobody seems to be offering me a refill, though I notice you've had one. And you keep saying it's value that counts, not money.'

A third glass of wine on Lucy's empty stomach produced a fair simulation of anger.

'No one else says I get worked up. Everyone in the office admires the way I act under pressure.'

'So you save it all to take out on me. Thanks very much. Don't get emotional. I don't want to know.'

This was cause for real indignation as she had been considering whether it was time to cry.

'I only suggested the Philips because you didn't like the Zanussi. I preferred the Zanussi.'

'How can you assume that if I draw attention to a minor design fault it means I don't like something? The Zanussi was by far the best option. You stopped us buying it.'

'If you want a cooker, go and buy a sodding cooker. It's my cooker we're using now.'

'Your cooker? Next you'll divide up the contents of the whole house.'

Her bottle was empty. She had to do something. And he'd thought of it.

'The wine glasses are mine for a start,' she said.

He pushed his glass across the table, stood up without a word and left the room, slamming the door behind him.

She began with the bookshelves. It was fortunate that she had written her name in all her college texts, but with other volumes she needed to recall the act of purchase as evidence. This took a while, but she had identified a good proportion by the time he returned with a half-pint mug. He poured wine into it, filling it almost to be brim.

'What are you going to do?' he asked. 'Put all your stuff in one room? What good will that do apart from making the place even more of a mess than usual?'

There was one threat she'd never made.

'Yes. I'm going to put it all in one room so it won't get in your way until I collect it. Then tomorrow I'll leave.'

The contents of the room trembled with a frisson quite unlike the angry vibrations of their previous engagements.

Everything in the room started to speak at once.

'Did you hear that?' a Paul Simon album sneered at the Joan Armatrading next to it. 'You're going to be out on you ear.'

'You were always in bad taste,' the Persian rug announced to the walnut coffee table. 'Poor value for what she paid.'

'So what? I never liked this dump,' snapped the Joan Armatrading album.

'Typical of you to judge everything by what it cost,' retorted the walnut coffee table.

'You think I invited you?' hissed the Paul Simon album.

'Her personal insurance won't cover you,' the video snarled to the music centre. 'You'll be in the cold.'

'That will be a refreshing change from the stiflingly oppressive atmosphere in here,' the music centre replied coldly.

Lucy had said it so she must mean it. Unprompted tears flowed down her cheeks as she went out to the hall where two suitcases and a blue sports bag climbed out of the cupboard and trailed after her into the living room. A Palgrave's *Golden Treasury* flung itself open at the frontispiece to prove that it had been awarded to her at school. 'Take me! Take me!' shrieked the twin lampshades on either side of the fireplace, uncomfortably aware of some internal activity on the part of their mutually financed lightbulbs. A small filing cabinet shrank against the wall, dreading a custodial dispute.

But Andrew raised no objection. He had opened another bottle of wine (whose was the corkscrew?) and he followed Lucy from room to room gulping from the half-pint mug. In each room he sat on an object he knew to be his, and watched.

The sports bag, now full, refused to leave Lucy's side. She tripped over it.

Even in the rooms she had not yet visited the word was out. The bathroom shelf was reverberating from the callousness with which the Brut gave the Impulse notice to quit. 'Bitch!' his sponge bag screamed at hers. 'Bastard!' it shouted back.

It was becoming difficult for Lucy to remember what she was doing, what with the tears, the bag bumping her shins and Andrew following her, sitting and staring. She found the wine on the dining table but not the wine glasses so she swigged, splashing, from the bottle and was about to take another step towards completing her task when the bag, still dogging her, wrapped its shoulder strap round her ankle and brought her down with a bump onto the carpet.

Examining her blurred surroundings she decided to take refuge under the table. It certainly looked more comfortable there than any other place she had been this evening.

What's more she was joined by someone who, she could have sworn, was on her side. 'Do you want to share the mug?' he said. 'Or have the bottle?'

'The wine glasses have gone.'

'I know. I couldn't find them either.'

'Who does the corkscrew belong to?'

'I think we may have bought it together. Why do we always fight about things?'

'We haven't got anything else to fight about have we?'

They drew closer and appreciated the joint good judgement

which had led them to purchase such a large oak refectory table.

'I didn't like to mention it before,' he said, 'but did you know you're wearing one of my shirts?'

It was unfortunate that the table hid what happened next or that the participants had not thought to post a notice of their truce, for all around them the battle reached new heights: in the kitchen the teacups were shaking with wrath upon their hooks; the knives in the cutlery drawer were doing each other serious damage; the plates were expressing their loyalty to Lucy in a series of suicide missions, dashing themselves against the inviolable orange walls of two of Andrew's Le Creuset pots.

Books which had not yet been segregated grappled, jackets flapping, tearing at each other's pages. A portrait of a delicate Edwardian woman flung herself, gibbering with rage, at Andrew's Modigliani print which, at six times her size, she would never dare to cross under normal circumstances.

It even reached the cellar. A hoard of plastic carriers, kept to hold the shopping of the future, rustled with ominous aggression. One Austin Reed bag rallied those which could easily be identified with its cause and led a foray of Lacoste and Paul Smith against representatives of Laura Ashley and Monsoon.

Soon the house rocked with screams and sobs and breakages. Debris mounted, silting against the walls. By dawn, Lucy and Andrew might have nothing left between them. In the eye of the storm they rocked in a far sweeter motion, moving slower and slower to extend their pleasure far into the night.

Mary Scott lives in London with a cat. A collection of her short fiction, *Nudists May Be Encountered*, is to be published by Serpent's Tail.

SANTIAGO

John Saul

Here comes the Minister now, it's another rainy day in Santiago. In their Paris flat just off the rue de Vaugirard Yvette and Victor pause to watch. Yvette breaks off from talking, Victor from dicing food. The chopping board is stained green from freshly cut marjoram. Victor wipes the knife on his apron and wonders how Yvette gets the television to stand on the vegetable rack the way that she has. She sits hugging her legs, he stays standing, together they stare at the Minister. The television camera light has made a mole of him, his face pushes up towards the light; his body leans forward, as all around him drizzles rain.

Not tropical but familiar rain thinks Yvette, so that is Santiago, disheartening drizzle on a grey, sullen evening. A sight which looks so familiar that soon the whole scene starts to play up, be familiar, it gets so she can't imagine it otherwise from how it is. That watching soldier looks just how he should, the Minister too, the sideboards and the fat lapels,

Only now does it register with Victor that Yvette is silent. She has been talking for half an hour about Zen, about cordon bleu, about his father back in their native Boston and what a love story her old affair with Naim would have made, if only it hadn't ended so weird, boy was that weird she said, him disappearing and her waiting and waiting and he just never came

those ridiculous, tiny
glasses.

Honey, turn up the sound
would you.

It fits to hear blustering
wind ruffle the microphone,
then rain beat hard on the
fabric of his umbrella. His
raincoat steams, his breath
steams, he's straining forward
to make the satellite pictures.
Again he is in a state of
shock. She must assume this
same state, it is attainable
with concentration. She wills
her skin, skin turn pale and
bloodless.

back. Victor, who suspects
that he himself is not so Zen,
and prefers his

He gives the sauce a hasty
stir, then goes over to the
television.

prefers his cordon bleu at the
end of a fork, was concentrat-
ing mostly on the Naim part;
not personally as they never
met, even crossed trails
within five years of one
another, but he was combing
his experience for parallels,
raking over Maureen, Lor-
etta, Eleanor and Sue, nope,
then he tried putting himself
in Naim's shoes, would he
ever disappear on Yvette and
why, he wouldn't, he might,
how fine it would be if she
learned to make a baked Alaska.
Despite the fish before his
nose he can imagine a taste,
an ice-cream texture, a warm
and cold against his tongue,
in addition he's wondering
what to make of the shells
Yvette has filled the hand-
basin in the bathroom with,
the cistern pipes she's painted gold and the blue and
orange hen made of porcelain
she has hung there on the
wall. When they go back to
staging dinner parties their
friends will love those
shells, what an imagination

that Yvette has, they will
turn on the taps and dig in
their hands like he did,
breathe in south seas, fruits
and palms and sweeps of
beaches, the moment will
hold its sweetness until they
discover there's no towel any
more and maybe in view of
the shells and the hen and
the gold paint it would be too
dull to ask for one. He
should ask Yvette about the
towels, and the pegs are gone,
but first he'll have to clear
the air of Zen, that weird
boyfriend, a backlog starting
with baked Alaska and what a
day he's had, wherever Yvette
found shells in the middle of
Paris. But not now, now she's
watching the news, look how
pale she's gone. This
Minister, Victor learned only
today, is responsible for the
Social Services in France,
and is right wing, and now,
buffeted by a sudden squall,
sheets of rain, he builds upon
his statement of the day before,
barks out a further denunci-
ation of the Pinochet regime.
Where has he just come from,
from seeing more relatives of
more people who have been
tortured, there clearly has
been torture and this has to
stop. Victor waits for words

Yvette, standing, reaches for the coffee beans, the grinder, tells Victor she'd like coffee before the meal, this is coffee from Nicaragua she adds. She gets a cup and stops to check the television schedules, would he like coffee too, she gets another cup, was that a yes or a no, he nods, she unplugs the set and puts it on the floor. Jean-Claude, she says, has a house in the Sixième. Yesterday Chilean women handed in bouquets of flowers there. She looks at Victor. He isn't listening again, what the hell's the problem. The television must go back to the bedroom. She realizes she has no hunger. Did you not hear me say, they took flowers to his house.

Abandoning the coffee things Yvette makes a balletic twirl, over to the hotplates; she takes over the pan, no recriminations, they are not Zen. She must concentrate on the sauce alone, stir it, the sauce has lost its elements and become one blended thing.

to tone this statement down; none come. Only rain and the Minister's jabbing fist, then more sharp reproaches, it's clear he's speaking from the heart. Yvette has switched off the television, how much is a pound of that, she's got the television programme. Would he like coffee too, he murmurs yes and nods, nods again when she asks again, she has unplugged the set and removed it from the rack, reducing Victor's backlog by one, because no longer does he need to worry how come the television stood there and stood there not crashing constantly to the floor, onions rolling, he looks in the sauce and doesn't like the way it's maybe clumping, are those lumps or bubbles forming. Is that so, Victor replies affably, would you take a look at this sauce a moment. He smiles dumbly, hands her the spoon and takes the coffee grinder, he touches the button and suddenly thinks again what a damn hard day at work it was. Deserving maybe a zabaglione, baked Alaska, there was an Indian one with curds and cardamom, all sweet melting cool things he'd never

She must become this
thing, this sauce, and swirl,
dive up upon a spoon.

Hot and steaming.

Soon spread and lay upon
the fish.

He sighs at small Yvette,
skipping cordon bleu and
switching courses, enrolled at
Zen, that was two dinner
parties lost already and gee he
misses the food experiments
and d'où vient ce vin si beau.
Yvette is strange again, look
at her, what is the matter
with her. He must have a pee.

The chain too has been
done in gold, he has dug deep
in the shells before remembering the towels. He comes
out shaking both hands at the
floor and thinking maybe next
year they should take a
holiday someplace south.
Now the smell of fish is
everywhere, television voices
are in the bedroom, the sauce
is under water in the sink. In
Santiago there's the man
again, stepping from a car to
a street, the reporter starts
talking, this morning, 3 pm
European time, General
Pinochet decided to offer
him an impromptu audience,
and there now is Pinochet,
this large, some say
avuncular man, beginning
now to show his age.
Victor constructs an irony
upon the contrast in their two
expressions; the one shocked
and shaken, the other equally
set but smiling, unruffled and

In Santiago the rain is the
same rain, at first just the
rain and then a commentary
begins, this morning, 3 pm
European time, General
Pinochet decided to offer
him an impromptu audience,
and there now is Pinochet,
this large, some say
avuncular man, beginning
now to show his age.
Filling a uniform, a chair,
but first Jean-Claude has to
shake the General's hand. At
the General's signal his guest
may sit, and Yvette sits, a

second sign and he may speak, he does, he speaks his mind. Pinochet appears to listen, smiles; across an awkward space of floor the Minister leans forward on the edge of his chair, this too looks right, it fits the way the rain was how it was, the leaning forward has grown into a natural characteristic. The satellite catches suddenly another drenched and forlorn street, out he comes again, having been to see still more people. Look Victor honey, isn't he just ashen. It's like he doesn't know it's television. He's looking lost, what day is it, what month, he doesn't know. Rain splashes down his face, he's going now to his hotel. The car drives off and Yvette draws the curtains, ready for her meditation, then sets a cushion on the floor.

serene. The interpreter too is locked into a certain look, a grave demeanour, unmistakably a little fear. Victor looks at Yvette to catch her reaction, she is leaning forward oddly, he might guess why, why, in empathy for the Minister. The Minister has become her *koan*, her task to meditate upon each day. He cannot discuss this with her as her *koan* is her riddle; he is not supposed even to know what her riddle is. Yet he is getting drawn in, or why does he stay in the bedroom and watch, adjust the screen and say, he sure is honey, it's like he's come from hearing things he never heard the like before. What's that he's saying, he intends to stay on extra day, tomorrow. The longer this has gone on, Victor is thinking, the less cordon bleu they have been having, and baked Alaska will disappear to the next life or the one beyond, perhaps the never never.

John Saul was born in Liverpool and now lives in Hamburg where he works as a translator for Greenpeace. His published work includes a novel *Heron and Quin* and stories in *Fiction Magazine, Stand, Panurge* and *Iron*.

MADAME REALISM

Lynne Tillman

Madame Realism read that Paul Eluard had written: No one has divined the dramatic origin of teeth. She pictured her dentist, a serious man who insisted gravely that he alone had saved her mouth. The television was on. It had been on for hours. Years. It was smiling. It was there. TV on demand, a great freedom. Hadn't Burroughs said there was more freedom today than ever before. Wasn't that like saying things were more like today than they've ever been. Madame Realism heard the announcer, who didn't know he was on the air, say: 'Hello, victim.' Then ten seconds of nothing, a commercial, the news, and *The Mary Tyler Moore Show*.

She inhaled her cigarette fiercely, blowing the smoke out hard. The television interrupts itself: A man wearing diapers is running around parks, scaring little children. The media call him Diaperman. The smoke and her breath made a whooshing sound that she liked, so she did it again and again. When people phoned she blew right into the receiver, so that she sounded like she was panting. Smokers, she read in a business report, are less productive than nonsmokers, because they spend some of their work time staring into space as they inhale and exhale. She could have been biding her time or protecting it. All ideas are married.

He thought she breathed out so deeply to let people know she was there. Her face reminded him, he said, of a Japanese movie. She didn't feel like talking, the telephone demanded like an infant not yet weaned. Anything can be a transitional object. No one spoke of limits, they spoke of boundaries. And my boundaries shift, she thought, like ones do after a war when countries lose or gain depending upon having won or lost. Power has always determined right. Overheard: a young mother is teaching her son to share his toys. Then he will learn not to share his toys, the toys he really cares about. There are some things you can call your own, he will learn. Boundaries are achieved through battle.

Madame Realism was not interested in display. Men fighting in bars, their nostrils flaring and faces getting red; their noses filling with mucus and it dripping out as they fought over a pack of cigarettes, an insult, a woman. But who could understand men, or more, what they really wanted.

Dali's conception of sexual freedom, for instance, written in 1930. A man presenting his penis 'erect, complete, and magnificent plunged a girl into a tremendous and delicious confusion, but without the slightest protest ...' 'It is,' he writes, 'one of the purest and most disinterested acts a man is capable of performing in our age of corruption and moral degradation.' She wondered if Diaperman felt that way. Just that day a beggar had walked past her. When he got close enough to smell him, she read what was written on his badge. It said BE APPROPRIATE. We are like current events to each other. One doesn't have to know people well to be appropriate.

Madame Realism is at a dinner party surrounded by people, all of whom she knows, slightly. At the head of the table is a silent woman who eats rather slowly. She chooses a piece of silverware as if it were a weapon. But she does not attack her food.

One of the men is depressed; two of his former lovers are

also at the dinner. He thinks he's Kierkegaard. One of his former lovers gives him attention, the other looks at him ironically, giving him trouble. A pall hangs over the table thick like stale bread. The silent woman thinks about death, the expected. Ghosts are dining with us. A young man, full of the literature that romanticizes his compulsion, drinks himself into stupid liberation. He has not yet discovered that the source of supposed fictions is the desire never to feel guilty.

The depressed man thinks about himself, and one of the women at the table he hasn't had. This saddens him even more. At the same time it excites him. Something to do – to live for – at the table. Wasn't desire for him at the heart of all his, well, creativity? He becomes lively and sardonic. Madame Realism watches his movements, listens to what he isn't saying, and waits. As he gets the other's attention, he appears to grow larger. His headache vanishes with her interest. He will realize that he hadn't had a headache at all. Indifferent to everyone but his object of the moment, upon whom he thrives from titillation, he blooms. Madame Realism sees him as a plant, a wilting plant that is being watered.

The television glowed, effused at her. Talk shows especially encapsulated America, puritan America. One has to be seen to be doing good. One has to be seen to be good. When he said a Japanese movie, she hadn't responded. Screens upon screens and within them. A face is like a screen when you think about the other, when you think about projection. A mirror is a screen and each time she looked into it, there was another screen test. How did she look today? What did she think today? Isn't it funny how something can have meaning and no meaning at the same time.

Madame Realism read from the *New York Times*: 'The Soviet Ambassador to Portugal had formally apologized for a statement issued by his embassy that called Mario Soares, the Socialist leader, a lunatic in need of prolonged psychiatric treatment. The embassy said the sentence should have read "these kinds of lies can only come from persons with a sick imagination, and these lies need prolonged analysis and adequate treatment."' Clever people plot their lives with strategies not unlike those used by governments. We all do business. And our lies are in need of prolonged analysis and adequate treatment.

When the sun was out, it made patterns on the floor, caused by the bars on her windows. She liked the bars. She had designed them. Madame Realism sometimes liked things of her own design. Nature was not important to her; the sun made shadows that could be looked at and about which she could write. After all, doesn't she exist, like a shadow, in the interstices of argument?

Her nose bled for a minute or two. Having needs, being contained in a body, grounded her in the natural. But even her period appeared with regularity much like a statement from the bank. Madame Realism lit another cigarette and breathed in so deeply her nose bled again. I must get this fixed, she thought, as if her nostrils had brakes. There is no way to compare anything. We must analyze our lies. There isn't even an absolute zero. What would be a perfect sentence?

A turn to another channel. The night was cold, but not because the moon wasn't out. The night was cold. She pulled her blanket around her. It's cold but it's not as cold as simple misunderstanding that turns out to run deep. And it's not as cold as certain facts: she didn't love him, or he her; hearts that have been used badly. Experience teaches not to trust experience. We're forced to be empiricists in bars.

She looked into the mirror. Were she to report that it was cracked, one might conjure it, or be depressed by a weak metaphor. The mirror is not cracked. And stories do not occur outside thought. Stories, in fact, are contained within thought. It's only a story really should read, it's a way to think. She turned over and stroked her cat, who refused to be held longer than thirty seconds. That was a record. She turned over and slept on her face. She wondered what it would do to her face but she slept that way anyway, just as she let her body go and didn't exercise, knowing what she was doing was not in her interest. She wasn't interested. It had come to that. She turned off the television.

Lynne Tillman lives in Manhattan. Her writing includes *Weird Fucks, Living with Contradictions* and *Haunted Houses*, and she wrote and co-directed the film *Committed*.

SCENES FROM THE LIFE: No 27

Living In

Janice Galloway

A *spacious room. One side is dominated by a wallshelving unit with a stereo, video, recording units, speakers and amps, some books and a HUGE TV. There are also some bottles and cans of lager as a 'cocktail' section. A modern armchair sits squarely in front of this unit, facing the glowing green lights of the sound system. A few open books on the carpet, an overturned (empty) wineglass, a rubik cube or some such 'adult' toy. Opposite these, a desk, a drawing board. Lots of crumpled paper and writing things on the desk. There is a large mirror and a cork pinboard above it. Some plants.*

Deeper into the room, a sleeping area with a large bed, wardrobe with set-in mirror, bedside table and a canvas chair. On the bed, a thick, dishevelled duvet. The fitted carpet is strewn with cast-off clothes: a pair of trousers hang over the chair arm.

Furnishings throughout are tasteful but pedestrian: everything self-coloured in subdued shades. Nothing is patterned; none of the plants are flowering or exotic. No cushions; no ornaments on the shelves. To one side, in a corner, is a sectioned-off bathroom with a permanently opened door; it should not seem too separate from the rest of the room. The sink and toilet bowl are clearly visible. There are lots of jars, bottles and tubes ranged along the back of the sink and on shelves. Behind the sink, an enormous mirror. The toilet seat is UP. There is a towel crumpled on the floor, and another draped untidily over the bath rim.

Light enters from a sloping skylight above the bed, angled to

*make visible a diamond of greyish sky. Light level should suggest
an extremely overcast day, twilight – something of that sort. The
same level obtains for almost the entire play.*

*Articles on the floor interjoin the different areas of the room.
There is also a telephone, coffee table, poster on one wall. THERE IS
NO KITCHEN APPARENT. Other minor properties will be indicated
in the text.*

Note for the ACTOR: *TONY is entirely suggested through
improvised movement. NEVER SPEAK. TONY is at all times a
presentable and pleasing figure, trim and tall (though not excessively
so), fashionably good-looking. His clothes and hairstyle are neat and
businesslike, but he wears them with a casual stylishness (or vice
versa). Maintain his neat appearance by occasionally checking that
cuffs, trouser-crease etc are as they should be, smooth down hair,
check shoulders . . . but keep this unobtrusive. TONY's movements
are graceful but masculine: even at his most relaxed he has dignity.
He is smooth and unhurried, never coarse or clumsy. His movements
and any noise he makes (humming or sighing, spitting out water, etc)
is restrained, almost self-conscious.*

*NEVER ALTER HIS EXPRESSION. The steady but eager blankness
of TONY's face throughout is essential to a correct interpretation of
the character. Never slip from character or acknowledge the audience
in any way.*

Act 1

Half-light. A fairly lengthy stasis before a digital watch alarm
begins to play *Clementine* thinly. The lumpy duvet twitches and
moves. Slowly, the head and hands of a man appear from the
top. It is TONY: his eyes still closed. The watch continues to
sing through his waking ritual. His feet find the carpet first,
then his torso rises to let him sit with his head hanging forward
over his knees, the corner of the duvet still hiding his crotch.
He reaches for the watch, silences the music, straps it to his
wrist. In slow stages, he rises, stretching a muscular body. He
has been wearing blue cotton briefs in bed. Only now does he
open his eyes. (He does not contort his face to wakefulness –
even newly emerged from sleep, he is a handsome man.) He

blinks a good deal on the way to the bathroom where he picks up the fallen towel at his feet and drops it over the edge of the bath before standing poised at the toilet bowl. With his back to the audience, he empties his bladder, soundlessly, and without undue disturbance to the blue briefs. Now he takes a few squares of white toilet paper to carefully wrap his penis and nestle it gently back inside the briefs. (Allow time and precision for these manoeuvres which are to be executed with utmost discretion; it should not be possible for even the most prudish member of the audience to take offence here.) Once this routine is accomplished, he carries on with the rest of his preparations: running the taps at full power to wash his face and dry it vigorously with the towel, sponge under his arms and across his chest then brush his teeth thoroughly. (NB a bearded actor will be able to take much longer over this part by spending time trimming the beard and moustache into the sink.) Once he has finished, the damp towel is once more relegated to the floor. TONY turns his attentions to the lotions and unguents on the shelves: he carries this out routinely. First, he applies roll-on deodorant to his armpits, then sprinkles some talc on his chest, rubbing it into the skin with firm, long strokes. Next, he selects a bottle of aftershave to dash some into his hands and slap onto his face and neck (neck only if bearded). He may also add a discreet touch to his pubic hair as an afterthought . . . gingerly. He examines his face for some time in the large bathroom mirror, flicking away a fallen eyelash, checking a dubious patch of skin, inspecting his teeth, etc. THE EXPRESSION ON HIS FACE NEVER ALTERS. After this, he turns back to the bottles and tubes, sprays something under his arms from an aerosol, adds a touch more aftershave, brushes his teeth again and strokes his neck. Fully awake now, he moves purposefully and decisively back into the main part of the room and begins an assault on dressing. He begins with the trousers over the edge of the canvas chair, putting them on as he stands, then adds the items strewn on the floor in turn: a white shirt, a dark tie, pair of dark socks. Last are the dark shoes at the side of the bed. Checks himself over in the wardrobe mirror: he looks GOOD. Now he rakes his hair with his fingers, combs it through into place (replacing the comb in his trouser pocket) and shakes his head to naturalize the effect to his satisfaction. A jacket from the wardrobe completes the outfit: he drapes it cavalierly over one shoulder. Expressionlessly triumphant, he gazes at his neat reflection (he does not smile).

Eyes still on his mirror image, he checks for wallet, keys and cash by patting at various appropriate pockets. He is ready. Erect, he marches out and off through the audience. He looks fine, assured, masculine. Fathomless.

Act 2

The room as it was left. Nothing is different. Street noise begins to filter through the skylight, making the room seem all the more still and quiet within. Then a series of distinct and discrete sounds, building in volume so the last in the series is very loud indeed.

1. General traffic noise, cars ticking over, etc.
2. A motorbike running, then revving repeatedly.
3. A car taking a corner too fast.
4. Drunken singing and cursing, indistinct obscenities.
5. A clicking of shoes on a pavement, then jeering: the banter of men catcalling. It becomes progressively more blatant and aggressive then stops. A burst of wolf-whistling.
6. Chanting (football slogans?) and a breaking bottle.
7. Some grunting and scuffling; the sound of running and angry obscenities.
8. Silence. An ear-splitting wolf-whistle.

The diamond of sky in the skylight glows and changes to a very bright blue then dims to its usual wash.

Act 3

TONY walks through the audience and back on-stage. His
jacket slung over his shoulder and his collar loosened suggest
a hard day. He throws down the car keys onto the coffee table
and drops the jacket on the floor before turning on the radio.
It plays soft music interspersed with long sentences – not
particularly audible. He selects a can from the shelves then
sits to peel it open. He spreads comfortably in the chair, the
can in one hand, sipping every so often with his eyes closed.
The radio plays and he eases into relaxation. The man, the can
and the radio make a soothing triangle for at least ten minutes.
Then he opens his eyes to press the button which activates
the HUGE TV. He sits up to look into the screen briefly and
finish the remains of the can. It shows discontinuous bits of
old films – Westerns, adventure stories, gangster movies, etc
– bits of detective serials, car chases and adverts, sometimes
cartoon figures and newsreel. The volume is very low. Rising,
TONY begins to wander about the room, picking up the odd
book, rifling through his record collection, etc. Soon, he takes
another can with a long glance at the part-nude figure on the
back before tearing off the ring-pull. He drinks from this
through his tour, making inspections, mental digressions. He
is at peace, relaxed in his ownership of the place: he is a man
in his own home. At some stage, he may put a record on the
stereo; again very softly. The combined volume of the radio,
TV and disc are never too obtrusive or harsh. Eventually, he
looks at his watch and settles into the easy chair, selecting
his favoured channel. It shows the same as the other one.
He falls asleep facing the TV and the green indicator lights
of the stereo deck. By turns, the noises of the machines fall
away, till there is only a soft crackle sifting from the TV. It
is then that TONY wakes, dropping the empty can on the
carpet. He looks around, rises, rubbing his neck, and goes to
the bathroom.

His evening ablutions are much less mannered and shorter
than those of the morning: he washes and dries his face and
brushes his teeth. Even the water runs less forcefully. He
slackens his trousers and pees noisily into the toilet bowl,

shakes his penis and discards the tissue from his briefs into the bowl before flushing. His flies undone, he comes through to sit on the bed where he undresses. Trousers return to the canvas chair, the shoes and socks, shirt and tie lie where they are dropped. Without rising, he swings his legs up to slot under the still dishevelled duvet, removes and sets his watch, then places it on the bedside table. He has finished with the day: he sinks well under the warmth of the duvet and rolls away from the audience to sleep.

Everything is still for a long time.

Next to the recumbent figure, the lumps in the duvet move. Minutely at first, then more noticeably they move toward TONY then undulate in small rhythmic patterns above his body. TONY inhales loudly: the movements stop: he turns abruptly from their direction, back to the audience. There is silence and motionlessness and TONY's eyes shut very tightly. Nothing happens for a few minutes. Another mild movement behind him. He sighs deeply, sets his mouth hard and rolls onto his face. Another period of immobility and stillness. TONY's form relaxes slowly, completely. He has fallen asleep.

Stars appear in the strip of sky above the bed. They glow very brightly as the set darkens until the shape of TONY in the bed has a silver outline. The bed pulses again: there is something under the lumps in the duvet – something in the lumps in the duvet. It moves again, then emerges in one sweep to stand at the end of the bed. It is a naked woman. Soundlessly she moves round to look down at the sleeping man, stroking the place above his head with one hand, taking great care not to touch. Then she moves more centrally to face the enormous mirror at the wardrobe. She stares and stands steadfastly, unblinking so her eyeballs shine in the dark and through the gloom; her skin looks very pale and downy, starlit. Gently, liquidly, with spread fingers, she traces her hands lightly over her body: lingering on her shoulders, over each breast caressingly in turn, stroking across her ribs and down, over her stomach, firmly and repeatedly across her thighs and hips: soothing strokes. This takes some time and cannot be rushed if the right effect is to be achieved. Her deep concentration, intensity and absorption in the task, the feel of skin under the fingertips are paramount. Then, nearing completion, one hand glides upward to clasp a shoulder and shield her breasts as the fingers of the other fan deep into her pubic hair. Head erect, she looks into the mirror, into the white contours of her body curving out of the darkness.

TONY sleeps.

ADDENDUM: Note to the ACTRESS.
Extreme stillness is demanded for the part. NO ONE is to know you are there till the moment comes. The audience must never be sure whether you are substantial or not.

Janice Galloway was born in Ayrshire but now lives in Glasgow. Her short stories have appeared in Scottish literary magazines and in anthologies and her novel *The Trick is to Keep Breathing* was published in 1989.

MY SOLE FEELING OF HAPPINESS LIES IN THE FACT THAT NO ONE KNOWS WHERE I AM

Rosalind Belben

I realise that if I think of you, I see you in your country, against a background of it; and either because of that background or because of you, I involuntarily smile. I think endlessly of you. I call you Therese Hellenstainer. It is a name I took from the stone of a grave.

Therese, the desolation of living underneath incontinent skies, which seem to spread skirts and legs, open up a flood; your heavens, on the other hand, weep; and, however tormented the tears, don't piss. A sourness in the world is palpable: I think, there must be a better place to live, and I am going to it. A matter of making one almighty effort. Torrents of passion, from the umbrella of an indescribable climate, for a blue sky and clean air, water. A place I have lavished my imagination on. There is a distant warm smell that could be spring happening outside, and hopelessly beyond, my house, my city. A dulling of the senses. I am consumed with longing, Therese, yet always I manage to hold back. A feeling that a body deserves relief; to leave all behind. How difficult it is, if I am in one spot, and healing springs are in another, to stay; exiled. What has befallen you? I imagine arriving, and being able to remember the names of all my friends. I imagine tears cascading from my eyes. I think: I could be whole. I could be made well. The high air and the water which has run from high mountains collecting life-giving properties will make me better. I see myself, endowed with sudden grace, shaking hands with all my friends. A lighter, and brighter, horizon, raising my eyes. A proper horizon: so many times imagined; and the tears falling out of my eyes. I am blind to everything; except that landscape in the mind's eye. I arrive a thousand times and see my destination around me like the rising tiers of an amphitheatre. I put a very tiny sprig of some plant I brought home with me into a drawer, contained in a matchbox, in which there were already a few matches and a small stone from the same ridge; and I dared it to lose its poor dried leaves. I knew that when all the leaves had fallen off something or somebody would be dead. It has lost three, but the other leaves cling quite tenaciously. I thought that perhaps one day I should visit your grave, knowing exactly where to find it; not that I'd return long, long before you lie in it. I know well, to speak an old-fashioned language, I've left my heart behind. I hadn't realised there is also, to retrieve, my soul. Which is more wrong: to have nobody but oneself in one's inner part; to hold somebody else there. I am a born recluse; it is you who have lived a recluse's life. What do I know of you? That you live in a place which is beautiful and I called paradise. It isn't easy, when one has been in paradise, to find the way back. I think: the Temptation. La via di ritorno. And, salva ero, I shall be whole, made whole? healed? Saved. The more I think of a place where I am not, and of people with whom I am not, like you, the more remote it becomes. It's an obsession. But also I can think with pleasure; see with pleasure; I am looking in my mind not at a place, people, you, but into the face of happiness, a sustained happiness. It frightens me. You will say, why didn't you come before? I have had, yes, these rare moments of extraordinary happiness, all my grown-up life; what I feel, have felt, grows more into a vision; I'm afraid I'll come and not find it again; and it's better to keep the vision than to lose it, risk losing it. It's important to me. Building a whole life, Therese, out of one very powerful feeling, my longing. There is no sanity, I think, no retreat, except inwards, the life of the mind; where the weather, like the ethereal unreality of the blue of the hurricane's eye, is quiet in the face of the whirlwind; enclosed; where there can be a feeling of safety; and an infinite at the core into which the miserable spirit pours, without finding the path blocked; absorbed and absorbing. To take a last backward look at the world. In which nightmare slips through the day, and dreams during sleep elide with wide-awakeness; both equally real. A wish to retire hurt. The earth's best resource, the human mind. Oh, the wish for a still centre, too easily interpreted as a wish for death. A still centre which is not dead, but which radiates life, health, calm. I shouldn't confuse such desires with the death wish. A closing-in, instead of an opening-out. The dream of trying to describe the early summer flowers of paradise to someone who not only has never seen them but who has no concept at all of what the sight might be. And then, in circling where you live, I saw the flood waters of your snow; filling the valley, the narrow gorge; so that all it was, held, was a violent river, and a fragile railway line two inches above the level of the water, clinging to one flank. The trees, with their roots helplessly in the air, running by faster than the train; and in a moment the river could have hustled and bustled the four carriages away too. I came no nearer. I draw my hand over my eyes, closing the lids as one might the eyes of a corpse. I say, hush, it's finished, it's all over, over. Hush. But it's not finished. I remember a path leading up through a copse, between stone walls and small, steep fields; an empty house, in the old traditional style, with long, heavy eaves, and much warm timber; a derelict fertile garden: here I install my god; it'll be my house, to live in when I come home to paradise. I circled like a lost soul around the object, the place, of my desire; sitting in silence, listening to death. I sat in a primitive café and heard the succulent, civilised voice of opera floating loud out of the radio. Totenstille. Totenmaske, mine. Therese, setting out to look at a dying world; I set out to look at the dying world. In your small spot, only, it didn't seem to be dying. The exhausted spirit. Beklemmt. Beethoven: may thy deafness be a secret no more, even in art. I thought I would be blind. To imagine music and its having to take over from seeking things out for the eyes. If one is going to see, there's not much point in not seeing everything. But if one sees too many things one doesn't want to see, in proportion to the gifts from art, nature and the gods, one begins not to want to see at all. Isn't it worse simply to hear things? I don't know; or maybe one would miss only the expression in one's own eyes. You smile, Therese. I slept in the ear of the sun. The sun rather terribly losing its strength. I waited three days for the wind to turn; for the širocco to cease; longing to do no more than take my clothes off and lie down on a plank a boat was moored from. An island so scented it sweetened the interior of the fumy bus; and glowing, with walnut, cactus, fig, juniper, heather, oak, myrtle, oleander, Aleppo pine, cypress, bay, rosemary, palm, marigolds, hibiscus, orange and lemon trees, pomegranate, and pretty electricity. With wind from the south, the lights on the mainland shore lost their tails, their reflections; they were cut off short, as if blown away. Oh, make the two halves of my life come together. The hunting dream. Cold in my soul, very cold. I wake with an amazing sense of unhappiness; but unhappiness as if from a dream; without any recollection of what the dream has been. And then the dream of having to go to a strange country; a country strange and unknown to everybody; and having to make arrangements to go into this unknown. Things that assail one's private self. Homing instinct re-directed, Therese. The relief that springs into existence from people's not-having-knowledge of where one is. It's not merely the fear of interruption; though it seems the mind is happiest in a contemplative state, like a garden growing; no, it's some magical hold others have, with this awful knowledge; one is gripped in place and time; the telephone can ring; they *know* one is there; and because they know it, one is; and for no other reason. The barometer of happiness, you say. Angst. It dawns, I have either too much imagination of what other people might be thinking, or a slightly enlarged, extra-sensory perception of what, it is true, they are thinking. I find it unbearable to hear the cogs in people's minds whirring while I speak. I can't bear being examined. I hate the sounds assumptions make. And sizings up. And being found wanting. To you, I don't have to be accountable. I am afraid of accountability. I am gnawed by having to account for my actions; and for my imagination. I can't rid myself of the feeling, Therese, that in having to talk at all I am losing, parting with, allowing access to a precious, secret self. The more hunted that secret self is, when it goes away to be by itself, the *closer* the hunters to me, the more frantic I become, guilty at their pique, bitter. I am less ready to expose myself, to be hurt, to give violence to my feelings. I am every so often assailed, abruptly, by an inexpressible sense of alone-ness; the structure of relationships seems to disappear, leaving me very cold. In heaven there would be no human relationships; and infinite foreign-ness of language. To step back into the landscape of the imagination, ah me. Those I have admired have been at ease in their own imagination-land. I would like a room, a room into which no one but myself can go, Therese. I think of coming to you, and saying: I want a room into which no one but myself goes; please, please, may I have a room which no one but I need go into. I want to throw off the shackles angrily, impatiently, as if bursting to free myself; as if there was only one end in sight, only one goal through which to propel myself; that, there truly is. What worries me, I think, is that one can become so profoundly unhappy as to be unable, almost, as it were, physically, to dwell on any other things than one's inmost sorrow, wound; Promethean, no? I feel I shall die; I point myself towards the place I can't bear not to see once more. I realise that the deep seat of my being has become detached; that to go to you means, in a way, a death; that I am ready to give up, burn boats behind me; that I would relinquish everything, even the state of mind that keeps me in this place, which is not the place of serenity and beauty I keep before my eyes like the reward of an earthly heaven; but as if with the river Jordan there would be no returning. At least I can say, I have woken up with a clear mind.

I imagine walking over the top of the mountain, and looking down into the mists and cloud; I imagine approaching so close I can touch you, almost come to your garden fence on the high plateau which sails like a fat boat in the river of the valley; imagine seeing what I have seen so many times, the city, the shining rivers and the setting sun; then I turn back.

To choose, finally, and to prefer imagination to reality, even though the imagination is derived from reality, is to lose grip entirely on reality and to be insane. All precisely the same; exactly as remembered, nothing has changed; the shadows on the mountains are familiar. The trees are taller. I realise at once that when I came before I was an invalid, as much mental as physical. I think, yes, when I was here I came ill. I was delicate; and, I suppose, hurt. The fragile feeling after an emotional upheaval, but compounded by months, not days, of it. That explains much. One arrives, and, trembling, receives the momentousness of the journey, like a visitor in the mind. The water leaks over the paths in the certain same places. It is wonderfully pretty in the twilight, with mist hanging over the mountains, the river grey-green, and the lights all twinkling. A tempestuous three years, emotionally. I could live here for ever, with no more to do; stupefied with pleasure. It is possible to see the turning world when the sun rises over the mountains. I thought I should one day be blind; it might have been soon; and I must, I knew, take another look. Content, knowing that if I climb up a thousand metres there will be mountains and mountains, and snow; schneebedeckt. All loving done; no passion left. I dreamt again of the dog, felt the grief; but knew it was in the past. Waiting for the words to come; wound up; such a rest from human relationships. A dream of killing. Living in the cloud; fresh snow on the mountains after the rain; the thing is, to stay calm, and not cold. The unhappy ghost, bumping home in a box; happy not to have to linger, and watch people making a mess of things.

You are baffled by my sudden change of mood. My sole feeling of happiness lies in the fact that no one knows where I am, Franz Kafka writes to Felice. The miracle of snow. Of a light near the top of a mountain. The austerity which is given by some grace, to turn back at the brink. The deathly stillness of the snow, the trees slack and helpless; even with voices, knocking, a woodpecker. Little cracks in the rock, echoing; pieces falling out of the high peaks; and falling somewhere; except one never hears the end of it. The mystical feel of that particular place; gentians; almost blood-red dandelions, not dandelions but like them; flowers drooping in the chill. A man with a small child standing on his shoulders, standing on a rock on which grows a tree; the child is taking a bird from the nest; the child is very small. I'd thought I was cured of being consumed with longing to see over the next brow, and the next. I felt at peace, and peaceful. It glows with the colours of the rain. Waiting anxiously for the clouds to be gone before the end of the ... Powerless to push at them. I didn't realise before I had the dream of edges that I was anxious about ... The entrance to the mountains, the opening, like an eighteenth- or nineteenth-century print, dark and forbidding yet inveigling; or something from the Romantic imagination; or how Goethe might have seen the Alps. How by following the dark road, the way becomes darker; and the mountains heavy with rain, wind and cold; and the road rises, and rises, and all the while it seems as if one is drawn into one's fate, into a dangerous region where the mind and soul will be risked. A narrow and slightly winding gorge, among very high mountains in a place which is already high. I thought, the great love of my life was a dog. The astonishing colour of the water, the mountain lakes in the Dolomites. A peculiar emphasis the spruce give the weather, like people standing very mute in drenching rain without umbrellas, knowing there's no point in lifting their arms. The trouble is knowing what it could be like, we know what life could be like. And feeling again that passionate ecstasy, in the warmth. The rain was beautiful. A sense of physical well-being; of sun on the skin; and a contentment; which is virtually unattainable in England. In the thinner air. The thinner air suits me. The assuaging of the soul. The sun's mark burnt into the throat. Beyond the confines, the border beyond which one is free, from which no postcards are sent; then one re-enters, as if the earth's atmosphere. I am separated from you. Privacy. I called you Therese Hellenstainer. I took your name from a gravestone. Alarmingly necessary to have had a private journey; the public visit at the end to buy presents and postcards, to establish the somewhere I've been. It's hard to recognise that I've become split into two parts; and one part is with you; the other with me in my own country; and that I have to live in my country, not yours. The dream of hearing your voice.

The dream of hearing your voice underneath my window, calling my name; I actually jump out of bed, in London, here, to draw the curtain away and look. And so, dear Therese, loving greetings from your Ralph.

Rosalind Belben was born in Dorset in 1941. Her novels include *The Limit* and also *Dreaming of Dead People* and *Is Beauty Good* published by Serpent's Tail.

GRADUATION BALL

Sandi Sonnenfeld

Let me explain why I took the job: I was twenty-two, I was broke, and I had no place else to go. There was another reason, of course, one that as a brand new college graduate I kept reminding myself of over and over again. I wanted to attach a significance to my work; I believed I had something to offer.

'Teaching dance to underprivileged kids in New Jersey?' my best friend Eloise said. 'It's more important that they learn to read.'

'Eloise always said things like that. It would never have occurred to me about reading. But Eloise was like that, practical.

But let me explain about New Jersey. If you are from the East Coast, you know about Jersey. Its smelly oil refineries start a few miles past the George Washington Bridge and the stench remains well beyond the Caldwells. Then the exhaust fumes from the cars, which are lined up bumper to bumper waiting to make that last right turn into the endless row of shopping malls, reach you instead. New Jersey, host of ugly sounding cities, Piscataway, Metuchan, Teaneck, and perhaps the ugliest sounding of all, Newark. Its very name tells you what it is; say it fast or slow it still sounds like the bastard child of the city that spawned it, New York. Newark, where eighty per cent of the prostitutes are said to carry the HIV virus. Newark, where drug addicts live in bombed-out housing projects. Newark, home of the underprivileged; the inner city.

There is, of course, another New Jersey, the neatly-trimmed lawns of the Princeton mansions, the farmland out past Anandale, the famed North Shore beaches. But despite this, very few New Yorkers can wipe the smirk off their faces when a native tells them where he or she is from. New Jersey: the Garden State.

I had come from a garden of sorts, an earthly paradise up in Western Massachusetts. In the town of South Hadley, there is a women's college known as Mount Holyoke. The oldest of the Seven Sisters, she shows her one hundred and fifty years beautifully. Nine hundred acres of ivy-covered buildings, of tennis courts and saunas, golf courses, riding stables, and not one, but two lakes, fully equipped with waterfalls. The college library, built in 1900, was modeled after St. Paul's in London. The college's nineteen dormitories serve milk and cookies to the students every night at ten o'clock, and those very same students are quite often seen going off to class the next morning still dressed in their Lanz nightgowns, Reeboks, and a single strand of milky white pearls. Mount Holyoke, with its own state motto: Excel or Die.

At Mount Holyoke, they taught us that Knowledge was infinite and therefore anything was possible. This idea pleased me. I was going to teach fifteen- and sixteen-year-olds the possibilities of Art.

The institute was supported by the New Jersey Council of the Arts. Through fundraisers held at those neatly trimmed Princeton mansions and with the cooperative funding of the public school systems, the program managed to offer places for around sixty students. The program was held at the state university in New Brunswick.

I arrived the first morning around ten, holding tightly onto my two dark red canvas bags, the contents of which constituted everything I owned. I put the bags down by the conference room door.

'My name's Carrie Lerner,' I said. 'I'm the new dance TA.'

'Yes?' a blonde woman with a clipboard said. 'Well, sit down. You're late.'

I sat down in a hard-backed chair.

'We were discussing the time schedule,' the blonde woman continued. 'Breakfast begins at seven-thirty and the daily meeting begins promptly at eight-thirty. All students must attend this meeting. One of the primary roles of the Teaching Assistants is to ensure that the kids get there. You'll take attendance and if anyone is missing I want to know immediately. The only excuse for a student not to be there is if he or she has been checked in by one of you at the nurses' station by eight o'clock that morning. The only excuse for a TA not to be there is if it is your day off.'

I leaned over to the freckled-faced woman sitting next to me. 'Who is that?' I whispered.

'She's the activity program coordinator. Her name's Lorraine D'Beire.'

'She's not the one who hired me. What does she teach?'

My freckled-faced colleague shrugged her shoulders, 'Nothing. That's not her job.'

'Carrie,' Lorraine said. She seemed to have a great aptitude for names. 'Do you and Melissa have something you want to share with us?'

I looked across the circle at Lorraine. Her white-blonde hair surrounded her perfectly tanned face like jagged icicles.

Her pale blue eyes stared at me and then at the eleven other faces sitting around in the circle. 'It's me you come to with problems,' she said. 'I will know everything that goes on here.'

I believed her. I had a sudden desire to run.

I want to explain about desire. Not that quick, explosive moment associated with wishes. Like wishing for a million dollars. I'm not talking about fantasy. I mean desire in its most complex form, perpetual longing, a dull, unceasing ache. I could never put the feeling into exact words when I was younger, identify exactly what it was that gnawed at me, made me itchy and restless. But there was never a time when the longing wasn't with me. It was a bleak loneliness that nothing ever satisfied. I describe it as a perpetual longing. There was also the perpetual hope that one day the longing would cease.

And then the year I was nine, it seemed that day had come. My parents had tickets for New York City Ballet's spring gala. My father, an industrial architect, was called away once again on business. It might have been to Khartoum. Or Kuala Lumpur. I had stopped keeping track. And my father had stopped sending postcards. And mother had stopped pretending that she cared. She simply dressed me up and took me with her to Lincoln Center.

The choreography was all Balanchine, the music all Stravinsky, and the dancers were all legs and arms. It was the most magnificent thing I had ever seen. I sat in a red velvety box seat and was transfixed by the perfect beauty of the ballerinas, and the costumes, and the lights. And then, from the recesses of the giant, multi-chandeliered theatre, beginning in the third balcony, and spreading through the entire theatre like a rippling wave, came the applause, loud, thunderous applause. And I felt that deep empty hole within me filling up with the noise, threatening to overflow. I didn't want to leave. I didn't ever want to leave. I knew then what I wanted, what I had to have, I wanted to dance effortlessly upon a stage.

Mother, in that way she had, that half-amused, half-contemptuous laugh, said that there were ten thousand other little girls who wanted the same thing. I didn't believe her. I hated her for saying it, but I didn't believe her. It was to be my dream only, mine, because it was the one thing that would eradicate my longing. It never occurred to me in the following years of dance classes that I might not have the talent. If the desire was there, the ability must be within me as well.

Desire is an odd thing; the closer one comes to its attainment, the stronger it grows. My need to succeed was vast, an empty, bottomless hole. Just dancing wasn't enough. Because I wanted to be better than best and beyond that. I wasn't and I knew it.

Perhaps that was why the sight of the students that first week at the institute upset me. We were the smallest department in the program; nonetheless, the dancers were terrible. They weren't dancers really, just teenagers. I was appalled.

'I was prepared to deal with anorexia, with jealousy, with competition, with bloody toes, and tears,' I told Theresa Larson, the dance instructor I was assisting, 'but how am I supposed to tell Maria that she shouldn't wear underwear beneath her tights?'

Theresa squeezed my hand. I knew she understood. Theresa had exquisite feet.

But I didn't understand. I didn't understand Lottie, who, dressed in a polka dotted leotard and shiny spandex tights, spent most of her time at the barre looking out the window trying to catch the attention of the boys practising in the music studio next door. Or Janice who wanted to know why I didn't have a boyfriend. Janice was fourteen. I had been a soldier doll, a candy cane, a flower, and a dewdrop. But I had never been fourteen. I didn't know anything about being fourteen.

Theresa told me not to worry about it, that it was only six weeks, and then it would be over.

But I did worry about it. One night, after I was sure that all the students on my floor were asleep, I pulled on my jeans and sweater and slipped out of the heavy grey door. I walked the ugly concrete campus. There were no trees. So I sat on a wall and stared out at a giant nearby parking lot. The uniformity of the white painted lines of the deserted lot was orderly and uncomplicated and silent. It reminded me of the Grecian orderliness of the large stone amphitheatre at Mount Holyoke. The night before my graduation, Eloise and I had made a last pilgrimage to the amphitheatre. Sitting on the wide, expansive stage, the tall, doric columns rising above us, we drank a split of champagne and silently toasted the college and ourselves.

'You shouldn't be out here alone,' a masculine voice said. The sound startled me. I looked for the person who matched the voice.

It was Andy, the music coordinator.

'Sorry,' he said, 'I didn't mean to frighten you.'

That's okay,' I said. 'I didn't think anyone else would be out so late.'

'That's why you shouldn't be either,' he said. 'Wasn't it you who gave the lecture last night at dinner about how the girls shouldn't ever walk around alone?'

I blushed.

'What were you thinking about?' he asked.

'Nothing. Just couldn't sleep.'

'Carrie Lerner,' he said, 'There was a Professor Lerner at Princeton. Any relation?'

'No. But it's funny you asked that. That was the first question my English lit professor asked at Mount Holyoke. I didn't know you went to Princeton.'

'Graduated five years ago. I've been teaching jazz at a prep school in Pennsylvania since then.'

'Are you any good?'

He laughed. 'At what?'

'At music. What do you play?'

'The trumpet,' he said. 'And yes, I think I'm good. How about you? Are you a good dancer?'

'I want to be. I want it more than anything.'

'Is that what you were thinking about? Sitting out here?'

'Sort of.'

Andy looked at me.

'Hey,' he said, 'are you okay?'

I started to cry.

'Hey,' he said again. He put his arms around me, 'Hey.'

I didn't cry long. A man I barely knew was holding me.

'I'm okay,' I said. 'Thanks. I mean, for asking. I should go in, check on the kids.'

'You aren't on duty now,' he said.

'No,' I said, 'but something might happen. You never know.'

'No,' he said, 'you never do.'

'Well . . .'

'Carrie?'

'Yes?'

'Nothing,' he said. 'I'll walk you back.'

He took my hand in his. His hand was very dark against my white skin. Strangely, the difference seemed even more great under the fluorescent glare of the parking lot lights. It hadn't registered before. That he was black. I mean, I knew the first moment I had met him, just as I knew that most of the students in the program were black, but I had never really been aware of it till now.

I was aware of something else too. Lorraine D'Beire was watching us. She was out on quad duty and she was watching. Her iced blonde hair was like a pale duty beacon in the semi-darkness. She was standing only a few feet away from us. On her face was a look of total disgust.

I want to explain about blackness, but I can't. Perhaps it is why I am now writing this down. I had studied, of course, at my self-proclaimed liberal college, my largely all-white, all-middle-class college, history, and anthropolgy, and sociology. So I learned about Afro-American origins, about slavery, about emancipation *de juris* but not in fact, about matriarchal kinship groups, about absent beaten men, about segregation, about the causes of poverty among the culture, about the Civil Rights movement of the 60s.

But how does one go about apprehending blackness? The act of being black. I didn't need to apprehend my own whiteness. No one ever talked about whiteness.

And I had only talked about dance. Despite what I knew intellectually, I had only thought about people in two ways, those who danced and those who didn't.

But now there was black. And there was white. The students, both in the dance program and the ones I was in charge of at night, still had the same names they had the week before; Maria still wore underwear, scrunched and bulging, beneath her leotard and Christine still cracked her chewing gum in the shower, but though I was with them daily for hours at a time, the first thing I noticed the following morning was the color of their skin. It hadn't been Andy's putting his black hand in mine that made me see this as much as Lorraine's reaction to his doing so. And I thought, 'Is this what they do? Is this what they see in me, not Carrie at all, but merely someone white?'

And then there was Andy. We would sit together at dinner,

and even though as a coordinator his work finished at five, he would come and stay with me during quad duty. Most of my time was not spent in the classroom, but in keeping track of all the students after classes were finished, making sure they were at the sponsored nightly activities, at the morning meeting, in time for meals. As a TA, I was never to let any student, whether or not he or she was in my cluster, do anything unsupervised. All the TAs tried to rotate schedules so it would be easier, but still our work day began every morning at six and did not cease until around eleven o'clock at night. The imposed rules and endless regimen made me both at once exhausted and restless.

So one night during the third week, Andy drove me down to the beach at Ashbury Park.

It was after midnight, there were no cars on the road, and Andy drove fast. I unrolled all the car windows, took my hair out from its ponytail holder, and let the night wind rush by me. It felt terrific.

Andy looked at me and smiled.

'If you could be an instrument,' I asked him, 'what kind would you be?'

He thought for a minute, 'Oh, God, I don't know. You ask hard questions. What would you be?'

'A piano,' I said, 'because it has eighty-eight different sounds. And that's before you even start to form chords and scales.'

I was well versed at this game, played it endlessly at college. Andy didn't seem to realize that my answers were just a bit too rehearsed.

'Yeah,' he said, 'I'd probably be a piano too.'

'Okay,' I said, 'if you were a color, what color ...' I stopped.

'Gold,' Andy said. 'Gold as a trumpet.'

The beach and boardwalk were surprisingly active. We had to walk a long time before we found a place on the sand that was free of beer drinkers and motorcycle gangs.

Andy talked about music. About jazz. And how he really was unhappy teaching at a prep school.

'I'm surrounded by boys twenty-four hours a day,' he said,
'I haven't had a girlfriend in months. I like being with you. I
like being with you a lot.'

'I like being with you too,' I said quickly.

'Kiss me,' he said.

'We only have three weeks left of the program. Then you're
going back to Pennsylvania. And I'm going, well, I'm going
wherever I'm going. Boston, maybe. Or San Francisco. It's
silly to get involved.'

'You could still kiss me,' he said.

I shook my head.

'Because I'm black?'

It was the first time he had ever referred to his color.

'I told you why,' I said. 'Don't you believe me?'

Andy was silent then.

'Andy?'

'Yes,' he said, in a choked voice, 'I believe it has nothing to
do with my color. But I don't believe your first reason.'

I sighed. I took his hand.

'Andy,' I said. 'God, god, god. You have been so good to
me. Aside from Theresa, you are the only person who talks to
me, who seems to care about me.'

'I care,' he said.

'I know. I like you. You're a good friend. I don't know why
I'm not attracted to you sexually. I don't know why, but I can't
pretend that I am. If I kiss you, you'll know I'm pretending. I
don't want to pretend.'

'I've heard this before,' he said. 'Do you know how many
times I heard this? That I'm a nice guy, but . . . I'm tired of
hearing it. What am I supposed to do to make you want me,
beat you up? It has been two years since I've made love to a
woman.'

His words came out hard. I thought he was going to cry.
'You could have,' he said. 'It wouldn't have hurt you to kiss
me once.'

I kissed his cheek.

'Don't,' he said. 'Just don't.'

And as he pulled away, an image of Lorraine's pale blonde

hair appeared before me. But I wasn't sure if it was her face I saw beneath it or my own.

'It's after three,' I said. 'We should go.'

We drove back to New Brunswick in silence.

The next day was Saturday. It was hot. Even for July. It was my favourite weather for dancing. The heat made it easier to warm up without strain. But I knew it would be hard to convince non-dancers of its benefits. And I had to do just that. It was my week to teach the workshop.

The workshop was a weekly event. Students were required to take one class in a medium other than their own. Carl, the institute director, may have known a good deal about developing the skills of the under-educated, but he knew very little about art. He thought that this one class would offer the students 'insight' into the other art forms. The workshops invariably went wrong.

I had prepared enough material for a two-hour class, thirty minutes longer than was necessary. I thought it was better to have something to fall back on, in case a couple of the combinations didn't work out. Unfortunately, I didn't even have the benefit of a live accompanist. The idea of using taped music defied everything I knew about dance, but I didn't have a choice. I also didn't have choice of a studio. There was none available on the weekends. I would have to teach in the gym, which could prove to be very dangerous to dancers. A gym floor was hard, usually built over concrete. It offered no flexibility.

I was nervous. This was to be the first class that I would teach alone. And these people were less than beginners. I wanted to talk to Andy about it and suddenly felt a strange loss, knowing that after last night I couldn't.

I met the class at the conference room as I had been instructed. We all walked over to the gym together. Eighteen kids had signed up for the dance workshop. All but two of the students were black. Most of them were in the theatre division.

'Okay,' I said, 'it's time to dance.'

I gave a very rudimentary barre. It took ten minutes just to teach the five basic positions. Pliés and tendus took another ten. Half of the students were boys. They kept making fun of each other, making faces, deliberately messing up the combinations. The girls looked bored.

'I want to do what they do on *Fame*,' one of the girls said to me. 'Can we do that?'

'No,' I said.

She stopped dancing.

I was losing control of the class. I wished that Theresa was there. I looked through my notebook, trying to find combinations that were easy and fun. I looked at my notebook and I had an idea.

'Okay,' I said, 'five-minute break. You can go get a drink of water down the hall, but then I want you all back here.'

Taking a sheet of paper from my notebook, I divided it into eighteen pieces. On each piece I wrote a word.

'We're going to do improvisation,' I said, when the break was over. 'Can anyone tell me what improvisation is?'

'Yeah,' one of the boys said, 'we do that all the time in theatre class.'

'But what is it?' I said.

'Well, Morty gives us a scene to act out. But nothing written. You know, no script.'

'Yes, well, I'm going to do something similar. In dancing, choreography is like a script. A dance is created by the choreographer, a person who has a specific idea or concept in mind. Sometimes it can be a story, sometimes just abstract movement.'

'What's that? Abstract?' the girl who watched *Fame* asked.

'Abstract. It has no meaning, or at least no particular narrative. You can see in it what you like.'

'What's narrative?' K.C. asked. K.C. was well known for causing problems. That's how I knew his name. Morty, the theatre coordinator, had told me about him.

'He likes to test you,' Morty had said. 'He's a smart kid, but he likes to test you.'

'Never mind,' I said. 'Let's just get to the exercise. There is a piece of paper here for each one of you. I've written a single word down on each. Some are actions, some are nouns. I want you to dance out your word. You can use any kind of movement at all, but you may not talk, nor act out the word like in charades. The rest of us will be the audience and we will try to guess the word from your movement.'

They had to talk among themselves about this. I think they were deciding whether it sounded like a good idea or not.

They must have decided it was okay because K.C. said, 'What's my word?'

I handed each of them a slip of paper.

'Don't show it to each other,' I said. 'I'll give you five or ten minutes to come up with something. Remember no talking. Only movement.'

To my relief, they set to work. They seemed serious about the task. I sat down in the corner and watched them.

A tall boy in cut-off shorts came up to me.

'What's this say?' he said, holding his slip of paper out to me.

'Eru-dite,' I said.

'What's that?'

I thought of Eloise.

'What does it sound like to you?'

'Nothing,' he said. 'It sounds like nothing. What's it mean?'

'Just dance out what it sounds like,' I said. 'It doesn't matter what it really means.'

He looked at me. Then he walked off angrily. I saw him throw the slip of paper to the floor.

I tore up a new piece of paper. I wrote the word 'Love'.

'Here,' I said, running after him, 'here's a new one.'

He looked at me. He didn't take it. I was suddenly very tired.

'Hey,' K.C. said, 'I'm ready. Are we going to go?'

I clapped my hands.

'Okay,' I said, 'everyone sit in a circle. Let the person do his or her movement completely before guessing. K.C. do you want to go first?'

I had given the words out randomly. I had no idea what each

of them would come up with. But watching K.C. I knew he had the word 'Happy'.

Because he sat there and smiled.

Everyone guessed it right away.

'Yeah,' he said. 'Right on.'

Everyone clapped.

'That was good, K.C.,' I said. 'Everyone got it. But that wasn't exactly what I meant.'

'Huh?'

'I wanted you to dance it out, make up steps, not just smile.'

'I didn't use no words,' he said. 'Like you said.'

'No, but you used a gesture, a sign. Gestures are good and facial expression is very important in dance, but it should be accompanied by body movement. We should get the idea from what your body says.'

'How do you do happy then?' a girl asked.

'Maybe a bouncy walk, swing your arms. Or turning around in a circle really fast. Dance movement isn't always obvious. Sometimes you might have to look at a combination or a dance a few times before you find a meaning. But anything, anything you feel, anything at all can be danced, expressed through movement.'

'Yeah?' K.C. said. I looked at the faces in the circle. They were listening to me.

'Who wants to go next?' I said.

'Why don't you do one?' Jessie said. 'To show how?'

Jessie was one of my charges in the dorm. I liked her. She was smart. And a bit of a peacemaker.

'I already know how to dance,' I said. 'This class is for you to learn.'

'Please?' Jessie said.

'Yeah, Carrie, you do one for us,' three or four voices said in agreement.

I looked at my watch. We still had a half hour left.

'Okay,' I said, 'give me one.'

'Well, go out of the room for a few minutes,' K.C. said. 'So we can decide.'

'No,' I said, ' I can't leave you here by yourselves.'

'All right. Then wait over in the corner.'

I know I shouldn't have let them take control like that. But I didn't know what else to do. They were interested at last. I went over to a corner of the gym. They put their heads together, whispering. I heard laughter.

'Okay,' K.C. said, 'we're done.'

He handed me a slip of paper, folded. I opened it. There was one word.

Negro.

The eyes of the boy to whom I had given the word 'Erudite' mocked me. On K.C.'s face there was merely challenge.

My hands began to shake. I knew I had to do this. I couldn't say no. How could I say no? Anything in the world can be danced. Any feeling expressed.

And so I began to move. I know the steps must have been ballet, but I can't tell you what they were. The movement began low in my body, a heaviness in my thighs, slow and weighty. And then the weight moved up my body diffusing into all my limbs, like a balloon filling up with air. I began to spin and turn with an urgency I had never before experienced. I was dancing for everything I believed in. For my longing. For the possibilities of Art. For the sorrow I had caused Andy. I felt like I had been dancing for an hour. It couldn't have been more than a minute. And when I was done, I looked at them.

Sixteen black teenagers. And two white ones. Inner-city kids. Underprivileged. Poor. And they cheered. They clapped their hands and cheered, a resounding wave that echoed off the walls of the cavernous gym.

My heart was pounding, like it had pounded thirteen years earlier when I had first gone to see the ballet. I felt like I was floating on air.

'All right,' I said. 'Who's next?'

I want to explain about . . .

I want to explain.

I want to tell you about the end of this story. I thought about leaving it with the black students cheering me, but I can't. It has been several years since I've walked the green, ordered campus of Mount Holyoke. And despite the fact that I now perform with a small ballet company in New York, the longing, that empty, inexplicable desire is still with me. So you see, I am not as sure as I once was.

The other day I was walking through Lincoln Center by 63rd Street. It was noontime and all the shoppers and businesspeople were out eating their fast-food lunches by the fountain. A stocky-looking man, over six feet tall, walked towards me. He was a black man.

'Hey, babe,' he said to me. 'Hey.'

Instinctively, with the quickest of steps, I crossed to the other side of the street.

Sandi Sonnenfeld lives in Seattle. Her work has appeared in magazines including *Ion, Written Arts* and *Sojourner*.

EQUAL OPPORTUNITIES

Tom Wakefield

Mr Garthwaite took a long drink of water from the glass which stood on the right-hand side of the papers in front of him. The interviews had gone well. Rather too well to give him much personal satisfaction. The best candidate had conducted himself even better than his inspector's report had indicated.

This type sometimes came a cropper at an interview and it was then that Garthwaite hatcheted them quickly. Yes, this candidate had come up to the standards of the inspector's report. The five governors had been impressed with the candidate's answers and were pleased with his general demeanour. The six people sat inside a warm oblong-shaped room that had olive green walls, whilst four people sat outside in a draughty corridor awaiting a decision. Lecturing posts (like any jobs) were difficult to come by.

All the governors had talked freely about all four candidates. From their discussions – which were fair and observant – there seemed to be a consensus of opinion that one candidate was not really suitable, that one had insufficient experience, that one was good but rather dull, and that one was very good indeed.

It was the latter of these candidates that Mr Garthwaite had taken one of his 'dislikes' to. Garthwaite had come across candidates like him before. Sometimes they showed a certain kind of flamboyance or originality which he invariably hated. If this one possessed these qualities he had not displayed them although he did look much younger than his thirty-five years. That was always a sign. Yes, he was convinced. It wasn't on the form now, but Garthwaite was sure that he was a bachelor.

His answers to the 'pastoral questions' had left him with few doubts.

Question: If you were appointed to this post, would you travel from your present home? It would take about one and a half hours by car. Probably longer by public transport.

Answer: I don't have a car. If I am appointed, I plan to move into or near this area.

Question: Ah, we encourage that. Will your wife be happy about such a move? It's always an upheaval – and don't I know it. A family move – what with children, dogs, house-selling – oh, I wouldn't envy you. We do offer some remuneration for removal expenses, of course. Selling a home is exacting, isn't it?

Answer: I'll be quite happy to take a change of scene. I haven't a home to sell and my belongings are all easily portable. I can't foresee any removal problems if I am appointed.

Question: I see that you taught abroad for six months. Greece *is* enchanting, isn't it? Although I expect that you would have liked to have gone further afield than Athens. Did your family enjoy it? It is so good for young children to spend some time abroad. They can sense other cultures rather than have them thrust upon them.

Answer: I was alone. I saw quite a lot of the country during the two holiday breaks. It was never my intention to settle there – but I enjoyed the experience and I feel it was useful.

Externally, Mr Garthwaite smiled as these answers were lobbed back to him. Internally, he snarled. The answers were direct, almost blunt – but they carried a hint of evasion. In the worst sense of the phrase; Mr Garthwaite had met his political match. He had smiled and nodded as if pleased with the answers. The candidate had smiled back as if convinced of Garthwaite's goodwill.

His nearest rival had introduced his wife and two children into the conversation without prompting. (They had always been good for a couple of votes.) 'I have two children of my own, one is eight and the other is thirteen. You could say that there is nothing like first-hand experience. I seem to spend almost as much time with them as my wife does – it's only fair that I am with them two evenings of every week. A woman's life shouldn't *all* be cleaning and cooking should it? She is chairman of our local Townswomen's Guild so she has quite a number of social obligations to fulfil – apart from our home. Oh yes, I enjoy my son and daughter, there is no point in being a parent if one doesn't take pleasure in it.'

A good solid candidate. Mr Garthwaite approved. Perfect family man – two children – one boy and a girl – sensible wife – only worked in two schools – eight years in one – seven years in another – nice tweed suit. A good solid reliable candidate, not innovative, not namby-pamby.

Yet now that the interviews were over Mr Garthwaite realized that he would have to use all his skills in his summary before the final vote was taken. It wasn't going to be easy, but he always enjoyed a challenge. Just as he always enjoyed being in the 'chair'.

He took another gulp of his water; smiled broadly at his fellow members and, like the talented puppeteer that he was, began to pull the strings. There were only two candidates in the running. He would leave his family man until last. Eulogies were always more effective at the end. He would open with the other one.

'Well, I must say that these interviews have gone well. To use a much vaunted phrase, we don't seem to have left a stone unturned – or a pebble. [Mild self-congratulatory laughter.] Clearly, Mr C. appears to be an outstanding candidate. No one could argue with regard to his ability, experience, and expertise. The inspector's report is quite clear on this, and his other references re-inforce it. He has a great deal of varied experience and is an excellent teacher. And yet, when I look at this form a second – no, a third – time, I ask myself a searching question. Is there *too* much experience?' Mr Garthwaite paused and allowed the appointments committee to sift through their notes to find and scrutinize the itemized section of the form. He gave them plenty of time to digest it before continuing.

'Mr C. has been teaching for eleven years and one could suppose that he is now at his peak. After all, he has had a lot of varied experience. Yet, when I look at this application form, I wonder. Has there been too much change? Over a period of eleven years he has worked in no fewer than five schools. Could he ever have consolidated ideas and method moving about as much as this? Why, on average he has spent little over two years in any one school. Where is the commitment in a wanderer? And I note for one month he was not working at all.' Like pigeons collecting crumbs the governors bent their heads and checked their forms.

'But surely that absence – the month's absence – was on his return from Greece. It would be highly unlikely for anyone to jump straight into a job after returning from a stay abroad. I have had that experience myself.' Ms J. Ventnor ventured an opinion. She was new to the governing body.

'Mmm-mm yes, I suppose that you are right. My wife and I have never had the inclination to take time off. "Dropping out" is the term, isn't it Miss Ventnor? Of course, you would know more about that than the rest of us would, I'm sure.' Mr Garthwaite smiled freely as he slashed at Jane Ventnor's credibility. The girl (and she was no more than that) was so untidy. Probably receiving money from the DHSS. For her part, Ms J. Ventnor felt that she could say no more at this time and in this place.

Mr Garthwaite's demolition of Candidate C. was both subtle and thorough. The gentle promotion of the 'Family Man' – Candidate J. – was put before the governing body with gradual sales appeal. The goods were duly purchased. Mr Garthwaite congratulated various members for their pertinent contributions and particular insights. In spite of detesting Mr Garthwaite's prejudices Ms Ventnor could not help but marvel at his skills in group manipulation.

'Oh, it is sad that we only have one post to offer. I am sure that Mr C. will be very disappointed and dismayed. He seemed so keen and enthusiastic. Opportunities don't arise so often nowadays do they? I just hope that he won't feel too depressed when he hears the result.' Lena Menton was a kindly widow;

she had voted for the 'Family Man' along with everyone else–
but she felt some sorrow now that she had cast her vote. Or
was it guilt.

'Well Mrs Menton, you know that only one horse can win a
race. The best horse usually wins. And in this case, we have
unanimously decided that Mr J. has won by a nose. If that is
the right expression. I'll let Mr C. know that it was a "close
decision". A photo-finish one might say. There will be other
races you know.' Mr Garthwaite smiled generously and closed
his file.

The rest of the governors left it to Mr Garthwaite to inform
the waiting candidates of their decision. He could always be
counted on to be tactful and pleasant in such situations. As
he left the room, he conveyed to all that were present that it
was a painful exercise for him – but that it was his duty. Only
Ms Ventnor was aware that it was a duty that Mr Garthwaite
relished. What the other members saw as minor heroics in
Mr Garthwaite, Ms Ventnor saw as spleen.

Ms Ventnor could hear Mr Garthwaite speaking in hushed
pious tones: 'Well after a lot of careful thought and much
discussion, we have decided to offer the post to Mr J. You
will be hearing from us formally by letter. I thought it better to
let you all know the result now. At least all the dreadful waiting
is over now, isn't it? I do hope that the unsuccessful candidates
won't feel too badly. It was a very difficult decision. Now, I'm
sure you will all want to go back to your homes. It's been a long
session with a lot of deliberation. My wife was expecting me
home over an hour ago. Really, you know, I feel that I have
hardly seen her this week. Thank you so much for coming
along. If you have filled in your travelling expenses form do
hand them in at the office on your way out.'

The performers in this everyday drama of British life now
wend their way homewards. And what of the principal players?
Did they measure up to the roles allotted to them?

Mr C. joined his girlfriend who had cooked a celebration
meal in anticipation of him getting the job. They had lived
together for three years now and they were good friends as
well as lovers. Perhaps it was time to marry? They were going

to talk about this if Mr C. got the job. ('I can't think where I went wrong.') Mr C. felt hurt and puzzled; his girlfriend wanted to enter his suffering. The meal set before them went cold, disappointment had destroyed appetite. They went to bed and fucked compassionately. No role-playing was required.

Mr Garthwaite let himself into his flat. The cleaning woman had been in and everything was neat and tidy, all in perfect order. He took off his hat, kicked off his shoes, broke wind and felt better. There was no wife to welcome him. Indeed, there had been no wife for the last ten years. She had left him long since. Gone off with some wisp of a man. A hairdresser if you please – a male tart smelling of hair lacquer. Filthy creatures – they couldn't have had anything in common – just sex. Dirty beast . . .

Mr J., our Family Man, felt the need of relief. The tension of the day had left him emotionally drained. He couldn't face going home immediately. That compartment of his life would not erase his present state of strain. He would visit Aldo for an hour. He always felt a lot more relaxed after visiting Aldo. Twenty pounds every three weeks was better than taking valium.

Aldo was an excellent masseur with just the right kind of idiosyncratic technique; he had such a light touch. He always knew what his regulars wanted. Yes, it was time for a little light relief.

Like any play, those taking part are not always what they appear to be. And like any play, comedy and tragedy vie with contradictions and injustices that will never be absolutely clear. Make your choice. Laugh or cry. Or do both.

Acknowledgements to Peter Burton

Tom Wakefield was born in the Midlands and now lives in London. His work includes a book of short stories *Drifters* and the novels *Mates, The Discus Throwers*; also *The Variety Artistes* and *Lot's Wife*, published by Serpent's Tail, as well as an autobiography, *Forties' Child*.

OTHER PEOPLE

Suzannah Dunn

Each morning at coffee break I changed Marion's sanitary towel because when she did it by herself she let the soiled one fall back into the toilet bowl and it slipped instead down her tights and stayed stuck to the back of her knee. And on several occasions I spoke to the Hygiene Instructor about Marion's teeth which were covered in green slime. The Instructor replied that Marion would have to attend the dental clinic at the mental handicap hospital and that there was a two-year waiting list. She suggested that in the meantime we avoid Marion if and when her breath smelled. This was particularly difficult at lunchtime when Marion pestered us for attention. At lunchtime we were all together in the big room: recreation for trainees; and supervision by staff. Classes finished each day at noon and began again at one o'clock. Lunch was served in the dining room and lasted for twenty minutes. Staff did not have a lunch break: we were employed by the Social Work Department to work a thirty-six hour week including a half-hour break in the mornings before the trainees arrived and a half-hour break at the end of the day when they had left.

Not long after I joined the staff at the Centre the Manager came to the Staff Room to address us.

Two things, she said: one, that there would soon be a new member of staff, on redeployment, and that she would discuss

this with us at a later date; and two, that she would like a word
with us about Elsa because Elsa's behaviour at lunchtimes
was grossly inappropriate. The Educational Psychologist had
therefore been asked to observe Elsa's behaviour and to
make recommendations for its modification. Elsa ran each
lunchtime around the big room rubbing the heads and faces
of those who swayed beside the record player, or stroking the
arms of those who were trying to knit, or screaming at anyone
having a temper or a fit, or singing loudly and tunelessly to
the Shakin' Stevens Christmas record played daily throughout
the year.

Several weeks after the Manager requested our cooperation
the Educational Psychologist arrived at the Centre to make her
observations; and several weeks later she sent the Manager a
report suggesting that we help Elsa to relax. She suggested that
when not starting the record player or switching it off, or lifting
the needle or lowering it, and when not soothing squabbles or
lifting the trainees from the floor or holding them down, and
when not dispensing medication or changing towels or clothes
or rescuing rows of dropped stitches, then members of staff
might like to take hold of Elsa's hands and ask her to breathe
slowly and to relax.

The big room had flock wallpaper. The building had been a
priory and then a children's home before it became a training
centre for women with mental handicaps. In each room there
was an electric bar heater switched on by the cleaning lady
when she arrived in the morning. When all heaters and lights
operated simultaneously the electric circuit would fuse. There
was no shower in the bathroom although the trainees were
supposed to learn how to wash their hair: instead there was
an attachment for the bath taps. The building had not been
refurbished because there were plans to build a new one. The
Social Work Department's Assistant Principal Officer told us
about the plans: he came from Headquarters one afternoon
and sellotaped drawings to the Staff Room wall.

'In three years' time,' he said, 'all this will be yours.'

He was responsible for the centres in the west of the
city, visiting ours whenever there was a crisis and taking

the Manager out to lunch. He tried when addressing us to remember our names but made mistakes.

The Hygiene Instructor peered at the plans. 'What's this bit here?' she asked. 'Well, Mandy,' he replied, although her name was Amy, 'that's a lovely new Hygiene Area; because when the patients come to us after the closure of the hospital, some of them might need help with the most basic of tasks such as changing their sanitary towels.'

The arrival of the Keep Fit Ladies on Thursday mornings represented the sole break from routine. Each group of trainees was instructed for half an hour: one lady demonstrating exercises and the other accompanying her on the piano.

'Today it's balls,' the demonstrator called to me across the big room one Thursday morning, holding a sackful of brightly coloured balls. 'And firstly we'll throw them into the air and then catch them again.'

But the balls when distributed were thrown behind the piano or into people's faces or out of the door. Hoops were not easy to manipulate, and scarves were not used because of the risk of entanglement or strangulation. Throughout the ballgames one of the trainees sat alone in silence: Paula rarely spoke unless it was to complain about pains in her back or leg or tooth; and whenever it was her turn to wash the dishes she was dragged to the kitchen by members of staff. She liked to sit on the toilet and if there was no toilet vacant she would enter a cubicle and sit on top of someone else. She had once almost been persuaded by the Keep Fit Ladies to participate in their game:

'But I can't,' she whined.

'Yes, you can,' they cajoled. 'Why on earth not, Paula?'

'I can't, she replied, 'because I'm a cripple.'

The Manager informed us one day that a woman named Jean was to join us following her redeployment from the children's home where she had worked for fourteen years. A rota was pinned to the noticeboard: she was to spend a day initially with the Social Education Instructor, a day with the Hygiene

Instructor, four days with the Domestic Instructor (two in the kitchen, two in the laundry), a day with me in Basic Education and then a day in the Special Care Unit.

'And then what?' the Domestic Instructor asked, raising her eyes to the ceiling, after the Manager had left the room.

On the day that Jean was scheduled to visit my classroom most of the trainees were crayoning: Jane, Lisa, Caroline and Doreen crayoned; but Jenny counted dots and wrote numerals beside them in her notebook, and Mary pieced together a five-piece jigsaw; and Christine took a magazine and waved it above her head; and Clare copied the letter 'C' into her notebook; Belinda threaded beads onto a string and dropped the rest from the table onto the floor; Lynda dragged cards towards her across the table and matched the pictures – a tree with a tree, a postbox with a postbox, and then unfortunately a banana with a car. There had been an argument: Jenny had ignored Jane and then Margaret had ignored Jenny; so Jenny had taken Margaret's Shakin' Stevens record and placed it in the cupboard; and Margaret had accused Jenny, and Jenny had denied it and cried. The argument had upset Lynda so much that she had dashed her chair against the wall, and upset the others so much that they collapsed cowering beneath the table. But when Jean entered the room at half past nine the trainees were peaceful once again.

I offered Jean my chair and handed her some typewritten notes to read whilst I retrieved Belinda's beads from the floor. The notes outlined the teaching of literacy – *recognising objects, naming objects, describing objects, matching objects, reproducing shapes, reproducing phrases, completing phrases, recognising name, recognising words, copying name, copying words*. After a minute or two Jean placed the sheet on the desk and rose from the chair. She crossed the room towards me and knelt beside me at Belinda's feet, scooping red beads into her hands.

'So what do you do in here all day long?' she asked me.

'Not much,' I replied. I dropped the last of the beads from my hand into a dish on the table and told her how I had arrived at the Centre six months ago to work for five days: on the Monday morning I had been shown into the classroom with a pile of scrap paper and instructed to ask the trainees to write down their names.

Jean stood up, her hands striking dust from her skirt. Her nails were painted a shade of pink identical to that of her handknitted jumper. I stood beside her and we glanced together around the room.

I told her that most of the trainees were unable to hold a pencil so that instead of asking them to write their names I had suggested that they crayon pictures of themselves.

'And then?'

'And then nothing: five days became four weeks, and four weeks became two months and then six months.' I shrugged and indicated the table at which Jane, Lisa and Doreen sat with their colouring books. 'And I'm still here,' I said, 'and they're still crayoning.'

Jean told me that when the children's home closed she had been guaranteed redeployment: same hours, same pay scale, but without the children and the night duty. She had been working nights for the past five years, knitting cardigans and watching late films in the Staff Room after the children had gone to bed. Then the home had closed and she had been offered a post in a Day Centre: the loss of overtime payments resulted in a large drop in earnings. As she spoke I bent to pick another bead from the floor; and when I straightened, she squeezed my arm. She reached into my hand for the bead and dropped it into Belinda's dish. Belinda reached across the table for it, so Jean lifted it and held it in one hand whilst reaching for Belinda with the other.

'Had you ever done this type of work beforehand?' she asked me.

'She cradled Belinda's hand, and Belinda gazed at her.

'No,' I said, 'although the Department knew me because I'd taught for a while on the evening class scheme; but otherwise no, not really.'

Jean shrugged. 'Well, that makes two of us,' she said.

It was then that I said something to her which the others had said on so many occasions to me: *it's not a qualification that you need, but the right attitude.* But many of them had come to regard Jean as someone with the wrong attitude. The Domestic Instructor was enraged by Jean's attitude to the laundry.

'It took me years,' she confided one day to me as we passed in the corridor, 'to teach Paula to attempt the ironing, and then Jean comes along and does it herself: *it's quicker, she says, and if you want a job doing, she says, then you should do it yourself.*' She raised her eyes to the ceiling. 'But if you ask me, she treats our trainees like children.'

But Jean had come into my room on the day of the spilled beads and she had taken Clare away: Clare who stood at my desk as I tried to mark assessment sheets and told me that her *dad was having a day off work, a day off, a day off work, and that he'd pick her up at the end of the day because he was having a day off work and that he'd take her out at the end of the day because he was having a day off work; and had I got a cat at home? had I got a cat? had I got a cat? because she had, she had, she had.*

'Yes, Clare,' I had replied throughout, the pen loose in my hand; 'Yes, Clare, yes; very nice, Clare, very nice; and I'm busy, Clare, please, Clare, can't you see that I'm very busy.'

Jean came across the room towards us, leaving Belinda at the table with her string of beads and two spare buttons taken from the underside of her cardigan. She took Clare's hands in her own. 'A cat?' She turned Clare towards her. 'How lovely: what's his name?'

'Timbo.'

'Rambo?' Jean raised her eyebrows.

Clare giggled. 'Timbo.'

She dropped Clare's hands for a moment and raised her own to her lips to moisten her fingertips with saliva; she then rubbed them gently over Clare's chin.

'Look at the mess you're in,' she said to her as she rubbed. 'Look at this lovely chocolatey moussey lunchtime mess. I think we should take a trip to the bathroom, you and I, don't you?'

From that day onwards Jean and I talked together of our plans to leave the Centre. Jean hoped for early retirement, and I had six weeks left until the end of my contract. One day I was walking along the corridor to the Staff Toilet with the cloth which had mopped Doreen's urine from the floor when the Assistant Principal Officer (APO) leaned from the Manager's office and beckoned me inside. I hesitated because I was not supposed to leave my class; but the APO was not aware of the rule, and in any case a few more moments should not have made a difference. So I entered the office: the Manager was not there. Perhaps she was at lunch alone or with someone else. Her cigarettes remained on her desk in their casee. I had been into her room once before for the annual review of one of the trainees: the review had been attended by a parent and a social worker as well as by myself and the Manager. The room contained a desk and a swivel chair, a phone and filing cabinet, and four low chairs around a coffee table. On the coffee table there was a potted chrysanthemum. The APO lounged in one of the low chairs and indicated that I should sit opposite him. He twinkled his eyes conspiratorially.

'Mandy,' he said, 'it's good to see you.'

My name is Mary but I sat down opposite him and attempted to return the twinkle. I remembered at that point what the other members of staff said about him: *humour him, he's harmless.*

'Mandy,' he said to me, 'it's always good to see you.' I worried about how I might return the compliment. 'These are difficult times,' he continued, 'for us all.' He paused and frowned.

'Yes.'

'Difficult times; because, as you know, we are so very understaffed.'

'Yes.'

He reached over to the Manager's desk and offered me one of her cigarettes. I told him that I did not smoke. He remarked, closing the case, that this was wise, very wise, and that young women were much more health conscious these days.

'Mandy,' he said, resuming his leaning across the coffee table towards me, 'you've been doing famously; you've helped us enormously, and you've turned out to be a very fine teacher.'

The urine-soaked cloth was heavy in my hands.

'And conditions here,' he continued, 'are of course far from ideal.'

I nodded.

'The kitchens,' he explained, 'are of course far too close to the toilets.'

Did he smell the cloth?

He leaned insistently towards me. 'But the people you are teaching, Mandy, would several years ago have been condemned to long-stay hospital wards.' He tapped the cigarette case onto the coffee table. 'But not now,' he said, 'not now, because now it's time for care in the community.' As I worried about what was happening in my unsupervised classroom he went on to tell me that these were challenging times, and to ask me if I might like to participate in them, if I might like to work for six months longer at the Centre.

No, I told him: *no, I would not like to work for six months longer or even for a day longer at the Centre because I am not a fine teacher but an under-qualified, under-experienced, under-resourced and under-paid teacher spending most of my time nursing the people I am supposed to train; the people who are supposed to learn how to lead independent lives in a community which denies them any independence; the people coming to the Centre every day for the rest of their lives and differing from hospital in-patients only by spending each night back at home.* And I shook the urine-soaked cloth at him as I spoke, of course, and dropped it into his lap. No, I didn't; of course I didn't; of course I thanked him instead for his kind offer and made an excuse.

But in the end I had the last word: shortly before leaving the Centre I was asked to write a report on Marion. I had been asked as her Key Worker to complete the report card when the others had commented on her specific skills. I had been asked to comment on Marion's *progress and areas of concern.* So one afternoon I sat alone in my room and wrote in biro under the appropriate heading that although the others had praised Marion's progress I had become concerned about her language skills: Marion had become isolated, sitting in silence day after day in front of the back-dated issues of women's magazines brought in bundles by members of staff; staring day after day at pictures of picnics and trifles and wedding dresses. In a classroom full of other trainees she could not speak for herself. I then signed my name at the bottom of the report and took it to the Manager who filed it in Marion's file in the filing cabinet where it stayed when her annual review was cancelled at short notice by a social worker with 'flu.

Suzannah Dunn was born in London in 1963. Her first book *Darker Days than Usual* is being published by Serpent's Tail.

THE LEAVING PARTY

Michael Bracewell

Barry in Buying was leaving.

There had been the usual memorandum announcing this piece of news; it was circulated around the building, from department to department, and it arrived on each desk fastened to a large brown envelope into which money could be placed towards the costs of a present and a small party.

Barry in Buying was a popular member of staff; everyone would be sorry to see him go.

'Where's Barry going?' asked Sonia from Sales.

'Head Office,' replied Maureen, her Supervisor.

Fairly soon – and all the while without Barry supposedly knowing – the brown envelope was bulging with money.

'We'll have to send another envelope round to Sales,' said Sam, the company's Head Messenger who lived in utter dread of the circulation of his own brown envelope.

'Sam says we've got to send another envelope round to Sales for Barry,' said Tom, the youngest boy in the Post Room.

'Oh,' said Dave, the Post-Room Assistant, who had always hated Barry. 'Better get on with it then hadn't you?' he continued, purposefully making the little task seem like an unwanted and cumbersome chore. Tom scurried off, his babyish round face flushed with excitement.

Over in Staff Conditions there was an anxious huddle of girls grouped about the typewriter of one of their colleagues.

'She's been sick,' said Sophie, by way of explanation to Karen, who had just come in from the lift with her sandwiches.

'Who?'

'Janet –'

A piteous moan came from Janet's bowed head, and the girls all moved back a few inches as the invalid reached out for another tissue from the box on her desk.

'Are you sure you don't want a taxi?'

'You look really pale . . .'

'I'll tell Louise you've gone home – all right?'

A sound of thunderous typing began in a far corner of the room as Irene – the only middle-aged lady in Staff Conditions – ended her lunch hour and returned to the monotony of work. It was two o'clock. Irene had not joined in with the drama of Janet being sick.

'She'd better go home then,' she had said, her lips pursed as she reached into a paper bag for an apple.

'God she's such an old cow,' muttered Sophie to Linda, more out of annoyance at the indifference to a welcome disruption of work than anything else. Irene – had she heard this insult – would have been unmoved. She was fifty-three years old, a spinster, and the graveyard where her parents were buried – both killed when she was just a little girl – had been hit by a stray bomb in 1944. There were few incidents in the lives of her young colleagues that Irene had very much time for.

And now it must be said that Janet in Staff Conditions was desperately and hopelessly in love with Barry from Buying. She had never admitted her passion to him, nor spoken of it to anyone, but now that he was leaving the flame which she had so tenderly nursed into a blaze seemed to be blowing out of control. She sat at her desk, with her brown hair hanging in disarray about the shoulders of her pale blue cardigan, and dabbed her nose. She didn't want to go home and she hadn't, in fact, been sick; when the note about Barry's leaving party had reached her desk she had simply fled into the toilet to cry.

And how she had cried. For over two years she had been in

love with Barry; first, because she thought him so handsome, and strong; secondly, because she knew from the way she had seen him behave that he was cheerful and funny; and lastly – and this was the most desperate symptom of all – because he was unobtainable. He was always to be seen with friends; his name was always on someone's lips ... And the girls in the company all flocked to him, flirting, laughing, asking his advice, and always so pretty. Janet was not pretty. She was short, and extremely thin, Her face was narrow and her nose too long. Her eyes were too small, and too close together, her cheeks had no bloom and her hair no lustre. All in all she dismayed herself, and she knew that men found her ugly because they were always so polite to her. She felt at her worst in the summer, when the city was so hot that she had to wear thin, revealing dresses if she did not want to roast to death on the tube. She would look at herself in the mirror before leaving the house in the morning, and wonder at the shapeless and unflattering way that her dress bunched up beneath its belt, flaring into voluminous pleats about her white legs, like sticks of wood, pressed into little grey shoes. She knew that she didn't stand a chance with Barry.

But Janet took her love to work with her every day – and every day she brought it home with her again, like an undelivered gift. She was twenty years old, lived with her parents in South Croydon, and was saving up for a deposit on a flat. Her love for Barry was her only connection with the world of romance, and desire, and so the passion grew stronger, with no rival emotion to weaken its power. Over the course of its growth this love had spread out – like flood water in a basement – to occupy every area of Janet's life. It rose in accordance with the constraints placed upon it, and so became threatening, and dangerous.

In moments of exhaustion Janet would try to stand back from herself and see exactly what kind of a life it was that she was living. On other occasions she sought to reason the thing out with common sense. 'This is just stupid,' she would say to herself; and then she would imagine the note that she would write to Barry, and the tone of her confession.

These efforts brought only further despair. 'I must be mad,' she would conclude, watching the bath water lap about her bony hips, 'I must be . . .' Words failed her. And now Barry was leaving; the god was quitting the shrine, and there was nothing that she could do about it.

The day of Barry's leaving party began to draw near. In comparison to the usual amounts of money collected for such occasions the quantity which had been donated for Barry's present and party was vast.

'Jesus,' said Tim, one of Barry's friends in Buying, 'there's nearly four hundred quid . . .'

'What sort of things does Barry like?' said The Other Barry, sitting on his desk and swinging his legs to try and kick the filing cabinet.

'We all know what Barry likes!' said Tim, and he looked about the office with a roguish leer.

'Why don't you get him a record token?' chipped in Boring Vic. Nobody took any notice.

'Where are they going to have the party?' asked Dave, who had just sauntered over from his end of the office. 'Board Room again?'

'No – too small, mate, too small – canteen!'

'The canteen! But that's –'

'There's over two hundred people coming you know, and that's not counting the lot from Head Office –'

'And Wigmore Street . . .' (It was Vic who remembered this small annex of the company. Nobody took any notice.)

By now the little group had formed themselves into an unofficial 'Party Committee'. The first task which they set themselves was that of deciding how much of the money ought to be put aside for drink.

'Well – there's twelve glasses in a bottle, and three glasses per person . . .'

'Leave it out! The lot from Production alone'll want half a bottle each – easy . . .'

'Is there going to be a pay bar?'

'Spect so . . .'

'Well if we get the bulk in then the real piss heads can use the bar . . .'

'What about music?'

'Steve.'

'Oh. Right.'

And so it went on, from half past five to nearly a quarter to seven, and then – it being Friday – most of the Party Committee went over to the pub.

At about half past ten, when a great deal had been drunk, and the personalities and ambitions of nearly everyone who was coming to the party had been analysed, found fault with, and dismissed, the conversation became obscene.

'. . .and her chair was all wet! Straight up! They'd just done it – he's still got his dick out and then old Woodward walks in . . .'

The group of young men all laughed, and leaned back with expressions of amazement on their faces, or leaned forward to try and make themselves heard as they thought of a story which they considered to be even more outrageous.

'No point asking Vic,' said Tim at one point, 'Dickless Vic . . .' And everyone laughed, even Vic, who was worried about travelling on the last train home. He hated Charing Cross Station so late at night, with its drunks and dossers and people who sat blearily opposite you on the train, chewing a hamburger and never once taking their eyes off yours . . . He would pretend to be asleep – it was only seven stops . . .

'One thing we've got to get,' said Luke, the Office Wally, 'is a strip-a-gram . . .'

The brilliance of the suggestion brought a silence to the table. Tim sat back and looked at a girl with long legs and a tight white T-shirt making her way towards the bar. 'Too fucking right,' he said, and threw back his head to down the remains of his beer. He misswallowed, and had to leave the table for a moment, coughing and spitting.

The Party Committee agreed that Luke should arrange the strip-a-gram.

'There's all those adverts in the giveaways – ring up on Monday and find out how much . . .'

'Yeah, and make sure you get one that'll go all the way –
don't want to waste a load of money just to see some tart take
her top off . . .'

Luke said that he would see to it.

Shortly before eleven o'clock the young men from Buying
all made their way to their respective stations. Vic alone went
to Charing Cross, and nobody shouted 'See you!' after him as
he said good night.

Down in South Croydon, Janet was standing in the kitchen
and making some cocoa. She was wearing a thick blue nightie,
and her face was all scrubbed clean.

Later, as she lay in bed unable to sleep, Janet composed
a fantasy in her mind about Barry's leaving party. In the
fantasy she was leaving with him, as his wife, and he wasn't
going to Head Office but abroad, to somewhere hot, and
colourful. All the staff had grouped around to see them
off and Barry said – as he held his leaving present in one
hand and Janet's hand in the other – 'Well, I've got the
thing that I want most right here!' And then he would kiss
her, in front of everyone, and they would all cheer, and
smile.

Eventually Janet fell asleep, and the light from the landing
came in through the crack in her door the way that it always
did, and caught on the orange stones of the necklace which
she never wore, but left hanging over the side of the mirror.

The big day finally arrived.

Barry arrived at work looking self-concious and cheerful,
and then he began to get on with his duties quietly, as if it
were just a normal day.

The other staff too all maintained a pretence that the day
was no different from any other. When they passed by Barry's
desk they said 'All right?' or 'Last day, eh?' and then went
smirking on, safe in the knowledge that the big party was soon
to happen, and that the afternoon would be shortened by the
presentation of Barry's gift, and the enormous card which they
had all signed.

The card itself was the biggest that Tim could find in

the shop. It depicted a cartoon office, where a party was in full swing. People dancing on desks, the 'boss' was looking lasciviously at a girl who was showing her knickers, and best of all there were spaces under each character for the real office workers who were presenting the card to fill in the names of those with whom they worked.

And then the card had been sent around for everyone to sign, beginning with Mr Woodward, the immediate boss. Soon the card was thick with signatures. These ranged from risqué in-jokes to formal expressions of farewell inscribed by people from distant departments who didn't really know who Barry was. 'Wishing you all the best in your new job' was the most common. Janet simply signed her name beneath those of the other girls in Staff Conditions.

There were two presents. Barry was well known throughout the company as 'Clint', this sobriquet being derived from his passion for American police thrillers. In a last minute flash of inspiration the Party Committee went out and bought their departing colleague an expensive replica hand gun.

'Fucking hell,' said Steve when the purchasing party, swollen with self-importance, marched back into the office bearing their parcel.

Everybody crowded around to see the gun before it was wrapped up. It looked like a real weapon, in dull steel and polished wood, with a long black barrel and a rotating chamber into which could be placed detonating caps.

'Nearly got nicked walking along with it,' lied Tim, and all the young men nodded.

'What did you get with the rest of the money?'

'Fifty quid record token.'

At half past five the party began in the canteen.

Barry inaugurated the event by pouring out glasses of sparkling wine for all his friends. A slight silence accompanied this first drink, with people saying 'Cheers' every now and then, and then feeling rather awkward. Nobody had accounted for the early part of the party when things were still 'warming up'. Everyone had simply envisaged the thing in full swing, with no intermediary period between sober work and drunken abandon.

The room began to fill up. Wine was poured more and more freely, the bar began a brisk trade, laughter rose in waves from one end of the room to the other and it was not very long before people had to shout to make themselves heard.

Barry showed off a little bit with his gun, and then he put it to one side on a small table where the crisps were. 'If anyone touches that I'll fucking shoot them,' he joked.

Shortly after six o'clock Janet came into the party with the rest of the girls from Staff Conditions. She was wearing a brown dress and a blue cardigan, and she walked with her hands folded in front of her, the better to guard her bag.

She had been feeling unwell all afternoon. There seemed to be a great distance between her sensations and her surroundings. Her head ached, and her body was tingling with pins and needles. She spoke mechanically when spoken to, and when she sipped her orange juice she was disturbed by an unpleasant burning in her chest. Her thoughts had become so deeply withdrawn that the noisy room seemed as silent as a church to her.

There was suddenly a great commotion, and a vast circle of people quickly formed around Barry, lowering their drinks and craning their necks to see. A girl in a beige raincoat, whom Janet had seen chatting cheerfully to Mr Woodward just a few moments before, was now facing Barry with her hands on her hips. Her mouth had split into a broad, lipsticked grin.

'Are you Barry?' shouted the girl, slipping off her raincoat as disco music began to blare out of Steve's hi-fi.

'Oh Christ!' said Barry, putting his hand over his eyes. 'You didn't!'

'Oh my God it's a stripper!' shrieked Sophie, half in amazement and half in triumph. One or two of the older guests left the room.

The girl began to dance around Barry, discarding her clothes in a deft, professional sequence. The men began to cheer.

'Yes! Yes! Yes!'

Barry gave the crowd a wink.

It was the wink which worked on Janet's mind; it hit her like a physical blow. 'How disgusting,' she said to herself, 'how stupid and pathetic and disgusting . . .' But there was worse to come. Having taken off all of her clothes except for a black G-string, the girl was now beginning to rub herself against Barry's chest. The men chanted louder. A lot of the women began to look at one another, shrugging their shoulders, as if to say, 'Now this has just gone too far . . .'

Janet moved closer to the centre of the crowd. Nobody took any notice of her. She saw the toy gun lying beside her on the table. 'Stupid disgusting little boys,' she thought, 'stupid disgusting pigs . . .' And then she felt the room go black.

It was Luke who saw what happened most clearly, and it was Luke who reported back a full account of the incident to Mr Woodward.

Just as the stripper was finishing her act, pretending to push her pelvis towards Barry's groin, Janet from Staff Conditions had suddenly rushed forward, a pair of small nail scissors in her hand. She had gone straight for the stripper's back, tearing down the exposed flesh with all her might. In an instant the dancer's back was streaming with blood, and Janet was pulled away, screaming.

'Slut Slut Slut – fucking Slag Slag Slag . . .'

Every syllable had been a slash of the scissors.

After Luke had left the office Mr Woodward sat back in his chair. 'What a terrible business,' he said to himself, reaching for the note to Janet's Personnel Officer. 'What a terrible, terrible business.'

Michael Bracewell, born in 1958, lives and works in Surrey. His novella *Missing Margate* was published in *The Quick End* anthology and his novels are *The Crypto-Amnesia Club* (published by Serpent's Tail) and *Divine Concepts of Physical Beauty*.

SMOG

Ian Breakwell

Thick, choking fog and smoke closed down on the city like a
blanket. Landmarks were invisible. Hundreds of trains were
cancelled. Traffic came to a standstill. Cars were abandoned.
People tried to get home from work as best they could,
walking uncertainly down once familiar streets now suddenly
strange and unknown, striving to recognize shops and side
turnings. They could not see their hands in front of their
faces. The smog got into their eyes, noses, mouths and lungs.
Everyone could smell it. It was difficult to breathe. Masks
were made out of handkerchiefs and scarves. All the sounds
of the city were muffled. Clocks stopped. Cars crawled along
with their headlights on full, following the pavement edges.
Buses crashed slowly into lamp posts. It was not safe to
cross the road even if it could be seen. Acetylene flares
were set up on traffic islands. Torchbearers walked ahead
of ambulances. Fires blazed unchecked while fire brigades
struggled through the blackness. Crime had a holiday. Cosh
thugs struck silently out of the murk, snatched handbags and
money, then disappeared. Countless houses were burgled.
Six police cars were overturned. Rioters stumbled blindly
through the shopping precincts. Bricks, stones and bottles
rained through the smoke. A number of people fell to the
ground, blood streaming from head wounds. A youth hurled
a fridge through the windows of a supermarket. Looting

broke out. Goods were grabbed. The dogs were brought in to sniff out their prey. Danger lurked at the docks. Eight people stepped off the quayside and sank without trace. Radio and television programmes were disrupted. Light orchestral music filled the airwaves. The smog crept inside. Pubs were half empty. Marooned in the cinemas, patrons sat in the front seats trying to see the screen. Outside, on every street, people leaned against walls, coughing and gasping for breath, unseen and unheard by each other. At home the linen, curtains and carpets were covered with black flecks of smut as the smog found its way through closed windows and under doors. Light bulbs grew dimmer. Rooms became colder. Nothing to do but go to bed. Nine months later the newborn babies lay wheezing feebly in their cots as the first autumn mists drifted in from the river.

Ian Breakwell lives and works in London. Serpent's Tail will be publishing an anthology on cinemagoing he is co-editing with Paul Hammond, *Seeing in the Dark*, and has published his books *The Artist's Dream* and *Ian Breakwell's Diary*.

NEVER A CROSS WORD

Fiona Cooper

Thirteen *across*: the day we went to 8, we went this way (8,4).

Alex had spent the entire evening thinking about that one. It was G.K. Chesterton, and 8 was Goodwin Sands. The day we went to Goodwin Sands by way of dum de dum. She couldn't find her book of Chesterton poems, and no one she rang had a clue. So she woke up with that dum de dum still nagging. And a voice like wasp-tunnelled rotten fruit fermenting across the airwaves.

Mornin', mornin', Jameson 'ere!

Straight into 'I Do Like To Be Beside The Seaside' by Mrs Mills.

'How can you wake up to that bloody awful man?' Jess put a pillow over her head, groaning.

'It's the only thing I can't sleep through,' said Alex, sliding out of bed so that Jess stayed warm. Into the kitchen and the misty view over London that almost made it worth being up. She could see right across to the Nat West building, where she swore she owned at least a brick in bank charges. The phone rang as she filled the kettle and lit her first cigarette. Click click whirr and an echoey voice came through the answer machine.

'Mother here, I can't seem to get you these days. When are you coming home? Give me a ring. Bye.'

That machine was worth its weight in gold, thought Alex, adding a guilty 'must call her later'. From work. She took

coffee and tea into the bedroom, wincing as Jameson 'ere
promised all you loverly people a nautical theme for the
show, wiv our Cliff and Summer Holiday – wot a star 'e IS!
It was seven thirty-seven and Jess was fast asleep again and
impossible not to kiss. So she did, and reduced Sid Yobbo to
the glutinous gargle of a blocked drain.

Downstairs the bathroom was icy, but the heat lamp felt
good. She added mineral crystals from the Dead Sea to the
running water for her health, and orange blossom bubbles
for vanity. Then Baby Bio-ed the much-neglected plant and
padded upstairs to sit by Jess and drink coffee.

'I ought to wake up,' said Jess. Always said it and never did
it.

Alex stroked her hair.

'You got another phone message. The Boss. Madame
Whiplash. Where are you? Meeting starts at eight-fifteen.

'Oh, shit! I spent so much time on that "by way of dum de
dum", I forgot. Start the day with an apology.'

The edge was off the chill in the bathroom and Alex lay back
to luxuriate for a careful ten minutes. Shot back upstairs with
dripping hair and rummaged around for knickers and socks.

'Brighton Pier,' said Jess.

'Chance would be a fine thing,' said Alex. 'Is Jameson 'ere
getting to you?'

'No, I just went down and got the paper. "The day we went
to Goodwin Sands by way of Brighton Pier!"'

'Of course!' Alex cut off 'Surfin' Safari' with the hair-dryer,
checked the clock, shit, eight-fifteen, time to hustle. Clean
shirt, clean jeans, jacket, an excavation of the laundry bag for
boots. So elegant! Jess was awake enough to be conversational
and there was no time . . .

She grabbed keys, tobacco and paper, stuffed a can of
Lucozade in her bag at the last minute. Knelt on the bed
and kissed Jess. And kissed Jess.

'Just so you think about me all day,' said Jess looking irresistible and knowing it.

'Later, later,' she said. 'Oo, my willpower does impress me!'

She hurtled downstairs grinning. Just a little lovin' early in the mornin' beats a cup of coffee for startin' off the day, yeah, Dusty! She started the car, twitchy at the time it took to de-ice windows, must remember not to park on that side again. And so into the usual line of cars trying to trickle out of the road and onto the main artery. The sluggish lifeblood of the city. Life was nothing but meetings and traffic jams these days.

Inch by inch it became her turn to make the break into the stream of cars. She tried a smile and a mouthed *please?* No good. Finally she slammed into first and risked her front bumper so far into the chrome caterpillar that the chauffeur-driven Mercedes to her right had to let her in with a sunglassed glare. She found herself inches behind a Renault Fuego. Which was fortunate. All Fuego drivers were macho, women and men. Glued to its burnished curves she'd whirl ahead like a foolhardy roller-skating bumper-rider, and simply carve her way through the traffic jam a.k.a. early-morning London.

If you were less than kamikaze with a Fuego on your tail, you'd be abused confused beeped flashed and cursed until it could tear past. No matter that its russian-roulette style of driving would gain it a mere two car-lengths at the next lights.

She hit the hospital car-park short cut just as the barrier dropped, adding at least ten minutes to her journey. She was stuck in neutral on the slowest lights in NW3. Add a one-person bus and a milk float, and there was time to roll a cigarette and light it, glance at the crossword and sip Lucozade, even jab a comb at her hair.

Into first and a kerb-crawl past the mums and dads and push-chairs at the nursery gates of the old gothic church where boards hung at the windows, bleached by age and weather, where the smoked Victorian red brick was splattered with pigeon-shit and green slime. At the lights, there was a choice of six directions, and an over-parked bike lane that lasted at most a hundred yards. And here came the skein of straggling high-school students re-playing the A-Team and the Muppet Show as they backed across the faint zebra crossing with its drunken belisha beacons bowing elegantly to the tarmac.

'Think they're bloody immortal!' snapped Alex as the red

lights stopped her again; the car behind yelled obscenities and she shrugged.

Five down: Edentate (if pink!) might drive topers to visit this thoroughfare, five went in here in pairs.(8)

Amber . . . green, she almost toecapped a red-faced youth, coke can glued in one hand, the other flung up into an automatic V. Five. V.

Waiting for a right turn she noticed the sky was clear blue. And the car-free run to Swiss Cottage gave her a chance to see buds on the trees, daffodils, geraniums in window boxes, scrubbed clean pink and blonde children in grey jerseys and shorts or skirts, bouncing along beside Jaeger mothers and Benetton fathers, satchels on their backs just like when she used to go to school. All them years ago, hundreds of miles from the great Metrollops. Ah, yes I remember it well.

The Scarlet City, looking almost fresh in the surprising sunshine. She didn't even bother swearing at the black cab and Porsche near-crash combination trying to make her economy city runabout wedge-shaped at the hidden crossroads.

Uh oh. The cars were still again; a crossing patrolled by a zealous ski-tan mother, Range Rovers, Volvos and BMWs angled anyhow while the uniformed babes were hand-held two by two into their private academy. Time enough to roll another cigarette, drive with her wrists, crawling one vehicle at a time past the shiny trappings of blithe affluence.

In pairs: two by two . . . the ark.

Topers: drunks, sots . . .

Edentate: some kind of animal.

Alex rounded the corner and was brought up sharp by a human chain of commuters rushing for the tube: the only place to cross three lanes of traffic. They high-stepped over a tangled web of metal ex-barrier, life and limb a game of chance: otherwise it was a long detour through a subway. No wonder they risked the lurching cars. Who'd walk through an underground gallery of vomit, graffiti and piss unless they had to? Besides, the woman crossing in front of her had a lovely smile, *and* the rest of it.

These are the things that dreams . . . thought Alex, oh, Jess!

She ignored the horn at her back, and glanced ahead to check the double lights. Best to hit the second lights the instant they went red, then at the green you could just roar across five lanes to take the road to Kilburn. Otherwise it was duck and dive, weave and herringbone within millimetres of buses and coaches and lorries and vans. Gratia Maria, gee it's good to see ya: she hit the red light and went into neutral. Perfect.

Now where would topers go if they saw a pink animal? A drying-out clinic? A.A? A thoroughfare? Street, boulevard, avenue . . . Maybe even to the huge pub on Swiss Cottage roundabout, an unfortunate marrying of fairy-tale gingerbread house and Clacton-pier souvenir musical box.

She slammed away from the lights into the extreme right lane and swept past the back of the ABC, now the Cannon and still playing mainstream Hollywood shit. Her lights were green, and stayed that way down to the curved hill where suddenly two lanes are one and a block of parked cars. Stopped at the crossing for a gaggle of small black children and real cool daddy-o, hands in lush leather swagger pockets. He smiled and saluted her behind his shades. She waved back.

The next right turn was dodgy. She slowed and was glad, for a young man was roller-skating across the road like a dancer. He made a mock terror face as he saw her and leaped to safety; she raised both hands and mimed a scream and drove on laughing. It should be a good day.

There was a building that always raised her spirits, gave her a smile from the heart. It was a simple white-painted warehouse, but in the sunshine it looked mediterranean, gave her the same lift as the first time she'd walked down the High Street in Brindisi and felt weightless in the solid heat and light. She almost expected to see the postcard-blue ocean around the corner, so it never mattered that it was just Kilburn High Road, and a phalanx of Post Office vans blocking road and kerb up to the slowest lights in NW8. If you really moved, if there were no dawn-dazed walkers and babbies, three cars could clear these lights. There were seven ahead of Alex.

Edentate. Typical crossword word. A.A. Street: ST. Avenue: Ave. And Ark. Arkastavea? Seven letters, idiot!

Left and determinedly right, she just slipped the green arrow as it vanished, passed the grey corrugated sea-scout hut that stood like a mammoth in a street half-yuppified, skips crowding the parking space. An underground station with its Koyaanisqaatsi clientele ignoring the zebra, come on, thought Alex, play fair, I stop for zebras. Not for stragglers making a long zig-zag, loping for that rare species, a 31 bus. Last seen in Chelsea! Three of them! Is this a record?

Arkastavea. Come ON! Vastea. Avast and belay there, matey, this car is made of metal and a little more resistant than flesh and blood!

Near where she worked, the young men walked like a steppin' razor, they were dangerous! Except that they held tiny babes tenderly by the hand, ushered adored daughters into the paper shop, bought themselves *The Sun* and the child whatever confection she wanted.

Junior, behave yourself!

And a tender whack to prime the babby for the Educational Experience ahead.

Hello, Miss!

Hi, baby, said Alex, wondering for the thousandth time why the tiniest children were corraled behind wire on climbing frames and rolly toys on tarmac; surely Esther Rantzen had made it clear that play space should be floored by something less likely to crack tiny skulls and smash small bones.

She leafed through the post, binned the catalogues, cash would be a fine thing. She put on the kettle. A.A. Asti, now that was a drink. Astiavea? Oh, pull-ease! Rara Avis?

In they came, Darren and Wayne and Natasha and Leroy and Sharon, she of the long pink nose . . .

OK. *Five down*:

Basic includes Santa's friend, a race and a party where love is lost but gains a high grade! (11)

''Ere miss can we do lego?'

'Nope,' said Alex automatically. 'Later. We're going to go over the basics. Starting with the Alphabet. Right?'

Right, miss.

Basic ... RUDI (Santa) plus MEN (race) plus (TORY minus O plus A) = RUDIMENTARY. Ha HA!

'Get your boxes out.'

Which put an R seventh in the Edentate ...

'A A A,' said Alex, 'like cat, bat, rat!'

'A A A,' said the children.

A thoroughfare ... a road: RD. Five: V. They went in pairs?

'Now sometimes, children, A goes AH,' said Alex in her best Joyce Grenfell, 'like ... AARDVARK!'

Fiona Cooper lives in London. Her short stories have appeared in anthologies *Walking on the Water* and *Passion Fruit* and she has published two novels, *Rotary Spokes* and *Heartbreak on the High Sierra*

Dreaming of Dead People
Rosalind Belben

This is an intimate portrait of a woman approaching middle-age, lonely, starved of love, yet avoiding the seductions of resentment. First published ten years ago and now reissued in paperback by Serpent's Tail, *Dreaming of Dead People* is a joyful, stark novel by one of the most distinctive voices of contemporary fiction.

'Rosalind Belben's eye for the movement and texture of the natural world is extraordinarily acute and she has a poet's ear for language. Her book, although apparently a cry of loneliness and deprivation, is also a confession of fulfilment, of endless curiosity for, and love of, life.' SELINA HASTINGS, *Daily Telegraph*

'[Belben's] heroine is a solitary woman who is suffering as she reconciles herself to loneliness and sterility. She tells of her past and recalls, often, the countryside, where being alone is not painful and, if there is no meaning to life, the call to the senses is immediate.' HILARY BAILEY, *The Guardian*

'So extraordinarily good that one wants more, recognizing a writer who can conjure an inner life and spirit, can envisage, in unconnected episodes, a complete world: one unified not by external circumstances but by patterns of the writer's mind.'
ISABEL QUIGLY, *Financial Times*

160 pages £6.95 (paper)

Is Beauty Good
Rosalind Belben

'A startling record of life preserved in the face of increasing desolation . . . Rosalind Belben's gift or burden is to press on to the painful edge of what is possible. It is an achievement to celebrate.'

MAGGIE GEE, *The Observer*

'In her work Belben gives us glimpses of such beauty that one can only choose, like her, to celebrate life.'

LINDA BRANDON, *The Independent*

'Spare, lucid prose, reminiscent of Woolf's *The Waves.*'
The Guardian

'Belben has an ability to tap deeply into the process of thought itself with all its fragmentation, puns, jokes, obscenities and moments of transfiguration . . . In this case beauty is certainly good.'

ELIZABETH J. YOUNG, *City Limits*

128 pages £6.95 (paper)

Faithful Rebecca
Janice Eidus

'Funny, clever, sexy, tender and tough, a real find.'
New Statesman

'Witty and unpretentious . . . sensuous and erotic.'
Sunday Times

'Highly entertaining and refreshing.'
The Pink Paper

'Eidus displays a wonderful ear for the text and subtext of the subversive talk of little girls.'
The Village Voice

'Eidus writes unpretentiously, without dropping names of products or MTV songs, and without having to resort to overdone street scenes.'
New York Native

176 pages £5.95 (paper)

The Artist's Dream
Ian Breakwell

'Like all surrealists worthy of their name, Breakwell never cuts his remarkable visions adrift from a very precisely observed social environment, thus making them all the more bizarre, outrageous and hilarious.'
New Statesman and Society

'Imagine Goya, Kafka, Man Ray, Alain Joubert, Timothy Leary, John Waters, John Cale and Joey Skaggs sharing a bath. You can almost imagine all this happening in the mind of Ian Breakwell — painter, video-maker, diarist, surrealist, television performer, possible lunatic.' *Fiction*

'One of the best writers alive; Ian Breakwell is also very funny indeed...He scares me. He delights me. I wouldn't miss one of his books, just as I wouldn't miss one by Ted Hughes or Angela Carter.'
ADRIAN MITCHELL

'Savage, searing . . . a poignant wit.'
The Guardian

120 pages (illustrated) £6.95 (paper)

Also published by Serpent's Tail

Without Falling
Leslie Dick

'A debut of great conviction and profound originality.'
New Musical Express

'A boldly overambitious novel . . . promising stuff.'
Blitz

'Thankfully a million miles from the rosily worthy world of seventies feminist fiction.'
Women's Review

'It is rare these days to find a novel which is so fresh, harsh, exciting and funny.'   *New Statesman*

'In a literary culture dominated by gentility and middlebrowism, *Without Falling* is itself something of a bomb.'   *London Review of Books*

160 pages £5.95 (paper)

The Crypto-Amnesia Club
Michael Bracewell

'Slips a razor-sharp knife into the ribs of London's Groucho gauchos and is as quick witted yet poetic a first novel as you are likely to read this year . . . in five years time when the Booker Prize winner is announced you'll be able to say, "Ah, but did you read Michael Bracewell's first book." '   *Over 21*

'More than leavened by a spiky and self-deflating humour . . . One of the most impressive British debuts in recent years.'   *Time Out*

'This flashy debut has a voice of its own.'   *TLS*

'A compelling read, especially for the cynical.'

Look Now

112 pages £4.95 (paper)

Forties' Child
Tom Wakefield

'Through his detailed, accurate and incisive observances and remembrances there exudes a natural unforced sentiment which proves both genuinely heartwarming and eminently readable ... It's one of those books that cannot be put down, and once finished demands to be read again.'   *Time Out*

'Beautifully evoked, touching and immensely readable.'   *Gay Times*

'He is able to touch base with the reader somewhere at some time and you know exactly what he means and why it is so important.'   *City Limits*

'A tender and original recollection of the way a child puts the amazing world together.'
EDMUND BLISHEN, *The Guardian*

'I greatly enjoyed Tom Wakefield's classic autobiographical account of a wartime Midlands boyhood.'
BEL MOONEY, *The Times*

'What disarmingly polished scenes they are. Tom Wakefield is one of our most engaging of novelists.'
VALENTINE CUNNINGHAM, *TLS*

176 pages £5.95 (paper)

The Seven Deadly Sins
Alison Fell (ed.)

'Seven fine writers, seven vices probed to the quick. Splendid.' ANGELA CARTER

'These seven writers represent . . . a newer and more knowing feminist strategy . . . Mischievous and exhilarating.' LORNA SAGE, *The Observer*

'Rich in experiment and imagination, a sign of just how far contemporary women's writing might go.' HELEN BIRCH, *City Limits*

'All of these stories cut deeply and with a sharp edge into the main business of life — death, God and the devil.' RICHARD NORTH, *New Musical Express*

'A rich but random survey of recent women's writing.' JONATHAN COE, *The Guardian*

'An exciting, imaginative mix of stories.' ELIZABETH BURNS, *The List*

'Witty, modern, female.' KATHLEEN JAMIE, *Scotland on Sunday*

'Extremely entertaining.' EMMA DALLY, *Cosmopolitan*

240 pages £7.00 (paper)

The Lizard's Tail
Luisa Valenzuela

'Luisa Valenzuela has written a wonderfully free ingenious novel about sensuality and power and death, the "I" and literature. Only a Latin American could have written *The Lizard's Tail*, but there is nothing like it in contemporary Latin American literature.' SUSAN SONTAG

'By knotting together the writer's and the subject's fates, Valenzuela creates an extraordinary novel whose thematic ferocity and baroque images explore a political situation too exotically appalling for reportage.' *The Observer*

'Its exotic, erotic forces seduce with consummate, subliminal force.' *Blitz*

'Don't classify it as another wonder of "magic realism": read, learn and fear.' *Time Out*

'*The Lizard's Tail* will probably sell far fewer copies than Isabel Allende's inferior *Of Love and Shadows*, and that is a great pity. [It] is a wild adventurous book . . . a gripping and challenging read.'
Third World Quarterly

288 pages £7.95 (paper)